"Do I have a reputation?"

"You mean, do people talk about the fact that you've dated every nice-looking woman in the county? Yeah, I can safely say you have a certain reputation."

His partner's obvious enjoyment of his discomfort was almost the last straw—but he had to speak to someone. "A volunteer from that cat shelter, Ten Lives, came to see me."

"So let me guess. She's single and attractive. And she turned you down."

"She told me she was tired of being judged on appearances."

"My, you must have been subtle."

"I asked her out to dinner!" Eric said in outrage. "I didn't say, 'Hey, baby, your place or mine?' "

"Look at it this way," his partner said. "You won't have time to date, anyway, not when your son gets here."

The dull ache Eric had been trying to ignore sharpened to a knife stab. "He doesn't want to come."

Dear Reader,

I'm sure it won't surprise you to hear that I, like Madeline in *Beauty & the Beasts,* have enough cats to make rolling over in bed at night a little difficult sometimes. Also like Madeline, I volunteer with a no-kill cat shelter, Purrfect Pals, which is the model for Ten Lives, although I've freely changed it to suit the story. Many of the cats in *Beauty & the Beasts* are real, in spirit if not details. Chevy and Ron lived in my fourteen-year-old daughter's bedroom. The older cats like Mittens and Dusky are the ones that break my heart—and give me the greatest satisfaction when we find them loving homes.

When I write a novel, I'm always in love with my hero, and I always identify with my heroine. But this time it was the cats who moved me to tears and smiles. I hope you feel the same. I hope, too, that you take my message to heart: please, please, neuter and spay your pets. And if you have the time, or just a few dollars, help your local shelters and animal rescue organizations, especially those like Purrfect Pals that don't euthanize unwanted animals.

Now go ahead, fall in love with Eric. Just save a soft spot for Chevy, Ron and the rest of the feline gang!

Sincerely,

Janice Kay Johnson

Purrfect Pals
230 McRae Road Northeast
Arlington, WA 98223

BEAUTY & THE BEASTS
Janice Kay Johnson

Harlequin Books

TORONTO • NEW YORK • LONDON
AMSTERDAM • PARIS • SYDNEY • HAMBURG
STOCKHOLM • ATHENS • TOKYO • MILAN
MADRID • WARSAW • BUDAPEST • AUCKLAND

ISBN 0-373-70758-4

BEAUTY & THE BEASTS

Copyright © 1997 by Janice Kay Johnson.

For Kathy,
with affection and admiration,
and for all the "pals."

CHAPTER ONE

"OKAY, GIRL, JUST RELAX," Dr. Eric Bergstrom murmured as he deftly parted the hair on the calico cat's foreleg in search of a vein.

"How do you know where to get blood from?" the teenage girl asked, eyes wide. "I mean, since she's got hair everywhere."

Eric smiled. "I know where to look. The tricky part is getting any blood from a cat as dehydrated as this one." He slipped the needle into the vein and eased the plunger out, allowing a trickle of red into the syringe. "Ah. Well, we're in luck this time. Often the vein just collapses."

"Is that enough blood?"

"I don't need much." He removed the needle. "This'll let me check her kidney function. If they're failing..." He hesitated.

The teenager's face crumpled in distress, but she squeezed her lips together and nodded. She'd found the cat huddled in the family's woodshed and rushed it straight to the vet. Her mother, she'd candidly told Eric, didn't know about the cat yet, but she was sure Mom would let her keep Callie.

"That's what I'll call her," she concluded, gently stroking the thin back.

Five minutes later Eric was surprised to find that Callie's kidneys were functioning well. In this case, then, they'd take a fecal sample and check for internal parasites—coccidia was a good bet, he thought—and get her on an IV and a massive dose of antibiotics.

The girl left Callie in his care, and June, one of the technicians, carried the pitiful animal to their isolation room in the back to get started.

Eric scrubbed his hands, then stuck his head around the corner and in a low voice asked the receptionist, "Who's next?"

She glanced around the waiting area, then turned in her chair. "Um...a Ms. Howard is here to see you. She says she's a volunteer from a no-kill cat shelter. She wants to talk about the possibility of us providing veterinary service for them."

He leaned a little farther around the corner so that he could see over the receptionist's head into the room. A mother and two children waited with a bulldog on a leash. Faintly amused, he noticed that the youngest kid and the dog bore a startling resemblance. Near them a cat grumbled in a carrier beside a heavyset woman. At the counter a young couple was picking up their newly spayed spaniel pup. He smiled and nodded at them.

Only one woman waited alone, sans animal, apparently absorbed in a paperback book. And damned if she wasn't a stunner, even in worn jeans and a sacky mud-colored T-shirt. Slender, with a mass of rich auburn hair she'd yanked back in a severe braid and the kind of swanlike neck that could make a model's career, she possessed a face to launch a thousand ships: incredible cheekbones, full lips and exotic thick-lashed eyes. She must be on her way to the shelter to clean; no woman who looked like that appeared in public without makeup and so unflatteringly dressed without a good reason. He'd give a hell of a lot to see her in a snug skirt and silk blouse, with her hair loose and tumbling over those slim shoulders.

He strode out into the waiting room. "Ms. Howard? I'm Dr. Bergstrom."

The auburn-haired beauty glanced up, then marked her place in her book. Rising to her feet, she held out a hand. "It's nice to meet you," she said pleasantly. "I wonder if you could spare a few minutes."

Her hand felt fragile in his. He let it go with reluctance. "Certainly. Why don't you come back to my office." He gestured for her to go ahead of him, wondering at the wariness in her eyes when she inclined her head.

With automatic masculine approval, Eric noted the sway of Ms. Howard's hips and the grace of her carriage. She appeared to be about five foot ten.

In his too-small office he lifted a heap of files off the one chair facing the desk. "Please, have a seat."

Her gaze took in the wall of veterinary reference books, the cabinets, the stacks of files—each with carefully squared corners—that covered his desk. Eric in turn admired her eyes, green flecked with gold. Her driver's license probably called them hazel, but no word so mundane could describe a color that made him think of shafts of sunlight touching a mossy forest floor.

He became aware that those eyes had settled on him in a way that made him suspect she was aware of his turn of mind and was less than pleased to have inspired it. Hell, maybe she was sick of men staring at her. He didn't like thinking he was just like all the rest.

"Dr. Bergstrom," she said briskly, "I'm a volunteer with a small no-kill cat shelter called Ten Lives. You may be familiar with it. There've been articles in the local paper, and we regularly do adoption days at some of the larger pet-supply stores between here and Seattle."

He nodded. "Yes, I've seen mention of the shelter."

"In the past, Dr. Heyer from Granite Falls has done our veterinary work. Unfortunately, as you may know, he's retired."

Eric cut to the chase. "I presume he gave you special rates."

"Yes. We simply can't afford to pay regular rates and keep our adoption fees reasonable." She made a face. "Even if we charged exorbitant fees, we couldn't pay your normal charges. We simply have too many cats that are living out their lives at the shelter. At best our expenses are steep."

When he asked, she described the facility: the cats had the run of a house and a generous area outdoors, as well, that was fenced with chain-link. A separate building that used to be a garage housed feral cats, who had their own outdoor runs. The bedrooms were used to separate newcomers and to keep kittens apart from the adult cats.

"We have cages, of course, to quarantine the cats initially and to keep sick ones isolated. The house has a small mother-in-law apartment where the woman who conceived and runs the shelter lives. We have a full-time housekeeper and quite a few volunteers who clean or take animals to the vet or whatever. I do a little of everything."

He nodded, savoring the unusual experience of being pleased on both intellectual and sensual levels. He was aware of Ms. Howard as he hadn't been of a woman in a long while. Damn, but she was lovely. Her wrists and hands were narrow, her fingers long, the movements they made graceful and unstudied as she gestured. The fact that she wore no fingernail polish surprised him, though he was more interested in the absence of a wedding or engagement ring. Her ivory cheeks flushed with her passion for saving these abandoned or mistreated animals.

But he took in what she had to say, too; he and Teresa Hughes, his partner, had been discussing how they could make a practical contribution to the reduction in the number of animals that ended up euthanized at the county shelter week in and week out. They tried to keep the cost of neutering down and offered the service free when they suspected that owners couldn't afford to pay. But beyond that, the practicalities had stopped them.

"I'll want to see the shelter," he said abruptly, "and I'll need to talk to my partner. Assuming she agrees and I'm satisfied with your facility, I can see my way to giving you a couple of hours free every week. I could neuter male cats on the spot, for example, doctor any minor problems, draw blood. We can set a reduced rate for those that have to come to the clinic and for medications and surgery. Is that what you had in mind?''

She blinked, and he knew he'd surprised her. "It's better than what I had in mind. I probably shouldn't admit this, but Dr. Heyer didn't volunteer any time free.''

Eric leaned back in his chair and linked his fingers behind his head. "His was a one-man practice. I know how that is. You work twelve-hour days, get called out in the middle of the night, and you're still behind all the time. I can afford the luxury of volunteering an hour or two because I've taken in a partner." He smiled crookedly. "Now I only work ten-hour days.''

"He was having a harder and harder time squeezing us in.'' Ms. Howard wrinkled her nose, an effect that her physical perfection rendered charming. Hell, she probably looked magnificent brushing her teeth.

Letting his voice become a shade huskier, he asked, "Do you have a first name?''

She stiffened. "Yes, as a matter of fact I do.''

For a disbelieving moment, he thought she was going to leave it at that. Evidently she wasn't interested in getting personal.

Apparently, however, she also remembered that she wanted him—in a manner of speaking—and she acceded with a stiff "Madeline.''

He tried to make his grin disarming. "Eric. You may see some of my partner, too, Teresa Hughes."

Madeline Howard's high brow creased for an instant before smoothing. "Oh! She's Jess Kerrigan's sister-in-law, isn't she?"

"You know Jess?"

She gave him a cool look and he had a sudden suspicion that she was aware he'd dated Jess Kerrigan briefly after her divorce. Good God, maybe Jess had given her a play-by-play. He seemed to recall, thank God, that the relationship hadn't amounted to much, dying a natural death from disinterest.

"Yes, we're friends." Obviously disinclined to chat, Ms. Howard rose to her feet. "I won't take up any more of your time. When would you like to see the shelter?"

She wasn't interested; he ought to let her off the hook. But he couldn't make himself. Stubbornness had awakened, along with awareness. If she was married or involved, okay, he could accept that. Otherwise, he wanted to know what she had against him.

He stood, too, hands flat on the desk. "When's good for you?"

"I don't necessarily have to be there."

Smoothly Eric said, "Look, I need to have one person to be my contact. I'd appreciate it if you are there, since you were the one who approached me. I may have questions."

He'd won another battle, if not the war, because after a brief internal struggle, visible on her face, she said with reasonable grace, "I can make myself available almost any time. One of the beauties of working for myself.''

Maybe she *was* a model. "What do you do?" he asked.

"I own a women's clothing store in Everett. Madeline's."

"I've driven by it." He wouldn't have noticed it at all, except that the clothes in the window and the delicate gold script above it whispered *elegance* in a way he might take for granted in downtown Seattle, but didn't expect to see in a blue-collar town like Everett. "How long have you been open?"

"Four years."

"So you know something about long hours, too."

Ruefully she nodded. "I lost money for a year, then broke even for another one. But I've built up a steady clientele, and the store is doing very well these days."

"Good for you." He smiled with deliberate lazy charm and circled the desk, going to the door. With one hand on the knob, he paused. "How would late tomorrow afternoon be? You could show me around the shelter, and then we could have dinner afterward."

Madeline's head tipped to one side and she subjected him to a disquietingly thoughtful scrutiny. "Are you asking me for a date?"

He leaned back against the door and crossed his arms. "Yeah, I think that's the idea. Are you married?"

"No."

Ah. "Then...?"

"Thank you, but no. I'm afraid dinner is out." Her gaze never wavered. "Tomorrow afternoon would be fine, though. Four o'clock? Five?"

"Five's good." He didn't move. "Why not dinner?"

"You're not used to a polite refusal?"

"It wasn't all that polite."

"Then I apologize. I'm afraid I'm just not interested." Her poise would have put a presidential candidate to shame. Except, Eric noted, for the pink that again tinged those aristocratic cheekbones.

He frowned. "You'd made up your mind about me before you came here. Is that because I dated Jess?"

She pressed her lips together. Even tight, they weren't any less kissable. "You do have something of a reputation."

Eric was stung. He grunted and stepped away from the door. In the act of opening it, he asked, "Do you always listen to gossip?"

Instead of fleeing, Madeline said, "Tell me—why did you ask me out?"

"Because you're beautiful and I'm attracted to you." He paused for only a heartbeat, although it was long enough for him to see he'd blown it. Frost had glazed her eyes. "Besides," he added, "I figure we have at least one thing in common—we both love animals."

She gave him a smile as chilly as her gaze. "If you'd said that first, I might have agreed to dinner. Unfortunately what you really judge on is appearances, and frankly I'm rather tired of that. Shall I see you at five o'clock tomorrow, Dr. Bergstrom?''

He could read her thoughts; she was wondering if his offer of veterinary service had been contingent on her willingness to go out with him. Knowing the possibility had even crossed her mind steamed him.

"Yes," he said tautly. "You will."

He walked her out, then led the family with the bulldog into an examining room. Kneeling, Eric stroked the dog's head. He was a handsome fellow, if you liked a face that appeared to have met a car bumper.

Madeline Howard, Eric reflected, would give him hell for that thought.

Somebody ought to tell her that men and women usually did judge on appearances when they first met. Sexual response was physical; goddammit, *sex* was physical. A man didn't get hard because a woman was generously endowed with compassion.

Maybe ugly men turned her on.

"Is something wrong with Soldier?" the mother asked anxiously.

He jerked back to the present company. Drool hung like an icicle from the corner of Soldier's mouth. Eric straightened and reached for a tissue.

"No, no," he said reassuringly. "Is he having problems?"

"I don't think so." Her youngest, who'd been attempting to scramble onto the windowsill, succeeded. Exasperation replaced the doubt in her voice. "Jeremy, you promised to stand right here next to me." With a firm hand she deposited the teetering boy back on the floor just in time to save him from falling one way or the other. Probably out, taking the new screen with him. To Eric she said, "Soldier just needs his shots."

Feeling like a fool, Eric carried on about what an outstanding example of his breed Soldier was. The dog's owner was too busy corralling Jeremy to listen. Only the older boy, perhaps five, listened solemnly. Eric made quick work of checking the bulldog's ears and gums and then slipping the needle under the loose skin at the dog's neck.

As he saw them out, he thought of suggesting that she put the leash on the youngest kid, instead of the dog. He needed it more.

"Yeah, Ms. Howard," he muttered to the empty examining room, "and the kid's uglier, too. Sue me for noticing."

Behind him one of the technicians coughed. "Doctor, your son is on line three."

"Here?" Jarred by alarm, he retreated to the phone in the dispensary. He talked to Garth once or at most twice a week, always evenings. The boy lived with his mother two states away, in the San Francisco Bay area. He had never before called Eric at the clinic.

Picking up the phone, he said, "Garth?"

"Uh, hi, Dad." The boy didn't sound in pain and his voice wasn't choked with sobs.

"You're okay?"

Sounding surprised, his son said, "Yeah, sure. Why wouldn't I be?"

"And your mom? She's not sick, or—"

"No. I'm...well, see, I'm calling from school so she won't know I talked to you."

"You mean, you're feeding quarters in?" Eric frowned and leaned a hip against the cabinet. "Why don't you let me call you back?"

"No, that's okay. I wrote down Mom's calling-card number. She won't mind."

"When she gets the bill, she'll know you phoned me."

"Nah," Garth said without hesitation. "She doesn't look at her bills that closely. I've made long-distance calls before."

Who the hell had Garth been calling long-distance without his mother's knowledge? But Eric didn't ask; he was in the awkward position of a divorced father who hadn't seen his son in almost nine months; he wasn't really part of Garth's life and he had no business interfering in the boy's relationship with his mother. Maybe, Eric thought, he was misinterpreting things, anyway.

"I've got patients waiting," he said. "What do you need to talk about?"

For the first time a small silence ensued. Then in a rush his twelve-year-old son said, "The thing is, there's all kinds of stuff happening here this summer. But Mom says I *have* to visit you. I figured, if I talked to you, you wouldn't mind if I didn't come. It's not like we had anything really special planned. I mean, what would I do every day? Here, I've got friends to hang with, and Mom needs me, you know. She just doesn't like to say that to you."

Eric's stomach felt as if the morning's stack of

pancakes, eaten at a Rotary Club breakfast, was turning to concrete. *Mom says I* have *to visit you.* God. He'd lost his son.

"Dad?"

He couldn't think of a damned thing to say.

"It's not like I don't want to see you. It's just, the whole summer..."

Eric found his voice. "Let me think about this. Maybe talk to your mother—"

That provoked some real emotion. Panic. "But you can't! She'll be mad I called you. Why should you have to talk to her? It's just between you and me, right?"

"Wrong. You know your mother and I don't make decisions about you without consulting each other." He and Noreen hadn't been able to salvage their marriage, but they'd continued to share concerns about their son. Until recently, Eric realized, frowning again; he hadn't spoken to his ex for more than a "Hi, is Garth around?" in quite a while. And something was clearly going on.

Or had she simply not wanted to tell him that distance had killed his relationship with his son?

Striving to sound dispassionate, he said, "I won't tell your mom what you said. I'll just discuss this summer in general, okay? But I've got to warn you, I was counting on some time with you."

"Yeah, but it's really important..."

"We'll talk in a couple of days. Now, get to class."

Feeling sick, Eric stayed where he was for a moment after putting down the phone. Because of his son, he'd hung on to his marriage longer than he should have. Even after the divorce, he'd stuck it out in a lousy job situation at a clinic in the Bay area because he wanted to be where he could see Garth often. Only when those overnight visits became unsatisfactory did he convince himself that having his son for the whole summer every year would be better, that it was time to make a change.

He couldn't win. Maybe there was no way a father who didn't live with his kids could be anything but irrelevant to their lives.

In frustration, he drove his fist against the wall just hard enough to hurt. The pain was a welcome distraction from the deeper anguish.

"Eric." His partner laid a hand softly on his shoulder. "What's wrong?"

When he lifted his head and turned to face Teresa, she let her hand drop. Snug black leggings showed under her white lab coat, which was beginning to strain just the littlest bit over her stomach now that she was four months along in her pregnancy. She'd remarried the year before, not too long after she'd bought into the practice and moved to White Horse. Today her dark hair was French braided, and she wore tiny gold studs in her ears. Her forehead creased with worry.

He said the first thing that came into his head— the first thing that had nothing to do with his son. "Do I have a reputation?"

"A reputation?" Teresa's eyebrows rose. "I hope so! My livelihood depends on it. If people don't think you're almost as good a vet as I am—"

"Not that kind of reputation," he interrupted. "I mean socially. As a lady's man."

"Ah." Humor warmed her brown eyes and she leaned comfortably against the wall, waiting until a technician had walked down the hall and gone into the nearest examining room. "You mean, do people talk about the fact that you've dated every nice-looking woman in the county? Yeah, I think I can safely say that you have a certain reputation."

He growled, "I never dated you."

"I would have said no."

"Why?"

"Because we work together," she answered immediately. "We'd have fouled the nest, so to speak. Besides...you weren't any more interested than I was, were you?"

She was right, but he'd never understood why. "I don't chase everything in a skirt," he said grumpily.

"No, only the pretty ones."

Her obvious enjoyment of his discomfort was the last straw. He uttered a profanity.

Teresa's grin faded. "Do you want to tell me what's wrong?"

"When we have a spare fifteen minutes."

"We have it right now. Not a soul waiting. I have some calls to make, but I can do that later."

They retired to his office, marginally larger than hers, and she ate a cup of yogurt and wistfully watched him drink a mediocre cup of coffee.

"My doctor insists that a little caffeine won't hurt the baby, but I don't like the way they keep changing their minds. When I was pregnant with Nicole and

Mark, it was taboo." She sighed. "I'll live. Now. Tell me what set you off."

"You know that cat shelter, Ten Lives? A volunteer came to see me." He told her what Madeline Howard had proposed and his own offer. "You have any problem with my giving away our services?"

"You know I don't." She set down her yogurt and leaned forward, face alight with enthusiasm. "We can offer care at cost—"

"Yeah, but what's that? We have overhead, staff salaries and benefits..."

After some amiable bickering, they settled on charges he figured wouldn't break the bank. He was half hoping she'd forgotten their earlier conversation, but no.

"So let me guess." Teresa licked her spoon, then smiled. "This volunteer is single and attractive. And she turned you down."

"She told me she was tired of being judged on appearances." He shook his head.

"My, you must have been subtle."

"I asked her out to dinner!" Eric said in outrage. "I didn't say, 'Hey, baby, your place or mine?'"

"When's the last time a woman turned you down?"

"For dinner?" He had to think. "I don't know, I don't usually ask unless I think there's interest on both sides..."

"Never," Teresa concluded with quick glee. "And your ego's bruised."

Maybe she was right. Maybe that was all that was

wrong. It wasn't as if he'd had a chance to fall for Madeline Howard's inner beauty.

Except, dammit, he *had* glimpsed it. He'd made up his mind to ask her out, not when he first saw her, but while she was telling him about the shelter and the cats the volunteers were able to save. The color in her cheeks, the sparkle in her eyes, the verve with which her hands shaped their plans. Inner beauty, or outer?

"Look at it this way," his partner said, pushing herself to her feet. "In another few weeks, you won't have time to date, anyway, not with Garth here."

The dull ache of loss he'd been trying to ignore sharpened to a knife stab. "He doesn't want to come," Eric said starkly.

"Oh, no." Real compassion in her eyes now, Teresa sank back onto the chair. "You didn't say anything."

"I just talked to him. I don't know what the hell to do about it."

But he did of course; the first step was calling Noreen and finding out what was going on in Garth's life that was so much more appealing than a summer with his father.

He waited until nine-thirty that evening, hoping Garth would be in bed so that Noreen could talk without an audience.

She answered right away, but when he asked if his son had gone to bed, she said wryly, "Bed? I doubt it. But he is in his room. Probably with earphones on."

"He's, uh, seemed a little different lately when

we've talked. Anything going on I should know about?''

"Nothing serious," she said immediately. "Otherwise I'd have told you. He's been in trouble at school a couple of times—a fight with another boy, talking back to a teacher—normal things for a boy his age. But his grades are still decent, and I figure it's just a stage." She was silent for a moment and he sensed she wasn't done. Her voice changed. "Eric, I'm remarrying."

Remarrying. He waited for a reaction more profound than mere surprise. They'd been divorced for—what?—six years now. No, five-and-a-half. But before that she'd been his wife for ten years. Shouldn't he be jealous? Resentful, because she'd moved on so completely?

"Congratulations," Eric said automatically.

"Thank you."

"Garth hasn't mentioned anyone. Who is he?"

Either he was numb, Eric thought, or he really didn't care. He felt mild curiosity at most.

Until it occurred to him that the advent of a new stepfather probably had something to do with Garth's desire to stay home this summer.

There's all kinds of stuff happening here this summer.

Like a new father.

Noreen was telling him about the man she loved. Chuck Morrison was a corporate type, something to do with plastics. He was kind, civilized, supportive of her career, tolerant of Garth's occasional sullenness.

Eric felt a burst of rage. Who the hell was Chuck Morrison to be with Eric's son more than he, Eric, was? And "tolerant" sounded goddamned condescending.

It was hard to make his tone civilized. "How does Garth like him?"

"Well..." Noreen sounded doubtful. "He seemed to like Chuck fine as long as we were just dating. Since we've become engaged, he's been a brat. I figure he'll get over it. It's normal for him to be scared about such a big change, right?"

"Yeah, I imagine so."

"In fact," she spoke faster, with more animation, "we've planned the wedding for early June so that Garth can be there, but then he leaves immediately to stay with you. That way, we can have a leisurely honeymoon and some time on our own before Chuck and Garth butt heads."

"I see," Eric said mechanically. For once he knew something about their son she didn't. Garth didn't want her to have a leisurely honeymoon and some time alone with her new husband.

But Eric didn't tell her. He wished her well, they discussed the airline tickets he'd be sending for Garth and said good-night.

His resolve hardened. He couldn't do a damn thing about Chuck Morrison, corporate executive, playing father to his son from September through May, but he wasn't going to give up his own time and his last chance to remind Garth that he already had a father.

CHAPTER TWO

"LILY, WILL YOU SEE if Mrs. Peterson needs a different size? She's in room three. I'll get the phone." Madeline paused only a moment; Lily, although just twenty-two, was a dream with the customers. When she smilingly complied, Madeline moved behind the mahogany counter to answer the telephone. "Madeline's. May I help you?"

The caller was her mother. "Madeline, did I get you at a bad time?"

Aware of a customer browsing a rack of suits only a few feet away, Madeline didn't allow herself to frown. Her mother, who lived in Southern California, often chose to call her at the store rather than waiting for evening. "No," she said, "although I do need to leave in five or ten minutes." She wondered how prompt Dr. Eric Bergstrom would prove to be.

"Oh." Her mother dropped the single word forlornly. Given their usually distant relationship, that was out of character for Gloria Howard. "Well." Her customary briskness returned. "I was simply wondering if a summer visit would be convenient for you. Perhaps in July. I thought I might stay several weeks."

Madeline turned her back on the customer. Several

weeks? They hadn't spent more than a week in the same house in the past fifteen years! Not that they argued or did anything else dramatic; it was just that they had little to say to each other. Or too much, which amounted to the same thing, as none of it *could* be said. Not if they were to maintain their pretense of a normal mother-daughter relationship.

"Several weeks?" Madeline said, letting no more than faint surprise sound in her voice. "Is this a special occasion?"

"No, not really." Gloria Howard hesitated. "I just thought...well, we see so little of each other. And I'm not getting any younger." This last was said lightly, as though she meant it as a joke, but Madeline heard the loneliness underlying her mother's usual attempt to hide any real emotion.

"Is there something wrong?" The strength of her fear caught her unprepared. What if her mother had cancer or a heart condition? What if she was dying? Madeline edged around again to keep her face averted from the customer who was browsing her way through the store. "Are you sick?"

"No, no, nothing like that. I'd enjoy seeing you, that's all." Her mother's voice cooled. "But if you already have plans..."

Madeline was being let off the hook. All she had to do was say, *Yes, I'm afraid I do.* Then make something up. Suggest a shorter stay. Or that they meet at a nice resort, like Rosario in the San Juans, for a pleasant weekend as they'd done before.

But the sharp fear and the thought, *What would I do without my mother?* had left a residue, an ache that made her feel like crying. The words "Oh, I'm sorry," wouldn't come.

"Mom, I have no plans," she heard herself say. "You're right. It's been ages. July would be great."

"I'll let you know exactly when I'll be arriving." Back to normal now, her mother sounded as if she were concluding plans for a business meeting. "And of course, I'll bring my allergy medicine." A pause. "How many cats do you have now?"

After a brief mental review, Madeline decided not to mention the six kittens currently in her guest bathroom. They'd be gone before July. "Seven. Only one more than last year."

"So long as I can keep them out of the bedroom…"

It was all Madeline could do to hide her irritation. "You know you can. Mom, I'd better go. I have an appointment."

Leaving Lily to handle the last hour and close up the store, Madeline hurried out to her Subaru station wagon, parked in one of two slots behind the building.

Several weeks. Dear Lord. She started the engine with an unusually vehement roar. How was she going to survive?

The drive took her about twenty minutes, which gave her plenty of time to brood. A year before she had bought her first house ever, in White Horse, a small town in the foothills of the Cascade Mountains. Today she turned off the highway before she reached the town limits and followed a narrow, winding country road to the shelter.

Where the gravel drive turned into an opening in a split-rail fence, a discreet hand-painted sign showed a black-and-silver tabby curled around the words Ten Lives. The shelter itself, housed in a large 1950s rambler, was hidden from the road by a stand of alders clothed in silver-green leaves that rippled in the breeze.

Madeline parked in front of the detached garage beside Joan's van, which had the same tabby painted on the side. No unfamiliar cars, thank God; she'd cut it close, arriving only five minutes early.

In fact, she was just closing her car door when a canopied pickup pulled in and stopped right behind her station wagon. Wearing brown cords and a khaki shirt, Eric Bergstrom climbed out slowly. She guessed he was no more excited about meeting her again than she was about meeting him.

Nervousness twisted in her chest, although she hardly knew its cause. He wasn't the first man to come on to her for no other reason than her looks. He hadn't even taken it all that badly when she'd turned him down.

No, it was something about the man himself. What made her feel like a hypocrite was her suspicion that she was reacting to his appearance.

Experience told her that the camera would find him magnificent. She hadn't met a man in a long while with his looks. Tall enough to make her feel petite, he was also lean and graceful, in the way of a natural athlete. Classically handsome, his face was all angles—stark cheekbones, with creases deepening the hollows beneath, and his nose narrow and aristocratic. In keeping with his Scandinavian name, his hair was light blond, silver and gold shimmering together in the sun. And his eyes, narrowed now as he scrutinized her, were a pale clear gray-green that seemed to see more than she wanted them to.

She immediately regretted the moss green suit that hugged her waist and hips. She should have taken a change of clothes to work.

"Dr. Bergstrom." She gave him a pleasant aloof smile.

"Ms. Howard." He sounded brusque; sulking, she thought with a mental sigh. Then he slammed the pickup door and winced.

She took a step forward. "Are you all right?"

"Yeah. Got kicked today. My own fault." His face was closed to her; his male pride demanded stoicism.

"We could have rescheduled."

"Unless you have pet cougars in there—" he jerked his head toward the house "—I think I can handle it."

Just once she'd like to hear a man admit that, yeah, he didn't feel so hot and, yeah, he wasn't up to being big and tough today. *Dream on,* she thought wryly.

"No cougars," she conceded. "Although Jackson comes close."

"Jackson?" He fell into step beside her.

"You'll meet him." She hesitated, one hand on the door. "I should warn you, although we do clean constantly—"

"It won't smell like my mother's rose garden?"

His look was ironic. "You ever done preg checks on a herd of Holsteins?"

"No." She opened the door. "*Does* your mother have a rose garden?"

"And a raft of prizes from rose shows. Cat shows, too. She breeds Abyssinians."

Madeline liked the picture his words created: sinuous golden cats sunning themselves by rosebushes in voluptuous bloom.

"I wish mine—" she blurted, and stopped just as quickly. Lord almighty, what was wrong with her?

They'd reached the entry, a tidy room complete with computer, phone and answering machine. Sliding glass doors separated it from the living room beyond. It served, in addition, as a safety net; the sliding door was never opened until the front door was closed so that inmates couldn't escape.

Eric Bergstrom didn't even glance toward the living room, where cats were draped on couches and windowsills and the tops of cages, while others paced or cleaned themselves or nibbled desultorily at dried food. Instead, his green eyes pinned hers.

"You wish yours...?"

"Never mind."

"Grew roses? Bred Abyssinians? Or just liked cats?"

"All of the above," Madeline found herself saying. "She's allergic to cats. She has no hobbies. She's visiting me in July. For *weeks*."

His mouth eased into a smile that showed in his eyes. "And how many cats do you have?"

"Now." At his puzzled look, she explained.

"That's what she always asks. 'How many cats do you have *now?*'"

"Ah." His smile was oddly comforting. "So how many *do* you have?"

"Seven." She paused. "Plus six kittens I'm fostering."

"That doesn't seem out of line." He finally turned to look at the legion of felines in the living room.

A man who didn't think seven cats was out of line? Maybe she'd been a fool to turn down his dinner invitation.

No, because he'd issued it for the wrong reason. Because… She closed her eyes momentarily. Because the very fact that she was tempted scared her.

"You must have some yourself," she hazarded.

"Only three." He flashed a grin over his shoulder as he opened the sliding door and adroitly stuck out a foot to thwart the black cat who shot forward. "But I have a horse. I lost two elderly dogs last year. I'm sure some more will find their ways to my door one of these days."

Wonderingly she said, "So you understand," and meant it in more than one way. He understood why she had so many cats, why she cared enough to volunteer here. Why all this *mattered.*

This time his glance was unreadable. "Yeah, I understand." His tone became bland. "So. Lead on."

She closed the sliding door behind them. "Joan," she called. "Are you here?"

No answer. The silence meant that Joan was either out in the feral building or had gone to start dinner in her own small apartment. Which *wasn't* cat-free;

eight who qualified as personal pets lived in the two-room quarters with her.

"Good God, what's this?"

Madeline laughed. Mudhen, who always made a point of greeting visitors, was wrapping himself around the vet's ankles. Perhaps ten years old, Mudhen had arrived several years ago, battered and hostile. His gray coat had a tinge of tan that made it look perpetually dirty; scars twisted his face, and only one eye had survived. But he'd decided the people here were okay, this was home, and he could manage it better than anyone else. Joan had never even considered putting him up for adoption.

"That's Mudhen."

"He's ugly as sin." But Eric had crouched, albeit with a grimace of pain, and was gently running his fingertips down the homely cat's broad back. Mudhen's permanent expression of malevolence didn't change, but a gruff purr rattled the air.

"We can't all be beautiful." It came out tartly, even as she knew that, in this instance, he didn't deserve her scorn.

His eyes narrowed, but he chose not to react. Instead, he rose to his full height and his voice became more distant. "Shall we get on with it?"

Biting her lip, she showed him the kitchen. "Joan has her own kitchenette in her apartment. We use this one only for medicines and preparing food for the cats. People donate chicken or fish sometimes that we cook, and of course a few cats are on special diets."

Eric made noncommittal noises and studied their

supply of medications, some in a cupboard and others refrigerated. Madeline chattered about individual cats as they progressed through the former family room and garage and out into the chain-link-fenced runs.

There the only comment she could think of was, "We can't really mow out here." As if he couldn't tell. Bringing a mower through the house would have been difficult to start with; no exterior gate had been installed, so that vandals couldn't let the cats loose with an easy snip of wire cutters. Inside the enclosure various wood climbers reached to the chain-link ceiling, with ramps and balance beams stretching like spider webs between. Thorny rosebushes and lilacs and rhododendrons grew around the perimeter. And everywhere cats of myriad colors and shapes sunned themselves on the rough grass.

"The cats probably prefer it this way." Eric scooped up a small gray-and-cream tortoiseshell that had plopped herself in front him to stare up beseechingly. "Who's this?"

"Hannah. She's ten, which makes her a little harder to place. Her owner went into a nursing home. We haven't found Hannah a new family yet, but we will sooner or later."

The small tortoiseshell burrowed her head under his chin and purred softly. When he followed Madeline to the bedroom wing, Hannah remained curled in the crook of his arm.

They visited the kittens in the first bedroom. A litter of tiny newcomers, no more than five weeks old, huddled in a nest of flannel sheets in one corner of a cage. Another cage was empty. A miscellaneous lot of leftovers from several litters ran loose, mewing and wrestling and poking tiny claws into Madeline's tights and Eric's corduroy pants.

"In the spring the kittens go fast at adoptions," she told him, plucking one off his pant leg. "But nobody wants the adult cats. By fall, everyone interested in getting a kitten has one, and we have a heck of a time placing the ones born from August on. We do better with adult cats in the winter."

He gently placed Hannah on the floor when they left the main house to visit the building where the feral cats lived. These unreclaimable animals had little contact with humans, other than the time it took to clean, change the litter boxes and supply food and water. They were all cats that had either been stray too long and reverted to wild behavior, or born to strays.

Madeline and Eric discussed the vaccination program, and he asked questions about the health of various cats, what medications had been tried and commented on what might be worth an experiment. Madeline was impressed by his knowledge and his kindness to the motley collection of animals. She'd approached several vets in the shelter's hunt for a replacement for Dr. Heyer. Most she'd talked to didn't seem to think these scroungy, shy or aggressive alley cats were worth the bother. Yet Eric Bergstrom's voice held affection as he talked to even the least prepossessing.

Her continuing awareness of him physically, of him as a man, however, was most annoying. He had wonderful hands, she noticed at one point: large, with long deft fingers. They were brown, callused in places, but also somehow elegant. He could have been a pianist. Or a surgeon, which of course he was.

Now, as he talked, she found herself thinking that the close-cropped cut of his hair suited the clean angular lines of his face, giving him a cool patrician look—until he smiled with the rakish confidence of a man who knew women would fall for him.

Don't be one of them, she told herself with a flash of panic. *He wants an ornament, a sexy woman in bed, not a friend or lover in an emotional sense.*

When they emerged from the feral building, Joan was hurrying across the lawn toward them. A tiny energetic woman, she invariably wore her unruly gray hair bundled into a knot atop her head. She talked and moved faster than a normal human being, which was a good thing since she worked six days a week to help support the shelter, while also doing much of the physical labor and generally being the authority and mastermind.

"You must be Dr. Bergstrom." She thrust out a rough hand, which he shook. "I don't know how it is that we've never met. Madeline, have you shown him everything?" She focused intensely on his face. "I wanted to talk about the possibility of equipping a small surgery room so we could haul fewer cats into your clinic. Although at least the drive will be shorter now. Your predecessor was unwilling to give us special rates, you know. We had to go to Dr. Heyer. Bless him."

"Dr. Heyer gave me plenty of advice when I

bought the practice in White Horse. Good thing, too, since I had a lot of questions. I hadn't realized Dr. Stewart intended to head for warmer climes the minute the check cleared the bank.''

Joan curled her lip. "That doesn't surprise me. He charged too much. And he was lazy. If your animal got sick at 5:02 p.m., you were out of luck. I have a friend who had to drive her retriever, who'd been hit by a car, half an hour into Everett on a Sunday just to find a vet to look at him.''

"It's difficult to be on call night and day seven days a week," Eric remarked diplomatically. "That's why I got a partner.''

"*He* wouldn't have wanted to share the profits," Joan said disdainfully. "You should have heard the lecture he gave me on how I ought to euthanize any cats who weren't adoptable. 'What's the point of keeping them alive?' he asked, as though they're no more than toys that ought to be thrown away if they aren't any good to some human.''

That had been Dr. Stewart's real offense; as far as Madeline could tell from people's comments, he'd been a competent veterinarian. And Eric was right: it was impossible for any one man to be available around the clock seven days a week no matter how dedicated he was. But Joan's only criteria for judging people was: did they care about cats? All cats. Preferably enough to make sacrifices for their sake.

Joan and Eric settled on the best hours for him to visit each week; he laid out the charges he and his partner had agreed on, and Joan's cheeks flushed with pleasure.

"Dr. Bergstrom, thank you." She pumped his hand again. "Now I must be going. Madeline, you'll lock up? A man offered a pile of wood shavings if I'd pick them up. We use them for kitty litter when we're short," she said as an aside to Eric.

"Dr. Bergstrom would like to meet Jackson," Madeline said. "Do you mind if we stick our heads in your place?"

"Of course not." With the speed of an uncaught feral cat, she whizzed away.

Several of the residents came to meet them in Joan's private quarters. One was Jackson, weighing in at twenty-five pounds.

"Good God," Eric said, with obvious awe. "He *is* a cat?"

With his huge head and magnificent plume of a tail, Jackson was probably Maine coon cat, perhaps even a purebred. Blueblooded cats passed through here just as the commoners did, none immune to the indifference or cruelty of humans.

Outside Madeline repeated Joan's thanks. "This is good of you," she said with more warmth than she'd let herself show him yet.

His brows drew together in what looked like impatience. "You're giving a hell of a lot more time than I will be. I don't deserve any more commendation than you do."

"I'm not a professional donating services I'm normally paid for," Madeline said.

"This is something useful I can do." He literally shrugged off her praise. "I'm happy to do it." He opened his truck door, adding brusquely over his shoulder, "I'm sure I'll see you."

"I gave you my home phone—"

"I have Joan's card, too." No more talk about a contact person. He settled behind the wheel and reached for the door handle.

Madeline backed away, feeling childishly let down. And why? Because she'd expected that he'd try to change her mind about that dinner invitation. He didn't strike her as a man who accepted defeat easily.

Unless he hadn't been that interested to start with.

He pulled the door toward him, then stopped just before it slammed. "Oh, hell." He looked at her with exasperated resignation.

Her heart began to drum.

"I'd like to adopt that cat. Hannah."

"Adopt? Oh." A flush spread across her face. God forbid he could read her thoughts. "Hannah. Are you sure? We...we do expect you'll be making a lifetime commitment."

"Of course I am. What do you require?"

"I have forms... They'll only take a minute. Naturally we'll waive the donation." She managed a smile. "You'll be working off the price of a cat."

Eric followed her back inside, where she dug the forms out of a filing cabinet. "I don't suppose you need the free exam at the vet," she said foolishly.

"I guess not." He reached for the pen she handed him and bent over the desk, filling in the blank spaces with vigorous dark script.

"I suppose you want to take her right now." This

comment struck her as equally idiotic, especially since Hannah was sitting right on the other side of the glass, gazing hopefully at them.

Eric lifted his head, and she expected to read mockery or impatience on his face. Instead, the crease in one cheek had deepened and a couple of smaller lines had formed between his brows.

He cleared his throat. "Unless you'd like to reconsider about that dinner. We probably will be seeing a lot of each other. It wouldn't hurt to get better acquainted. Besides... I don't know about you, but, uh, I wouldn't mind somebody to talk to while I eat."

Was this sudden suggestion of vulnerability just a ploy? He might simply be changing his tactics, confident charm having failed. Madeline studied him warily.

If he was acting, he was darned good at it. Right now she saw only a man who was tired, probably in pain—she'd noticed him rubbing his thigh several times—and a little lonely. If, she thought with a mental sniff, a man with his kind of appeal to women was ever lonely.

She froze, hearing herself as though she'd shouted the last thought aloud. She'd fought that kind of stereotype all her life! If you were beautiful, your life must be perfect. *You* didn't have the problems other people had. Sheer beauty moved you into another plane of existence where teeth were always pearly white and everyone was blessed.

And now it turned out that she, too, was guilty of

harboring, somewhere deep in her subconscious, the same idiotic delusion.

Of all people, she ought to know that physical beauty didn't guarantee that you were never lonely.

"I..." Madeline blinked, gave her head a shake, saw immediately that he'd interpreted it as a refusal. "No! I mean, yes. I'd like that. I mean, dinner. Eating by myself tonight doesn't sound very appealing to me, either."

His eyebrow had gone up as she babbled. But instead of saying something sardonic, he smiled with a warmth that took her breath away.

"If you really manage to eat by yourself, you've done a better job teaching your cats manners than I have."

His smile tugged one from her. "'By myself' was an, um, intraspecies reference. I do tend to have a feline audience. Barely restrained from joining me."

His grin widened. "Do you ever wonder if they're speculating on what you'd taste like, assuming you deny them that last bit of chicken or pizza?"

"They're smart enough to know they can't turn a doorknob or operate a can opener. My two main functions in life."

Eric laughed, and her heart did a crazy flip. Turning, he crouched and opened the sliding door enough to stick his hand through. Hannah scooted under the curve of his fingers. Stroking her, he crooned, "I'll be back, little one. I promise."

When he withdrew his hand, the little gray cat opened her mouth in a silent meow of protest.

Madeline didn't know what effect this appeal had

on Eric, but it worked on her. "Why don't we take my car or your pickup?" she suggested. "Then come back here so you can take Hannah home right after dinner."

"Good idea." He shook his head. "All I need is another animal. This place could be dangerous."

And so are you, she thought. What she said was, "There's a reason I have seven cats. Hannah might have become number eight if you hadn't just bailed me out."

"You can't have her."

Another smile, crooked and sexy, sent panic spurting through her. Meeting him at the restaurant would have been safer. Less like a date.

But it was too late, because he gave Hannah one last pat, closed the sliding door and rose to his feet. "Shall we?"

"Sure," she said, "but it'll take me a moment to lock up."

"No problem." His eyes met hers, held them with something close to a challenge. "I don't mind waiting for you."

And if *that* didn't have a double meaning, she was a foot tall and had four paws.

She should have been mad that he'd suckered her into accepting this invitation. Instead, excitement quivered in her stomach and tiptoed up her spine. Maybe, just maybe, the fact that he'd repeated his invitation meant he was interested in *her,* not just her face and body.

What did it hurt to give him a chance?

CHAPTER THREE

"SORRY." ERIC HURRIEDLY lifted a box of used ampules from the front seat of the pickup. "Let me just stick this in the back."

"We could take my car."

Madeline Howard stood there looking like the Ice Queen, poised, cool, perhaps a tiny bit impatient. Petty of him maybe, but he wanted to be the one behind the wheel, to have some sense of control.

"Petty" wasn't the word. "Adolescent" came closer, he realized with a flash of amusement. Nonetheless, he unlocked the canopy of his truck and slid the box in. After locking the canopy again, he gestured toward the open passenger door.

"Madam, your chariot."

He was looking forward to seeing her hitching that tight skirt up enough to clamber into the truck. He had been so distracted by her deliciously long legs and the tantalizing curves just above them that he'd missed half of what she'd told him on their tour. To his disappointment, she ascended now with a ladylike grace and modesty that avoided exposing even another inch of those legs, clad in hose he'd have bet his last dollar was silk.

He slammed her door, shook his head—win some,

lose some—and circled to the driver's side, where he levered himself up easily onto the high seat. Starting the engine, he asked, "Where would you like to eat?"

"I like almost anything." Her nose crinkled, and a flash of mischief wiped away the Ice Queen image. "The starchier and fattier the better."

"You mean, you're not a fan of tofu and lentils?"

"I like those, too." She grinned unabashedly. "But I like Italian better. And Chinese and Thai and deep-fried fish and chips, and pizza and designer ice cream. So far, my cholesterol has stayed low—good genes—and I haven't worried."

He'd meant to avoid any remarks that might suggest flattery, but now he couldn't help it. "A woman with your figure doesn't diet?" he said incredulously. "My ex-wife counted calories in her sleep."

"I guess I'm lucky." Madeline looked down at her long legs, demurely crossed, and a small frown touched her face. "I'd rather not be overweight." Damned if she didn't sound doubtful.

Eric studied her curiously. What the hell was going on in that beautiful head? Every woman he'd ever met would kill to look like she did! He had to be misinterpreting, not hearing the profound gratitude she must feel at being able to eat however she wanted and not put on pounds.

His curiosity went beyond the idle; he vowed he'd find out even if it required the patience of a cat waiting for a mouse to emerge from a woodpile.

"How about Gianni's, then?" he suggested. "You can clog a few arteries with fettuccine Alfredo."

"Sounds good to me. If you like Italian."

"Only thing I don't eat is raw fish." He released the emergency brake and looked over his shoulder to back out. "Although in the interests of avoiding a heart attack at forty, I do watch the fat content."

"How far away is forty?" A smile enriched her voice. "Or is it rude to ask?"

"Not if you'll answer the same question." He didn't mind finding out that she was curious about him on a personal level. "I'm thirty-eight."

"Thirty-one," Madeline said promptly.

Older than she looked with that smooth skin. Eric was just as glad. He was starting to feel uncomfortably as if women much under thirty might well be from another generation. If they were closer in age to Garth than him, he figured he wouldn't have much in common with them.

As he turned toward Everett, they passed the Forland farm on the right; with an approving eye Eric scanned the peacefully grazing herd. A three-generation concern, it had a lower incidence of infection and disease than any other dairy farm around. As a result the Forlands were less profitable to their vet, but it wasn't as if he and Teresa weren't plenty busy, and he liked to see things done right.

"You take care of their cows?" Madeline asked, apparently noticing his interest.

Next thing he knew, she'd asked pointed enough questions to get him talking about mechanical feeding systems, the design of loafing sheds and the evils of manure ponds.

They were on the trestle crossing the river plain,

and the city reared against the skyline ahead when he broke off. "You shouldn't have gotten me started. I've probably ruined your appetite."

"Nothing ruins my appetite," she assured him. "I was interested."

She looked like she meant it. "Have you ever been married?" he asked abruptly.

Her gaze flicked nervously to his and then away. "No. Not even engaged. Why?"

"Just curious."

Out of the corner of his eye, he saw the expressions come and go on her face. She lost her internal struggle. "How long have you been divorced?"

"Five-and-a-half years," he answered willingly. "I just counted. My son called the other day. The...subject came up." And he still hadn't called Garth back.

"How old is he?"

"Twelve. He's coming for the summer."

He felt her gaze, heard the tentativeness in her voice. "Are you looking forward to that?"

"Sure I am," he said. "I miss him." Pride didn't let him admit that Garth apparently didn't miss him.

"Where does he live?"

They chatted about San Francisco. She owned to having spent most of her youth in Southern California and said that her mother still lived there.

"I sometimes go down there for Christmas."

Her tone was particularly inexpressive, as it had been when she mentioned living in L.A., and Eric wondered why. Obviously her relationship with her mother wasn't close, but more seemed to be going on here. He made no comment, however; it was too soon to pry.

Conversation over dinner stayed casual. They talked about the shelter, about the regular adoption days Madeline took the cats to, about the people who abandoned cats and the ones who took them in.

"We have a lady who must have rounded up twenty-five strays over the past couple of years. They were all in apartment complexes. People move and just leave their cats." Anger and sadness mixed in equal measure on her face. "We lend her a live trap sometimes. Mostly she spends hours feeding them and making friends until they let her catch them. She pays to have them neutered if they're not already, and then we take them in. Nearly all of them have been adoptable. A couple had been declawed, which made them especially defenseless. Most were sweethearts. To think that somebody just climbed in the car and drove away, leaving them sitting in the parking lot."

Eric shared her feelings. He'd had to euthanize a stray only the day before who'd been hit by a car. He'd have liked to smash the nose of the bastard who'd dumped that poor animal.

Eventually Eric worked the conversation back to the personal. "Had you ever had your own business before you opened Madeline's?" he asked.

"No, but I'd been a buyer and department manager in a big store." She named a pricey Northwest clothing store that had expanded into a dozen or more malls in the more upscale suburbs of Seattle and Portland. "Finally I got frustrated with decisions that weren't mine to make. I shared a house in the Greenlake area with a couple of other women, and that got old, too. I decided to strike out on my own, preferably not in the city. I wanted to live in a small town." She spread her hands. "Voilà. Truthfully I'm lucky it worked. Most ventures like mine don't."

As a small businessman of a different sort, he'd had many of the same problems and experiences she'd had. Probably they shared a few of the same clients. A couple of women who dressed elegantly were regulars at the animal hospital.

Madeline seemed happy to talk about business taxes, parking problems—the handful of slots on the street in front of her store weren't enough—and amusing or annoying clients. It wasn't until he steered the subject back to her that her animation became evasiveness.

"No, I didn't start as a clerk. And, to tell you the truth, I don't even have a college degree. I wish I had one in business or accounting. Actually—" she was no longer looking at him "—I was a model."

"New York? L.A.?"

"L.A." She glanced at her watch. "Oh, dear. I really ought to be going. Do you mind…?"

Subject closed. "Of course not," he said obligingly, and signaled for the check.

Conversation stayed light on the drive back to White Horse. At the shelter she produced a cardboard carrier for Hannah, who unhappily allowed herself to be ensconced in it.

Eric waited while Madeline locked up again, then strolled beside her out to their vehicles. Days were growing longer, but by this time of the evening dusk had painted the sky purple-gray. He deposited the carrier in his pickup, then turned back to Madeline, who'd hurriedly unlocked her car door and was using it as a shield.

"Thank you for dinner." Her voice was light, quick. Nervous. "Really. I enjoyed it. But I do wish you'd have let me pay my own way."

He shook his head and took a deliberate step closer. "I'm the one who wouldn't take no for an answer."

She ran a finger along the metal edge of her car door. Head bent, appearing to concentrate on the back-and-forth movement of her finger, she said, "I was rude when you first asked. I apologize."

"No. You were polite enough, despite what I said at the time. I made assumptions." According to Teresa, what he'd assumed was that any woman favored by an invitation from him would leap at it. Dammit, he wasn't *that* cocky.

Madeline apparently didn't want to talk about his assumptions. "Well, um, good night." Her shaky smile died when he took another step.

"Can we do this again?" he asked, voice deepening.

Now her fingers gripped that car door. She swallowed hard. "Again?"

He didn't usually have this effect on women. And he'd been so careful tonight.

He backed up a step, made his tone soothing. "Yeah, why not? The food was good, and I thought the conversation was, too."

She relaxed immediately, he guessed because of his physical retreat. "Yes, it was. Dinner again sometime sounds nice."

He knew better than to say, *What about tomorrow night?* Patience, he told himself. Take it slow.

He smiled easily. "Good night, then. Thanks for your company. And the cat."

"I'm sure we'll be talking," she said dismissively. A moment later she'd climbed into her car, started the engine and with a wave of her hand backed out.

He got into his pickup. Hannah uttered an inquiring mew. Eric poked a finger into one of the holes in the cardboard so that she could rub her soft nose against it.

"You want to know where we're going? Is that what you're asking? You'll like the answer. Home."

He used his signal, then turned out onto the road. Ahead red taillights flickered. To the cat he said, "Do you know why that lady is scared of me, Hannah? No? Well, I'll tell you what. I'm going to find out. When I do, I'll let you know."

Patience, he reminded himself.

HE'D INTENDED to shut Hannah in Garth's bedroom for a couple of days, to give her a chance to acclimate, but when he let her out of the carrier, she tested the air with her pink-and-gray nose, then hopped up on the bed and surveyed the room with quiet serenity. She wasn't going to hide under the dresser for a week. Eric decided to see what she'd do if he left the door open.

What she did was follow him. She wasn't completely confident; she crouched, ready for flight if necessary, and she oozed around corners, but she still came.

She slipped around a glass-fronted bookcase and almost tripped over Mannequin, who'd earned her name by rarely moving. If she hadn't occasionally wanted food and the kitty litter, he could have kept the cream-colored ball of fluff on a shelf like a stuffed animal, with no one the wiser. Now Mannequin lifted her head, blinked her magnificent blue eyes and allowed herself to be sniffed. The newcomer's tail puffed, but otherwise she didn't appear alarmed. She'd apparently read Mannequin's nature immediately.

The other cats seemed to be outside, which was just as well. Hannah could explore without fireworks. Leaving the two to get acquainted, Eric went into the kitchen, grabbed the cordless phone and dialed Garth's number. He might as well get it over with.

His son must have snatched up the receiver after the first ring. Sounding surly, he snapped, "Yeah?"

"It's Dad," Eric said mildly. "How are you?"

"Oh, I thought you were... I'm okay." His voice turned eager. "Hey, did you think about this summer? You didn't say anything to Mom, did you?"

"About your not wanting to come? No." Eric trailed Hannah, who'd lost interest in Mannequin, into the next room. "She told me she's remarrying. Chuck something?"

"Morrison," Garth said gloomily. "He looks like he's wearing a tie even when he isn't."

"You don't like him?"

"Not especially." Garth let out a heavy sigh. "As if how *I* feel makes a difference. *Mom* likes him. That's all that counts."

Eric watched the small gray cat explore. "Your mother thought you got along with him better before you found out they were getting married."

On a burst of anger his son said, "Having him around once in a while was okay. I don't want to live with him, all right?"

"You've got to take that up with your mom," Eric said. "And it sounds to me like it's too late. The wedding is only a few weeks away."

Garth sank back into gloom. "Tell me about it."

"I've sent the plane ticket to your mother."

"Well, I guess I have to come while they're on their honeymoon, don't I? Honeymoon," he sneered. "It's not like they waited for the wedding night or anything."

Eric forgot the cat. "What? You haven't been spying—"

"Dad," the boy said with exaggerated patience, "Chuck spends the night. It's obvious, don't you think?"

Yeah, he did think. On the other hand, it wasn't as if Noreen had had a string of boyfriends doing the same. After five years of life as a single mother, she'd met a man, gotten serious and was marrying him.

"Does that bother you?" Eric asked.

"You mean that she's having sex?"

Eric gritted his teeth. "Yeah, that's what I mean."

With the nonchalance of modern youth, his son

said, "Nah, not really. It's just that he's all she *thinks* about anymore. Everything I say she pops up with something Chuck said. It's like he's some expert on every subject. And she's always on the phone with him. She *giggles*."

Noreen had giggled when they first fell in love, too, Eric remembered suddenly. They'd had a lot of fun in bed that first couple of years. Out of it, too. For the first time since Noreen had broken the news, he felt a stab of loss.

"She must be happy."

"Shouldn't she care whether *I'm* happy?" Garth asked.

Had he ever been that self-centered? Eric wondered. He'd have to ask his mother.

"Of course she cares. She's just caught up in her new feelings." He took a deep breath. "That's why she needs this summer with what's-his-name. By fall, she'll be your mother again."

"They're dumping me on you, right? I'll bet you'd get out of it if you could," the boy said rudely.

"Your mother is *not* dumping you." Eric's mouth twisted. "And I wish you were here all the time. I'm your father. I don't want to give up this summer."

The silence fairly pulsated. "So I have to come!" Garth burst out. "Nobody cares what I want!" The phone crashed down.

Eric winced and turned his own off. That hadn't exactly been a success.

He thought back to the boy who had happily spent the summer with him the year before. Garth had been eleven then, but he didn't look much different than he had at ten or nine or even eight. He hadn't yet had a real growing spurt and was being left behind by his classmates, about which he'd become sensitive. He was skinny, thin-faced, his blond hair cut short by his mother. His blue jeans invariably had grass stains or rips at the knees, and he liked T-shirts with funny sayings.

In his school picture, taken last September, he'd looked a little older, but his blue eyes still held the solemn quizzical expression he'd had since he was two. Noreen and Eric used to tease him that his first word was "why?" Unlike some kids, he really wanted to know. His best quality, though, was his empathy. He always thought about other people first. He was the one to worry about the squirrel running across the power line, or the dog down the street whose owner left him chained outside twelve hours a day.

Still brooding, Eric went looking for Hannah. The family room was quiet and still. When he opened the garage door, he heard a scrabbling sound. Poking his head around, he saw her tidily burying something in the kitty litter. Good. She'd found it and knew what it was for.

She hopped out and headed straight for the food bowls, in another part of the big garage. Eric let the door quietly close. Obviously she was comfortable with kitty doors, too.

Garth was a terrific kid, he told himself. Okay, he was nudging adolescence, and he was having a hard time dealing with his mother's remarriage. It was normal for him to be pretty much fixated on himself for a few years here. That didn't mean he'd really changed, not inside where it counted. The boy had been blowing off steam tonight, that was all. Give him a month or two, and he'd accept his mother's new marriage.

Any lingering uneasiness Eric put down to his own anxiety, which rose like a barometer every year at this time as he worried about whether he and his son could take up where they'd left off. His nervousness invariably vanished the second Garth popped out of the airline passenger tunnel and gave him a grin so incandescent it would have glowed in the dark.

They'd always gotten along great. No reason this summer would be any different.

MADELINE PUSHED her grocery cart down the pet-food aisle. The damage to her budget mostly came here.

Thinking about pet food turned her mind to the shelter and then to Hannah and logically to Eric Bergstrom, DVM. Amazing how often it had worked that way. She'd be embarrassed for anyone to know how frequently she went over their dinner conversation, replaying every glance, the couple of brief touches, his suggestion at the end that they do it again.

Again? she'd parroted, as if she had no idea what he was talking about. She still blushed, thinking about her gaucheness. It would be amazing after that—especially considering her response to his first invitation—if he really did call.

Of course, she didn't care that much one way or the other.

"Madeline!" A female voice brought her out of her brooding. The pretty dark-haired woman pushing her own loaded cart wasn't going to distract her from thoughts of the veterinarian, however; Jess Kerrigan had dated Eric a couple of years ago and was sister-in-law to his partner, Teresa.

"Hi, Jess. I've been meaning to call you." Meeting Eric had made her think about Jess and realize they hadn't gotten together in a while. "Would you like to have lunch someday?"

"Love to," her friend said promptly. "How about Tuesday?"

They arranged a time and place. As Jess moved past, Madeline began to select flavors of canned cat food from the shelf and stack them in her basket.

Jess stopped her cart so suddenly toilet paper toppled out. She swore as she bent to pick it up, then apologized. "If I'd been behind the wheel of my car, I'd have probably rear-ended someone. But seeing you just gave me an idea. You guys have kittens right now, don't you? Steph's birthday's coming up and it occurs to me I could get her one. We only have Atlas, you know, and he's fifteen if he's a day. Not much fun for the girls. I'm sure he'll hate a newcomer, but all he does is sleep and eat, anyway."

"Could I talk you into two?" Madeline asked. "Kittens are so much happier with another one to play with. Especially since they'll be alone in the day while you guys are in school and working. Raised together, they'll stay friends all their lives. Besides, even though it's Steph's birthday, this way the girls could each have their own.''

"Thus avoiding squabbles." Her friend gave her a look. "You're good at this."

Madeline widened her eyes innocently. "Finding the right homes for cats?"

"Suckering people into taking one. Or in this case, more than one."

"They really *are* better off in twos."

"The grocery store and the vet will be happier, too." She sighed. "I've been trying to talk Teresa into offering a family rate. Doesn't that seem just?"

"Absolutely." Careful to sound casual, Madeline said, "I did persuade them to give the shelter a special rate. Dr. Heyer retired. Yesterday Eric came for the grand tour." She smiled. "He adopted a cat."

"You *are* good," Jess said admiringly.

Madeline's grin broadened. "I know." She laughed. "Actually Hannah managed it on her own. She courted him very affectingly."

"Smart cat."

Even more casually Madeline said, "Don't I remember that you dated him?"

"Uh-huh." Jess leaned comfortably on her cart. "Two or three times. I think it was too soon after my divorce. He'd smile—you *have* seen him smile?—I'd get goose bumps, and then I have this horrible attack of guilt. It was like I was still married and contemplating an affair. Really strange. Somehow we didn't hit it off that well, anyhow." She shrugged. "He's great with the horses, though. Best equine vet around. And very nice to look at."

"I'd never met him before."

Jess grinned. "Let me guess. He asked you out."

"I said no." Madeline edged her cart out of the way of a grandfatherly type shopping with two pre-schoolers. One was singing in a piercing voice. The other stuck out his tongue as he passed.

Jess turned her head to reciprocate as soon as Grandpa's back was turned. Then, expression unrepentant, she said, "He's a brat. Steph baby-sits him." She gave her head a shake. "Did I hear you right? You actually rejected the gorgeous Dr. Bergstrom? You *did* get a good look at him first?"

"Yes and yes." Madeline hesitated, then confessed, "But I'm weak. He asked again yesterday and I succumbed. We had dinner."

"And?"

"I had a good time." How tepid that sounded, she thought in disgust. Should she admit she got goose bumps, too? "He was nice. Not what I expected."

Surprisingly Jess nodded with apparent satisfaction. "You haven't dated anyone since I've known you." She made a face. "Not that there are very many single men around who I'd even get in a car alone with. Never mind ones who are glorious, heart-stopping, hormone-zapping—"

"I get the idea."

Jess's blue eyes were suddenly serious. "Just so you know—he's kind of a playboy. I mean, don't bother getting serious."

"Warning duly noted." Madeline gave a careless smile. "He may not even call again."

"Now that he's set eyes on you?" Her friend patted her arm. "He'll call."

She thought about demurely saying that her looks weren't anything special, but was afraid she'd sound like she was fishing for a compliment. Besides, it would be less than honest; she knew she'd been blessed with great bone structure, flawless skin and eyes and hair that pleased the eye. She could still be modeling if she wanted to. If she hadn't grown to hate being valued for nothing *but* her cheekbones and skin and eyes.

"Maybe," she said, and wondered if Eric Bergstrom was capable of seeing beyond those features. Or were they precisely what he, too, valued in a woman?

CHAPTER FOUR

"I'M HOME," Garth called, slamming the front door behind him.

Nobody answered. Had Mom gone somewhere? That'd be surprising; lately she didn't trust him—her words—to be home alone. Just because she'd caught him lighting up a cigarette in his room. He'd done that because he knew it would make her mad. Why not? At least then she noticed him for a minute or two.

Their San Francisco town house was narrow and tall. The bedrooms were on the third floor. As he bounded up the stairs, he heard voices drifting down. Women's voices. Mom was in her bedroom with someone else.

Instead of going into his own room, Garth moved quietly down the hall and stopped just outside her door, which stood a few inches ajar. He couldn't see anything, but he heard a long breathy, "Oooh! Noreen, it's glorious! Chuck'll think he's the luckiest man alive when he sees you coming down the aisle."

His mother giggled like a junior-high-school girl. "Oh, Frances, I hope so! *I* feel so lucky."

Garth gagged. So she'd found some guy willing to marry her. What was so lucky about that? Chuck

Morrison had money, but he was balding on top and getting a paunch that hung over his belt—he really, really liked to eat. He took Mom to these fancy restaurants, and the rest of the time she fussed in the kitchen so she could surprise him with some gourmet delight like *blanquette de veau*—which was still eating a big-eyed calf, even if the name was French. Or—get this—squid in ink sauce. Mom had actually sat there in the kitchen on her tall stool, humming under her breath and squishing ink sacs in a sieve and then making a sauce out of it. And she called him picky because he wouldn't eat it. Chuck, of course, had exclaimed in delight and dug right in. Mom told Garth that she was trying to cook more seafood because she was worried about Chuck's cholesterol. Big surprise. And she was *lucky* to have him?

"I'm home," Garth repeated, and pushed the door open.

One of her closets had mirrored doors. Mom stood in front of them in her wedding dress admiring herself. She'd spread it on the bed for him to see a few days before, but on her it was different, not just stiff fabric. Rose-colored—at least, that was what Mom called that dark pink—the dress was really simple and shimmery. Long and straight, it sort of molded to her waist and hips and thighs more than he liked noticing when they were his mother's. Her best friend, Frances, who Garth used to think was okay until she introduced Mom to Chuckie, sat on the edge of Mom's bed, her hands clasped in front of her as though she was gazing adoringly at a Monet or a

Picasso. Frances didn't even turn her head to look at Garth.

Mom didn't ask how his day was, either. She held out her arms and rotated gracefully on tiptoe. Her cheeks were flushed and her eyes shone. "So, what do you think?"

He would never have admitted it to his friends, but he knew she was beautiful. He'd been proud of her when she picked him up at friends' houses or went to school functions with him. But he'd never seen her like this. She…glowed. Because of Chuckie.

And because she was ditching her son for the summer so she could be alone with the love of her life. All she'd do was cook. And go to bed with Chuckie, something he didn't want to think about.

He jerked his shoulders and said in a bored tone, "It's okay."

Her face dimmed a little. "Sweetie, I wish—"

"That I'd call Chuck 'Daddy'?" Garth curled his lip. "I suppose we're having something gross for dinner?"

"I thought…since it would just be the two of us…"

Chuckie must be busy. Otherwise, she couldn't have lived without him long enough to have dinner alone with her son. She'd even brought the guy to a school parent night.

Garth gave her a flat stare. "I'm going over to Dave's."

"Why don't we go out to dinner? Your choice." Her smile was as bright and fake as the gold-painted poster-board crown he'd worn in a school play. "I'll pick you up about six?"

"I'm not that hungry."

Mom's eyes became steely. "I'll pick you up, anyway."

He shrugged and left, throwing his book bag in his bedroom as he passed. Maybe he wouldn't *be* at Dave's when she came at six. That'd show her how much he wanted to spend time with "just the two" of them. Like he was supposed to be excited because she might actually talk to him for once, instead of to Chuckie with an occasional vague question his way when she remembered he existed.

He bumped his mountain bike up the basement steps and out the front door. What would happen if he scared his mother enough? Would she call Chuckie and weep in his arms? Or would she be so glad to find him she'd change her mind about shipping him off for the summer?

Garth figured it was worth a try.

A DOZEN HORSES, ridden English-style by solemn-faced teenagers, pranced as they waited for the gate to the arena to be opened for their amateur class. Among the shades of cream and dapple gray, the few chestnuts and blood bays stood out. Yesterday's rain had left the ground muddy enough to splatter the gleaming hooves and slender legs of the Arabians.

"Hot dog?"

"Hmm?" Madeline turned from admiring the horses to Eric, who'd paused in front of the concession stand.

"Are you hungry?" he asked, nodding toward it.

She realized that mixed with the smells of manure and sawdust and mud had been the seductive aroma of hot dogs and warm pretzels and mustard.

"I'd love a hot dog. Or even two. And maybe a pretzel. And, um…" She contemplated the offerings. "A licorice rope—I love those, have you ever had one?—and a lemonade."

He grinned, that slow mischievous smile that twirled her stomach on some kind of internal spit. "And I thought you'd be a cheap date."

"I warned you I like to eat," she reminded him.

"So you did."

As they stood in the short line, the gates opened and out loped a Western class, bits jangling and Stetsons worn low. In went the English horses and riders, numbers pinned crookedly to their backs.

A few minutes later, loaded down with food, Eric suggested they go in and sit down while they ate. "We can watch a few classes, see what's coming up, then wander through the barns."

Madeline smiled happily. "This was such a good idea."

She wasn't sure why coming to a horse show at the Evergreen State Fairgrounds in Monroe hadn't inspired the same anxiety in her that a dinner date would have. It just seemed so much more relaxed. More like something friends would do together. And they didn't have to stare at each other across a candlelit table and think of witty things to say.

Even the topics they'd covered on the drive here had been uncomplicated. Jess Kerrigan was showing one of her Arabians later this afternoon in a class for amateur owners. Teresa Hughes and her kids planned to come. That subject exhausted, Eric talked about doctoring horses, more his specialty than Teresa's, although she'd become increasingly interested, he said, as the whole family got involved with 4-H and cow penning.

"I wish barbed-wire fences would go the way of bell-bottoms," he'd said, shaking his head. "I treat more cuts than anything else, it seems. A horse will paw at the fence and rip his foreleg open, even get the damned wire wrapped all the way around the pastern."

"I hate to tell you this, but bell-bottoms have come back in style."

"What?" He'd shot her a glance. "You're kidding."

"Regrettably, no."

"All right, I wish barbed wire would go the way of...oh, hell, how about disco?"

"That's probably safe. For a few years."

Now they found a seat partway up the bleachers overlooking the arena. They watched as the teenagers and their horses trotted and cantered on command from the judges, who stood in the center with clipboards in hand.

"Reverse," the announcer said, and the riders dutifully swung their horses in neat U-turns so that they were cantering the opposite direction around the perimeter of the ring.

"I like that dapple gray," Madeline said between bites of her hot dog. "The one with the boy—that one." She pointed as the pair passed in front of them, the canter perfectly collected, the horse's neck arched and the pale mane foaming over the boy's quiet hands.

Eric took a swig of his coffee and nodded. "And the bay."

The gray took home the huge blue rosette, while the bay inexplicably got left out of the honors. Eric grumbled amiably while they argued about who ought to win out of the next batch, a yearling halter class. The lanky youngsters fidgeted and rolled their eyes and flared their nostrils as the judges solemnly circled them and made notes on their clipboards.

After studying the program and agreeing that they wanted to be back in time to see Jess and the costume class afterward, Eric and Madeline followed the yearlings out, watching them dance skittishly on impossibly slender legs while their trainers or owners made soothing noises.

"What fun," Madeline said a little wistfully. She'd been as horse-crazy as any other girl, but instead of having a chance to indulge in her dream, she'd spent her childhood as far from green pastures as you could get: among the concrete building blocks and freeway cloverleafs of Southern California. She'd spent it, not on horseback, but in front of a camera.

"Do you ride?" Eric asked.

"I've only been a few times," Madeline admitted. "You know, rent a horse for an hour. The kind of thing where you plod along a trail in a dutiful line behind the wrangler. Or do I mean baby-sitter?"

"Want to learn?"

She studied him warily. "Do you mean it?"

"I have a horse, you know. A quarter-horse mix, nothing fancy, but she's easygoing. When you get a little more confident, I can borrow one of Teresa's or Jess's and we can go trail riding. The real thing, not a plod."

Excitement bubbled in her, as if she were a girl again being offered this same chance. But she wasn't a girl anymore; his offer sounded so long-term, as though she'd be over at his place—or wherever he kept his horse—often. As though he took for granted her compliance.

And she still didn't know why he wanted to spend time with her. Was it only her face and figure that interested him?

"I...wouldn't mind trying it," she said, figuring she wasn't committing herself to anything.

"Good." He smiled, took her hand and drew her into the first long barn.

She'd always liked the smells of manure and wood shavings and hay and leather soap. Absurdly conscious of the warmth of his hand engulfing hers, she wandered with Eric down the aisle lined with stalls. Horses popped their noses inquiringly through the bars, and Madeline used their lure as an excuse to withdraw her hand from Eric's. Wary of the horses' big yellow teeth, she tentatively stroked velvet muzzles.

Show ribbons festooned some stalls, and a few silver bowls were proudly displayed on wooden chests. Owners groomed the handsome animals cross-tied in the sawdust-floored aisle. A few of the riders, wearing flowing robes, were tying ribbons into their horses' manes and loading them down with jeweled tack and tiny silver bells and colorful satin draperies for the costume class to come.

Eventually they found Jess, already leading a dainty gray mare out of the barn.

"Hi!" she called. "Did you come to cheer me on?"

"Absolutely," Madeline said warmly. "Are your girls here? Oh, there they are. Hi, Sarah. Hi, Steph."

Teenagers now, the two dark-haired girls smiled and said, "Hello, Ms. Howard. Hello, Dr. Bergstrom."

"Either of you showing?" he asked.

"I am tomorrow," the older and taller of the two said. "It's my first time in anything bigger than the Stanwood Fair." She made a face. "I'm really nervous."

"I've seen you ride. You'll do great." His smile would have brought a blush to the cheeks of any female between ten and eighty. It didn't fail with Sarah.

"Thanks, Dr. Bergstrom."

This time Madeline and Eric sat with Jess's daughters and Teresa Hughes and her kids. Jess rode with flair and dignity and left the ring clutching the blue ribbon.

Almost immediately the ten entrants in the costume class swept into the arena, the horses moving in a high-stepping trot that made robes and manes fly. The crowd cheered. Madeline found herself smiling, although she couldn't imagine any self-respecting Arab nomad wearing purple satin or robes in a rainbow of velvet. The riders might have looked silly, had the horses not been so magnificent. They cantered and galloped and pranced, ducking their heads and preening as though they knew well their own beauty.

The rider and snow white stallion in purple satin won; second place went to a bay bedecked in brilliant green and black.

Madeline sighed in contentment. Eric smiled. "Once you learn to ride, the world's your oyster. You, too, could don ten yards of gaudy fabric and gallop around the ring."

"They were more artistic than that," she protested. "But no, thank you, I don't think it's for me. I'm too shy and retiring." Not entirely true, but she'd come to dislike the idea of putting herself on display for any reason.

Eric opened his mouth as though to say something, but changed his mind. She almost pressed him, but refrained; she was afraid she knew what he would have said. *You'd look beautiful.*

Steph popped up with a comment just then, and they left the arena with the girls, any private conversation impossible. On the way home Eric put Madeline at her ease by asking when she was doing the next adoption day. Here she was on confident ground; as he'd said himself, the way they felt about animals was the one thing they did have in common.

"Tomorrow," she told him. "That big new pet-supply store in north Everett, near the Safeway. They don't sell animals, bless their hearts. Eleven to three. I'll be surprised if I don't place eight or ten kittens and turn down half a dozen people who want one just because it's little and cute. You know, the kind that lose interest when the poor animal has the nerve to grow up.''

''Yeah, the ones who dump their pets out on a deserted road and figure they can take care of themselves.''

''I'd like to 'take care of' the former owners,'' she said.

He looked at her with interest. ''Do you think you're successful in screening out that kind of person?''

''Reasonably.'' She wrinkled her nose. ''I know we mess up sometimes, because someone I thought was really nice will end up bringing a cat back for the worst reasons. But most of the time...well, I hope. The best way to judge is by asking about the animals they've owned in the past. If their nineteen-year-old cat died of kidney failure six months ago and now they're done with their mourning enough to be ready to choose another one, I can be pretty sure they'll be good owners. On the other hand, if they used to have cats but are vague about what happened to them, I tend to make excuses.'' She sighed. ''I just hope that tomorrow a few people come along who are willing to consider an adult cat. I have a couple of especially nice ones.''

His mouth crooked. ''I'll bet you always say that.''

''Well—'' Madeline laughed ''—maybe. The

trouble is, we always have a dozen or more waiting for adoption, and I like them all. People dump the sweetest animals. I just don't get it.''

"I don't get it, either.'' He was silent for a moment. "Maybe I'll stop by. I'm off tomorrow. Can I bring you lunch?''

A shiver of something between fear and anticipation traveled up her spine. He was pursuing her. And she still didn't know why.

"I usually skip it when I'm doing an adoption. Too busy talking. But that would be nice if you keep it simple. A bagel with cream cheese or a hamburger....''

He gave her a sidelong amused glance. "Oh, come on, you must want the milk shake and fries and onion rings and apple pie to go with it, don't you?''

She punched his arm. "I'm not that big a pig!''

"Did I use that word?''

"I know I ate a lot today. But I don't *always*. I'm like...like a big cat in the wild. When I eat, I stuff, then I go a long time before I eat again.''

"Right.''

"You don't believe me.''

He grinned. "Yeah, actually I do. If you ate like you did today all the time, you'd be built like that cat at the shelter.''

Not beautiful was what he meant. A hot spurt of temper made her retort too sharply, "Jackson is handsome. Stately.''

"From a medical standpoint, obese.''

"So he's ugly, I suppose.''

Eric raised a brow. "I didn't realize we were talking aesthetics here. I didn't say he wasn't handsome. Sure he is. But he's still fat. He eats too much. You obviously don't. I wasn't implying anything else."

He sounded exasperated and she didn't blame him. She'd gotten paranoid, assuming the entire world was focused on appearances because the part of it she'd grown up in was. And, she reminded herself, because most men seemed focused on women's figures and faces. Including Eric Bergstrom. Still...

"You're right," she admitted. "He's fat."

"Saints be praised! The woman conceded a point!"

"Do I detect some sarcasm?"

"Never." He put on the turn signal. "This street?"

A moment later they pulled up in front of her tiny old house, a source of great pride and joy to her. Like the others on this block, it had been built as company housing by one of the giant lumber mills in the early years of the century. The houses had eventually become shabby, mostly rentals; a few had been razed to make way for bigger houses or, down at the corner, a five-unit apartment building. But now most of the ones along her street were being restored to their former charm by young families or single professionals who commuted to Bellevue or Seattle daily. Madeline had painted hers sea-foam green with white trim. A white picket fence marked the boundaries of her front yard. She loved that white picket fence. She'd always wanted one.

Today it represented refuge.

"Thanks," she said, hand on the door handle. "I had a great time."

Formidably handsome, Eric smiled. "I'll walk you up."

A flutter of panic raised her voice an octave. "Oh, you don't have to."

Now that smile had become implacable. "I want to."

He was going to kiss her. She knew it. And she wasn't ready, hadn't the slightest idea how she'd respond, how she *should* respond. Dear God, how had she let herself get so out of practice, so...*naive?*

But it was too late to argue; he was already out of the pickup and circling the front. Hastily she scrambled down. Heaven forbid that he think she was waiting for him to help her out. By the time she slammed the passenger-side door, Eric had opened her front gate, which passed under a white-painted arch covered with a tangle of honeysuckle and royal purple clematis.

On the way up the walk, Madeline unzipped her waist pack and grabbed her keys. She had the door unlocked and open before she turned to face Eric. One cat hopped from the porch railing to rub her ankle and go in; two others shot out of the house and down the steps as though they were convicts escaping the joint.

Only peripherally aware of the feline activity, Madeline said, "I really did have a lovely time today. Thanks."

He took a step closer; as if they were dancing, she took one back. Creases formed between his brows

and then he inclined his head, as though acknowl-
edging her wishes.

"Unless something comes up, I'll see you tomorrow."

Madeline agreed and, refusing to let herself watch
him as he headed down the walk, gently closed the
door. Safely alone, she let out her breath with a long
shuddering whoosh.

He was a stubborn man. She hadn't deliberately
set out to be difficult, but she knew she was. Why
wasn't he calling one of the many single women out
there who would be delighted to date Dr. Eric Bergstrom, who would be eager for his kisses?

Why her?

And how would she feel if he did give up, if he
didn't show tomorrow and didn't call again?

ERIC OPENED his door to find Hannah sitting just inside, gazing up at him with patient eyes. Waiting.
There was something so trusting about her and yet
also so vulnerable that a rush of painful feelings
filled his chest. He knelt and picked her up.

"I'm home, Hannah," he murmured. "It's okay.
I'll come home every day and you'll be here every
day. Forever and ever. I promise. Got it?" All the
while he stroked, his fingers finding the places that
brought forth a contented purr.

"You know something, sweetie?" He set her on
the floor.

She looked up at him, the end of her gray-and-
cream tail swishing, as though she were asking,
"What?"

"Madeline Howard reminds me of you. It's the eyes. She wants to trust me, too, but she doesn't. And she's less willing to try than you are."

Damned if he knew why he cared, why he was fighting his way through her occasionally thorny defenses. The easy answer was that he wanted her; she was a beautiful woman, and his body reacted to the very sight of her—a smile, the way she tipped her head, the long graceful line of her back—with a hunger that went deeper than it ought when he hardly knew her.

But there was something else. Pity, maybe, he thought, but felt disturbed at the idea. Sympathy might be a better way to put it. She seemed lonely. Occasionally she'd start talking, as she had that day about her mother, but he sensed that she rarely opened up about herself.

Or maybe, he conceded wryly, he just liked the idea of being her savior, as he was Hannah's.

Whatever the reason, he wouldn't let a few scratches keep him from trying to get to know her. Tomorrow was as good a time as any. Besides, he looked forward to seeing her work her magic on the innocent pet owners who set out to shop with no intention of acquiring another cat.

He arrived, lunch in hand, just about noon the next day. The setup at the store was terrific, he saw immediately as the automatic doors glided shut behind him. Just inside to the left was a glassed-in room with cages, much like those used by pet stores that sold cats and dogs. This one was for the exclusive use of shelters like Ten Lives.

A dozen or more cats filled the cages. A banner that proclaimed the shelter's name draped a long table outside the glassed-in room. A volunteer sat behind it, earnestly talking to a young couple who had a Sheltie on a leash. Madeline was inside the glassed-in room, her back to him, a cat slung over her shoulder. She was simultaneously petting and gesticulating, and he saw the balding man she spoke to laugh.

Twenty feet away from the table the greyhound-rescue organization had set up for their own adoption day. Five of the large elegant dogs lay peacefully on blankets, while their handlers sat chatting with shoppers interested in knowing more about the racing greyhounds culled from the track. Eric had done some vet work for the organization; he admired the effort they made saving these dogs that would otherwise have been euthanized when they didn't run fast enough.

Eric nodded at the volunteer behind the table, who smiled brightly and said, "Go right in. The cats love to be visited."

He didn't correct her impression that he might be the next sucker to take a cat. No, he thought, amused, he was the last sucker. He'd already taken his cat home.

He pushed open the door, and Madeline spotted him immediately. She gave him a quick smile, flashing dimples, but her gaze returned to the balding man, her hand never stopping its stroking of the Russian blue that lounged in her arms. Lucky cat.

Even the black jeans and the T-shirt that, below the picture of a grumpy cat, said, "I *am* smiling," couldn't hide her subtle curves and natural grace. Her hair was wound into a knot on the crown of her head, but tendrils were escaping to curl over her forehead and along her slender neck. Eric's hands itched to brush them back, coincidentally feeling the silk of her skin and the pulse beneath.

The balding guy, his back to Eric, was still talking. Eric tuned in at the point where he was saying, "That cat spent every day on the back of the couch staring at the bird in its cage. Worried us, I can tell you. But darned if we didn't come home one day from work and find that bird loose and the cat cowering under the bed. He never went near the cage again. We figure the bird spent the day dive-bombing him."

Madeline's laugh rang out and Eric smiled in pleasure at the sound. How had a woman who liked people and animals as much as she did become so guarded much of the time?

"Well, I'm not sure Misty here would ever bestir herself enough to contemplate eating a bird. If you want a lap cat, she's for you, but don't count on her chasing toys or mousing in your garden shed."

"You say she's five or six?"

"That's our best guess." Madeline handed over the cat, who wrapped her front legs around the man's forearm and settled in cozily.

He bowed his head, looking down at her. After a moment he said in a low gruff voice, "Since the wife passed away, my place seems so empty. Our last cat was hers more than mine. He was nineteen when he died. Her health wasn't too good by then, so we didn't replace him, but now…"

"Cats are wonderful company," Madeline said gently.

"Well...all right." He turned and Eric could see his face. He smiled ruefully down at the gray cat, which was purring nonstop. Misty knew which side her bread was buttered on. "I'll take her."

Madeline reached for a flattened cardboard carrier and said, "You won't be sorry. She's a honey. Let me set this up for you to take Misty home in. I do have some paperwork for you, but it won't take long."

The fellow, perhaps in his midsixties, filled out the form, wrote a check and took a shopping cart off to load up on cat food and litter. In her carrier, Misty went with him, presumably so she could be consulted. Eric suspected that some catnip and a plush bed and maybe an elaborate carpeted scratching post would be included in the final tab. Love made a man want to open his wallet.

Madeline introduced Eric to the other volunteer, a young woman named Linda, who then left to run a quick errand. Things had quieted down, so once Linda was gone Madeline and Eric sat down behind the table and opened the bags he'd brought.

"You did buy a milk shake!" She sounded delighted.

"Chocolate okay?"

"Chocolate is nirvana."

They'd adopted out two cats already, she told him, a six-month-old kitten to a couple who wanted a companion for one they already had, and now Misty.

"Misty liked him, I could tell," she said content-edly. "Nice guy. He's stopped to look at the cats and chat before. I knew that eventually he'd fall for one. He gave us a hundred dollars."

A skinny blond girl, maybe ten years old, darted in the automatic doors and up to the table. "Do you have any kittens today?" she asked anxiously.

"A whole litter." Madeline pointed through the glass behind her.

"Oh!" A radiant smile lit the girl's face. "I'll be right back!"

Sure enough, in less than a minute she was hauling her parents through the doors. They looked willing enough, however, and a younger girl clutching Mom's hand was bouncing in eagerness. They all poured into the room, followed by Madeline, who gave a last wistful look at her half-eaten cheeseburger.

Eric watched through the glass, unable to hear the conversation but able to tell what was happening. They picked out one kitten right away, a playful black one with white feet that he remembered neutering just that week. It appeared that the girls liked an orange tabby, also, but the mother preferred a second black-and-white one. The kittens got passed around between family members, while Madeline hovered protectively. Eventually they settled on the black-and-white female, and Madeline gently deposited the two kittens in another carrier. Her hand lingered inside for a moment before she closed the top.

"And you've already bought everything you need?" Madeline was asking as she pushed open the door and came out with the family behind her.

"Yes, we've been looking for kittens for a couple of weeks. A farm had some, but they had runny noses," the mother said, "and so I wasn't sure…"

"Probably just a cold, but you never know." Madeline sat down beside Eric and began explaining Ten Lives's procedures and expectations. "We do ask that you not declaw cats you get from us, but I already told you that, didn't I?"

The mother began filling out the form. "Yes, but we wouldn't do it, anyway. It must be painful."

The youngest kid squatted and poked her finger in a hole in the side of the carrier. She giggled. "His whiskers tickle!"

"You'll have fun with them," Madeline said, smiling at the child. "These two are really playful."

Linda arrived back just then and went into the glassed-in room with a man in a business suit.

The family left with their kittens, and Madeline shot to her feet. "Tell Linda I'll be back in a minute," she said, and hurried away. Her voice had sounded a little choked, and after only a brief hesitation, Eric went after her.

Already well down the aisle between displays of dog toys and bowls, she turned and disappeared. At the back of the store, he saw a hall that said, "Rest rooms," and then beyond, "Employees Only." On a hunch, Eric pushed through the "Employees Only" door. Inside was a huge stockroom, deserted but for Madeline, who stood with her back to him.

"Are you okay?" he asked.

She swung to face him, and he saw she was crying. She wiped her eyes, blew her nose firmly, then nodded. "I fostered those kittens, you know." She sniffed. "It's dumb, but I cry every time I place one I've had at home. I feel like I'm giving away my own cats."

He stepped forward and carefully wiped away some fresh tears that clung to her lower lashes. "Yeah, but thanks to you they have a chance at a good life."

"I know." She blinked hard. "It's worth a few tears. But I'd just as soon no one saw."

"Including me?" With a will of their own, his hands closed on her shoulders, but he resisted drawing her into his arms.

She gazed up at him, eyes huge and shimmering. "No." Her voice was just audible. "You understand, don't you?"

"Mmm-hmm." Now he did pull her close.

She laid her head on his shoulder and wrapped her arms around his waist. For a moment she relaxed completely, and he moved his mouth against her hair, reveling in its life and vibrancy, in her momentary trust.

When she lifted her head, she didn't step back. Triumph and wanting surged in him, but tangled with nervousness he didn't understand. He didn't stop to try. Instead, he bent his head and kissed her.

CHAPTER FIVE

MADELINE STIFFENED momentarily, but couldn't make herself back away. He brushed her mouth again, moved to her eyelids where he kissed away the tears, then went back to the beginning. The way he nibbled gently at her lower lip felt amazingly sensual. It made her want more—more pressure, more heat, more...something. She hardly knew what.

With a sigh she relaxed and parted her lips. A groan vibrated in his chest; she felt it as powerfully as if it had come from her, perhaps because her breasts were flattened against him. His grip shifted so that he no longer held her as a friend might, but as a lover would. One hand was splayed on her lower back, pulling her more tightly against him. His other hand wrapped around her neck, his thumb persuading her to tilt her face upward, his fingers caressing, stroking, seeking out the suddenly frantic beat of her pulse.

And his mouth hardened, captured hers. She felt his teeth against her lip; his tongue touched the tip of hers. Her knees almost buckled. Warmth flooded her belly, and for the first time in her life, she understood the urge to have sex.

With a whimpering sound she pulled back, frightened by this new awareness. For a moment his hands tightened, as though he wouldn't let her go, and her panic grew like a fire worked by bellows.

Behind Eric, footsteps came down the hall. One of the double swinging doors whooshed as it opened. Madeline heard the sounds, but her brain made no effort to figure out what they meant. Eric lifted his head, and she thought only that he'd finally sensed her resistance.

It wasn't until a young male voice said awkwardly, "Uh... I'm sorry, but customers aren't supposed to be here," that awareness parted the fog.

Her cheeks flooded with heat. Discovering she was gripping Eric's shirt, Madeline let it go and took a quick step back, grateful he released her so quickly.

"It's...it's me," she said inarticulately.

The twenty-year-old in the orange vest blushed as fiercely as she did. "Madeline! Oh. I didn't know...that is, I'm sorry. You can...I mean, I shouldn't have interrupted." He backed away, eyes bulging. "I thought..."

Eric kept a hand on her arm. It steadied her, for reasons she didn't want to analyze.

"That's okay, Jon. I promise we weren't back here necking." Yes, they were, her conscience objected. She ignored it, forcing a shaky smile. "I just placed a couple of kittens I was especially fond of. It always makes me a little weepy. Eric was...was being nice."

The young man stopped backpedaling. "I'm sorry. I know how that is. We had a litter of puppies once— our dog is a purebred Dalmatian, see, and we took her to this breeder. Only then when it came time to sell the puppies, it was really hard. I mean, I'd named them all, and—'' He stopped and blushed again. ''I'm sorry. I came in to get something, but I don't have to.''

''I'm leaving,'' she said with a more natural smile. ''I just needed a minute. That's all.''

Jon stood back to let them pass. Madeline couldn't look at Eric. They walked silently side by side to the front of the store. Linda was in the room with the cages, engrossed in a conversation with two older women. Madeline's knees gave way, and she dropped into one of the folding chairs behind the table. There, right in front of her, sat her half-eaten hamburger and milk shake.

Eric didn't sit, just leaned over the table, his hands flat on the top. His voice had an undertone she couldn't identify. ''I feel like I'm fourteen and the principal just caught me making out with my girlfriend behind the gym.''

A giggle came out like a hiccup. Madeline clapped her hand to her mouth, but she couldn't stop. Soon she was laughing so hard it hurt.

Finally she managed, ''I feel like my kid brother caught me.''

He winced. ''Ugly thought.'' But the deepening of one crease in his cheek let her know he was suppressing amusement, as well.

Her laughter died. ''Oh, dear. Are you hopelessly embarrassed?''

''Not me.'' His gray-green eyes held an intensity that shook her, even though there was something peculiarly reassuring about it. "I'll kiss you in public anytime."

Because of how I look? she wanted to ask, but chickened out.

"Thank you, kind sir," she said, instead.

One eyebrow went up. "My male ego will be wounded if you don't reciprocate."

If she wasn't scared to death of men, relationships and herself, it would have been a great kiss. Maybe, just maybe, if he kissed her again she would have the courage to find out where it led.

How to express any of that? "Ditto," she said a little shyly.

A smile lit his eyes, softening the intensity. He leaned farther across the table. "Is that an invitation?"

She licked dry lips. "I—"

A man stopped beside Eric. Over her shoulder, he scanned the glassed-in room. "You got dogs?"

"I'm afraid not." She sounded almost normal. "Ten Lives is a shelter for cats only."

He grunted and moved toward the greyhounds. But Linda was coming out, followed by the two older women.

"I'd better get going," Eric said, straightening. His expression was bland, but his gaze lingered on her face. "Like to try riding tomorrow after work?"

So soon. Her pulse leaped. She'd seen him yesterday and today, and now he wanted them to get together tomorrow, as well. He was pushing hard. And she could feel herself toppling. A somewhat worrisome analogy, considering what men and women tended to do prone.

"Sounds good," she admitted, trying for breezy and coming up breathless. "Do you want to give me directions?"

"I'll pick you up this first time. Five-thirty?"

"I can manage that."

"Good." His smile was almost as sensual as his kiss. His mouth was so darned sexy. "Tomorrow." He nodded and walked out.

Thank God the door was close or she would have made a fool of herself staring at his retreating back. And a very nice sight it was, with his lean hips and long legs in worn jeans and his broad shoulders covered by a faded gray T-shirt.

She let out an unconscious sigh when the doors swallowed him, and then reluctantly turned to the two older women.

"They'd like to adopt Fiddlesticks," Linda said.

Madeline ignored the knowing looks on all three faces and drew the binder toward her, saying briskly, "Oh, that's wonderful. Now, did Linda discuss our policies?"

IN THE CAR, utter silence reigned. Garth fidgeted and stole glances at his mother, who drove without once looking at him, her face set in rigid lines. It wasn't like her. When he hadn't come home last night or called to let her know where he was, he'd figured that today she would weep or storm at him or *something*. Not thank Will's mother for keeping him, then quietly tell him to get in the car, they'd talk about this later.

"Did you call Chuckie?" he asked, putting a sneer in his voice.

"I said we'd talk about this later." Her voice was cold enough to make him shiver. "I meant it."

She turned into their parking garage, smiled at the attendant as though nothing was the matter, then drove up three levels to their spot. She got out, locked her side and started toward the elevator.

"My bike—"

"Leave it," she snapped.

From habit he locked, too, then hurried after her. He wanted to saunter, pretend he was cool with whatever was bugging her, but he couldn't. He was scared. He hadn't known you could do something to your parents that was unforgivable, unless maybe you murdered them with an ax or drowned your baby brother, but he had this sick feeling that his mother wasn't going to forgive him for what he'd done.

The elevator took them to street level. The Walk sign showed a red hand, but Mom marched across, anyway, even though a car had to slow for her. She went up the steps to their town house without once checking to see if he was behind her.

He guessed she didn't care if he ran away. Maybe he should. That'd show her.

His steps slowed, and he thought he might puke. It wasn't like he had anyplace to go. Will's mother had thought he had permission to spend the night. Next time she'd check. The parents of most of his friends would, and they sure wouldn't let him stay without permission.

He'd seen kids living on the streets; San Francisco was full of them. They had tattoos and sneers and a way of swinging their hips when they walked, but they were also dirty and skinny. He knew the stuff they had to do to get money to eat.

"Go to your room, please."

Jeez, he'd followed his mother in the front door like he was some little puppy dog. But he didn't know what else to do.

"If you want to yell at me..." he said desperately.

"I don't want to speak to you at all right now." She almost looked like she hated him. "Do as I ask."

Garth stared at her. She stared back without cracking. He opened his mouth to beg, but pride wouldn't let him. Without another word, he whirled and took the stairs two and three at a time. He slammed his bedroom door so hard a pile of CDs fell off the shelf above his desk.

Anger and fear and nausea all balled up inside him, as if a huge tumor was growing in there, swelling and eating him up. He hated it, hated his mother, hated Chuck, hated his father. Hated himself.

A word came out of his mouth, one he'd never said before because even he thought it was kind of disgusting. But saying it felt good. He said it again, more loudly, then shouted it. At last, in anguish, he threw himself on his bed and cried.

"HERE." ERIC CUPPED his hands. "Give me your left foot and I'll boost you up."

Madeline stroked the quarter horse's powerful brown flank. The horse turned her head to gaze at this new human with one thoughtful eye. Tentatively Madeline said, "She's awfully tall."

"So are you." Eric's grin was heartless. "Think of it this way. Your feet will only be—" he flattened one hand next to the stirrup "—this far off the ground. You could easily hop down from something that height."

"Most somethings that height are inanimate. They won't throw me off." Madeline took a deep breath. "Okay, okay. It's just that the whole idea is a little scarier than it seemed when I was fifteen."

He didn't give her a chance for second thoughts. She'd barely lifted one foot off the ground when he scooped his hands under it and threw her up. Desperately clutching the saddle horn, Madeline swung her leg over the horse's back. The mare shifted and Madeline squeaked.

"Relax." Eric wrapped a hand around her booted ankle. "Honey's a big baby. You're safer on her than you were driving over here."

How true, Madeline decided a moment later, after Honey had proved her kindness by patiently waiting for some signal from her rider. Madeline's heartbeat slowed. Looking down at Eric's silky blond head, she had no doubt that he was the biggest danger here to her.

She'd been absurdly nervous about today's date. They would be alone at his place. Now that he'd kissed her once, would he expect things to progress from there? But so far, he'd been friendly, not touching her unnecessarily. Only an occasional glint in his gray-green eyes warned that he was aware of her as a woman.

"You said you'd been on a horse a few times?" he asked.

"Uh-huh." She made a face. "Years and years ago."

"Well, Honey neck-reins. To go right, you gently lay the reins across the left side of her neck." His big hand closed on hers and demonstrated. A tingle traveled up her forearms. "To go left, vice versa."

She nodded, and to her secret disappointment, he took his hand from hers.

"To stop, pull back. Not hard—you don't want to hurt Honey's mouth."

Another docile nod.

"To go forward, you squeeze your legs. Harder if you want to trot. Give her a boot if you have a good grip on the saddle horn and plan to gallop. Maybe pen a steer."

She shot him a look. "Sure."

That wicked grin flashed across his lean face. "Go for it."

"All right." Madeline took a deep breath, looked around from her position high atop the horse's back and thought about what she would have given for this chance not so many years ago. Well, now she had it, and she was determined to enjoy the experience.

She softly clicked her tongue and squeezed with her heels. Honey ambled forward along the fence line. The sunlight was warm, the rocking gait relaxing. By the time the two had circled the entire pasture, Madeline's confidence was growing.

"Can I trot?" she asked, when she arrived back where Eric was now sitting on top of the split-rail fence, his heels hooked on the bottom rail.

"Damn straight." He instructed her to let her body stay loose, her hips move with the lurch of Honey's back. "Sort of like—" He stopped abruptly, a crease deepening in his cheek. "Never mind."

With a jolt Madeline realized in what activity a woman's hips went with the flow, so to speak, and a flush warmed her cheeks.

Eric pretended not to notice. "Don't worry if you bounce around at first. It's really not as easy to fall off as you'd think."

"How comforting," Madeline said, her embarrassment fading. She knew how to do sex, the mechanical part at least. With luck, riding the horse would be more fun. Which wouldn't necessarily be saying much. As she urged Honey into a trot, she felt a flicker of amusement, imagining what Eric would think if he knew how she rated the two activities.

Amusement didn't survive the first meeting of her rear end with the hard saddle leather. It snapped her teeth together. Her hands frantically gripping the horn felt slick with sweat. Nothing would have made her let it loose long enough to pull back on the reins. Oh, God. Every bone in her body was rattling. The ground was so far away, and she knew she was going to hit it any minute. She almost wished she would— at least it was standing still.

But she didn't do a swan dive for the grass; after a while she realized she was basically bouncing straight up and down. Okay. She squeezed her eyes shut. What had Eric said? *Relax. Let your hips move with the horse's back.* Still holding tight to the horn, Madeline eased first one muscle, then another. She let her lower back go loose, felt her hips flex forward, back. Eric was right. It was rather like...

She opened her eyes. Hey, this wasn't half-bad! Not smooth, exactly, but not bone-crunching any-more, and...well, exciting. If a trot was this much fun, imagine what cantering would be like!

Did she dare?

Honey took the decision out of her hands. The reins were lying slack, and she apparently felt frisky. Or maybe *her* joints were rattling, too. With a lurch that rocked Madeline back in the saddle, the mare swung into a canter that whipped Madeline's hair about and stung her eyes.

Honey went right on by Eric, who'd jumped from the fence. Her eyes watering so that he was blurry, Madeline unclamped one hand from the horn and waved. She saw the flash of white teeth as he laughed. She grabbed the horn with both hands again and let exhilaration rip through her.

By the time she'd made it around the pasture yet again, she felt like a seasoned horsewoman. Poised in the saddle, back straight, in control. She did, how-ever, have to let go of the horn to pull on the reins. Honey obligingly came to a stop right in front of Eric.

He took hold of her bridle and grinned up at Madeline. "You're a wild woman."

"That was...it was...it was fun!" How inadequate that sounded.

"Walk around one more time, and then we'd better call it quits for today, or you'll be too sore to get out of bed tomorrow."

"Walk?" she said in disappointment.

"Walk," he repeated firmly. "Honey needs to cool down."

"Oh, all right," Madeline said.

"Try putting your foot back in the stirrup first, though," he suggested.

So much for the seasoned horsewoman.

She and Honey ambled around the pasture, enjoying the sun and the view of White Horse, still snow-covered, at the head of the valley. *What a heavenly place to live!* she thought, without letting herself analyze whether she meant White Horse or this particular spot—Eric's home.

To her surprise, when she slid off the mare's back, her legs wobbled and she leaned gratefully against Eric when he came up behind her and wrapped an arm around her.

"I haven't been on her that long!" she protested.

"Half an hour. The inside of your thighs will feel it tomorrow."

Was he kissing the top of her head? If so, she didn't mind. She felt...carefree. Young and foolish and reckless. Wisps of exhilaration still floated through her like memories or dreams. She should live a little, shouldn't she? If Eric kissed her, this time she was going to find out if she could feel anything more than she had the few times she'd experimented with men after achieving adulthood and independence from her mother.

He turned her, one hand still holding Honey's reins. As he looked down at Madeline, a smile warmed his eyes.

"I think you're a natural."

"Really?"

"Really." His voice roughened. "Your body moves beautifully."

She ought to hate his choice of words. Captured by the heat that had burned away the smile in his eyes, she hardly noticed. "Thank you," she whispered.

His head bent. "May I kiss you?"

"Oh, yes," she breathed, and lifted her mouth to meet his. Naturally.

LIFE CHANGED. Madeline felt like Sleeping Beauty, awakened by the prince's kiss, and the comparison frightened her. Even as a girl, she hadn't liked fairy tales where the princess was passive. Helpless. Needed rescuing by a prince. Yet the comparison was apt; she'd been in a kind of deep freeze, and Eric had thawed the ice that trapped her. And just as in the fairy tales, he had kissed her only because he found her beautiful. Or so she feared.

What the tales didn't say was that the thaw hurt. She was filled with churning emotions: regret, renewed anger, apprehension and outright fear. She'd missed so much by holding herself aloof, too much ever to make up for. And this thing with Eric was an idyll, not a forever-after. That knowledge was a knife edge, even though she didn't know yet whether she even wanted forever.

After that first riding lesson, she had a second on Thursday and a third longer one on Sunday. Of course, each time they'd had dinner together, and they'd had to talk about something, so she found herself telling him more about her life than she could remember sharing in years. About her mother and the distance between them—although she didn't admit that she'd deliberately chosen the distance to avoid the alternative: confessing to her anger and bitterness.

Late Monday afternoon Eric called her at the store to cancel their lesson. "A pickup pulling a horse trailer got in an accident," he said briefly. "It's pretty bad."

"I'm sorry," she said. "Phone me later if you'd like."

Feeling at loose ends, Madeline went to the shelter. Joan and the cleaner were gone for the day, and the place was the next thing to spotless. Notes on cards taped to cages let her know that all the cats who required medication had received it. In the kitten room she got out a toy—feathers at the end of a string tied to a stick. Only a couple of the older kittens even looked interested.

She picked up October, a five-month-old orange tabby, and kissed him. He turned his head away and squirmed in her arms.

"Well, phooey on you," she said. "I'm going home."

She'd eaten out so much this past week her cupboards were well stocked, but nothing she saw inspired her. Finally she decided she wasn't really hungry. She popped a grape into her mouth and picked up the TV guide.

Spring was the season of reruns. A trip to the library sounded like too much effort. She ended up vacuuming and mopping the kitchen floor, then paying bills. All the while she imagined the scream of injured horses, splattered blood, flailing hooves. Had people died? Would Eric have to put down any of the horses? He hadn't said how many there were. She wished he'd call.

By bedtime, he hadn't. Madeline was dismayed to realize how empty the evening had seemed without him, how aimless she felt. But her life had been complete! She'd been contented. Now she needed a man to fulfill her? Toothbrush poised, she glared at herself in the bathroom mirror.

The face that looked back at her photographed superbly, although she knew much of that had to do with peculiarities of the camera lens and tricks of light. To her own eye, without makeup she was more the ugly duckling than the swan. Her cheekbones were too prominent, her lower lip annoyingly pouty, her forehead so high it left this big blank space above the arch of her brows. Why did men find it so seductive? Lord knew, at heart she was more like the cliché of a spinster librarian with mouse brown hair pulled tightly back into a bun.

It scared her to think that all Eric saw was the image the cameras captured. In the midst of teenage angst, she'd actually considered scarring herself or doing something else equally drastic to mar the facade, to make sure people saw *her*. She was grateful she hadn't acted on her desire to deny that she was what people saw. Even so, she'd never become comfortable with her own face or body. The little girl who'd reveled in being told she was pretty had grown into a twelve-year-old who'd come to the painful realization that her only value as a human being was her looks. It had to be, if her looks were all even her own mother cared about.

She closed her eyes so that she could no longer see herself in the mirror. Memory of that kiss—the one after her first riding lesson—flooded through her, followed by memories of the others: the times his mouth was wholly gentle, the times his fingers bit into her arms and his hips shoved urgently against hers, the times he looked down at her and smiled. At her? Or in satisfaction at the prize he'd captured?

How would she ever know?

Madeline opened her eyes and stared fiercely at herself. She was more than a face that had appeared on the cover of *Seventeen* and *Mademoiselle*. More than a body that had pirouetted for countless photographers. More than the girl whose mother had ruled against the junk food other kids ate, the sleepovers where the girls giggled far into the night, the sports where they challenged themselves, all based on how they would affect her appearance. She couldn't put on weight. Heaven forbid she get a pimple. No sleepovers; why, she might look tired for tomorrow's shoot! Soccer was out; she might get bruised or even break a bone. She had to take enormous care to avoid sunburn or too much tan. She had to look perfect, because only her beauty—and the money it brought in—counted.

Madeline brushed her teeth in a hurry and braided her hair. Bedside lamp on, she moved Peaches off her pillow and climbed under the covers. Maggie grumbled at her intrusion, then snuggled cozily against her legs. Madeline was just reaching for the lamp switch when the phone rang.

She made herself wait for a second ring, then picked up the receiver and said cautiously, "Hello?"

"Did I wake you?" Eric's voice was rougher than usual, without its customary insouciance.

"No." She sat up to the accompaniment of more grumbles from the fat tortoiseshell and wedged a pillow behind her. "Did you just get home?"

"Yeah." His tone was flat, the weariness almost tangible. She imagined it weighting his shoulders and carving lines into his face.

"Was it…was it bad?"

"We had to euthanize two." He took a ragged breath. "It was a big rig, Thoroughbred mares and foals. We set a couple of legs—got the horses in slings. It'll depend on how patient they are. Teresa came out, too, and Dr. Lee from Lake Stevens. He's an equine specialist."

Madeline made an inarticulate noise and listened as he described the horror. The decisions had primarily been theirs; the driver, a trainer, had been in shock at the hospital where his wife had been taken with internal injuries.

"The foals?" she asked.

"One died. Whole damn rig rolled. One stall was just...crushed."

Eventually he talked himself out. He sounded less sick and more leaden, tiredness fogging the sharp colors of the scenes he described to her.

"Good God," he said finally, "this was just what you needed! A cheerful bedtime story. I shouldn't have dumped on you."

"Isn't that what friends are for?"

His voice quieted. "Is that what we are?"

Everything went still inside her. "I hope so."

"I have a little more in mind."

"And...does the 'little more' rule out friendship?"

His answer meant too much. It was too long coming.

"No." He sounded surprised. "No. I used to wish—"

He broke off, and she heard nothing but the sound of his breathing. She prodded, "You used to wish what?"

"You don't want to hear about my marriage."

Actually she couldn't think of anything she'd rather hear more about. "Yes," she said firmly, "I do."

"Noreen didn't like me to talk about anything sad. She'd just cry and what was the point? she'd say. If I vented anger, that upset her. We communicated fine about practical stuff—still do—but we didn't just *talk.* Too much was forbidden.''

"That's sad.''

"Yeah.'' Eric was silent for a moment. "Doomed our marriage, I guess.''

"Of course it did!'' Feeling indignant on his behalf, she spoke more vehemently than maybe she ought to have. "If you can't really, really talk to your husband or wife, who can you talk to?'' As if *she* was any expert!

"Yeah, well.'' Another pause. "Noreen's getting married again. Next week.''

Madeline reached for Benjamin, her soft flame-point Siamese, and began stroking, needing the contact. "Do you mind?''

"Nah,'' he said promptly. "Too many years. I hope it works for her.'' Not even the tiniest bit of regret colored his tone.

"I'm glad,'' Madeline said softly.

His voice lowered. "It's nice to know you care.''

Oh, God. Panic came on a burst of adrenaline. This was getting too serious, too fast. *Do something!* she ordered herself.

She tried to sound teasing. "Oh, I don't know if I'd put it that strongly.''

In the silence that followed she would have liked to see his face. She was also glad she couldn't.

"Okay,'' he said at last, agreeably. "You don't care.''

She squeezed poor Benjamin too hard. He squeaked and wriggled free of her arms. "I didn't say that!''

He laughed, a genuine warm chuckle. "I'll tell you what—I won't pin you down on what you did say. Or more to the point, what you meant. We'll let it go for a while."

Time to end this. Before she said something *really* stupid. "Then...good night."

"Pleasant dreams." He must be mocking her, the huskiness in his voice a way of making sure her dreams were about him.

Which, of course, they would be. Since, despite common sense, she did care.

CHAPTER SIX

THE BROAD WING of the 747 tipped to reveal Mount Rainier below. Garth pressed his nose to the thick glass of the window. He used to think the volcano looked like a Sno-Kone without the flavoring: a huge snowy white dome. He'd imagined licking it, the icy crystals tingling his tongue. Now he thought maybe a woman's breast, white and cold. He'd been noticing breasts a lot lately; the girls in his class were definitely getting them, some faster than others. Mary Aiken looked practically like Dolly Parton. When she went by, every boy's head swiveled.

Slowly the 747 straightened, and Garth couldn't see Mount Rainier anymore. In hardly any time, though, the plane began its descent toward Sea-Tac, the airport south of Seattle. Dad would be waiting. He and Mom had probably arranged it: the captive handed over to the attendant, who wouldn't take her steely eye off him until his father gripped his arm on the other end.

Every other year, he'd been so excited by this time that, when the light blinked on, he could hardly bear to fasten the seat belt and just sit still as the engines roared and the plane banked. He'd be craning his neck looking out the window, fidgeting, hands on the belt catch so he could be the first to free himself and race down the aisle. In the terminal, he'd throw himself into his father's arms.

What a little kid he'd been, Garth thought disparagingly. Like coming up here was some big treat. As if anybody gave him a choice. He'd even had to have a baby-sitter, for Pete's sake! Some days he'd go with Dad on his farm calls or hang around the clinic, but sometimes Dad couldn't take him, or Garth didn't feel like it.

Last year he'd become friends with Mark Hughes, the son of Dad's partner. Garth wondered what Mark was like now. Did he listen to cool music and wear shorts so big they hung down practically to his ankles? Or was he still the good little boy, into soccer and school? Like Garth was going to spend *his* summer kicking around a dumb ball or riding bikes as if they were eight years old.

With a faint thump, the wheels touched the runway and the pilot applied the brakes. Before the plane even stopped, people unclicked lap belts and began stretching. Garth stayed in his seat when everyone else jostled into the aisle, heading toward the exit or reaching for stuff in the overhead compartments. Let Dad wait.

He still hadn't moved when the attendant paused by his seat. "Are you okay?"

Garth gave her a flat stare. "Why wouldn't I be?"

She returned a sunny smile. "Can I get anything down for you?"

He wondered what her boobs would look like with

her arms stretched above her head. "Uh, yeah. I think my bag's up there."

The two little Mount Rainiers on her chest lifted and flattened when she stood on tiptoe and groped overhead. After a moment she peered down at him. "I don't see anything up here."

"Really?" He played dumb. "Wait a minute. Gol. I guess it's down here. Sorry."

"No problem." She turned sideways to let a couple of people squeeze past. "I'll bet your father's waiting eagerly."

Hidden message: she wanted to hand him over. He rolled his eyes and shrugged. There wasn't any point in sitting here, anyway. Unless they'd let him stay on the plane and fly wherever it was going next. Hawaii, maybe. Or Alaska. He briefly fantasized getting off in some exotic place all by himself, his mother's credit card in hand.

But the attendant was still waiting. And probably the plane would just be parked for the night, or else it was going to someplace deadly, like Kansas City or Chicago or Dallas.

So he slouched out of his seat and down the aisle. He was the last one off the plane, except for the crew. Up the long tube to the terminal and then he popped out. And there was Dad, a big fake smile on his face.

GOD ALMIGHTY. Shocked, Eric stared at the boy, who stared back. Garth? Could this kid really be his son? What the hell had happened to him in the past year?

His jeans were about ten sizes too big, the crotch bagging around his knees, the tattered dirty hems dragging on the floor. The sneering face of a rap singer known for his particularly violent lyrics adorned the front of a T-shirt just as sacky.

Well, okay, Eric knew oversize clothes were in style for boys. Garth was twelve, old enough to care about such things.

But sweet Lord, what about the head, shaved bald, and the earring in one lobe? And the expression that echoed the rap artist's?

"Garth?" he said uncertainly.

The kid's lip curled. "You expecting someone else?"

Yeah, my son, Eric wanted to say. He settled for, "You've changed."

Jerking his shoulders, the boy said, "So? It's been a long time."

"You've grown," Eric said. That seemed safe. Garth must be five foot eight now, an alarming leap toward manhood from last year's child.

"Mom says I'll be taller than you." The idea seemed to give the boy pleasure in a disquieting way, as though stature would give him superiority.

"Maybe. She's tall, too." When Garth didn't say anything, Eric shook his head. "Why are we standing here? Let's go get your luggage. Want me to carry that bag?"

The boy grunted something that might have been no.

"How was the wedding?"

"It sucked."

Eric glanced at him. "What? Your mom tripped

on her train and fell flat on her face? The groom didn't show?"

"I wish."

"She'd tripped?"

"That *he* didn't show." They entered the subway-like people mover, and the doors glided shut. Garth grimaced. "But Chuckie always shows. As long as Mom feeds him, anyway."

"Is he overweight?" The image of Chuck Morrison, ideal man, as obese held a certain appeal, Eric was ashamed to discover.

"Just...soft." His youthful state of fitness without effort allowed Garth to be disgusted. "He likes to eat."

"Your mom's a good cook."

"She *used* to be!" Garth burst out. "You ought to see the stuff she cooks now! It's all weird. Like—" He broke off suddenly, his expression closing. Apparently he'd realized he was being confiding.

Eric pretended not to notice. "She always did like to experiment. You didn't mind when you were little."

"Yeah, well, if she'd put squid in ink sauce down in front of you, would you have eaten it?" the boy challenged.

Parents should stick together. "I would have, uh, taken a bite. You never know..."

"Oh, right." His son sneered.

Glad of an excuse to change the subject, Eric nodded toward the revolving belt that carried a planeful of luggage. "Which is your bag?"

From then on, Garth answered Eric's questions in

monosyllables. An hour later, just breaking free of
Everett's rush-hour traffic, Eric flexed his fingers on
the steering wheel and glanced at his son, whose face
was averted. The boy was slumped in the passenger
seat, nibbling on one fingernail and staring out the
window. A few minutes ago he'd pulled a Walkman
from his pack and put on headphones, shutting out
Eric's increasingly desperate attempts at conversation. Despite the headphones, a monotonous bass
beat thudded through the pickup cab.

Why the hell hadn't Noreen warned him? Eric
wondered, his anger growing with every mile that
passed. Had Garth changed so slowly she hardly noticed? Or was she afraid he'd opt out of his parental
responsibility if he knew what a fun summer lay
ahead of him?

"Goddammit," he muttered, "she should have
known better."

And he couldn't even call her. She was off on her
honeymoon to Tahiti. No phones in the grass hut
presumably. Although something told him that
Chuck Morrison, CEO, had booked a somewhat
more upscale room. The new wife just wanted to be
incommunicado. Eric looked again at their son. Who
could blame her?

Actually she *had* left an emergency number. But
he didn't figure this was an emergency. Yet.

At home he carried Garth's suitcase to his bedroom, unchanged from last year. The seemingly per-
petual sneer never left the boy's face as he looked
around at the books he'd left on the shelf, at the
mountain bike Eric had put in here the day after

Garth went home last August, at the sports posters he'd reverently hung two summers ago.

"You don't care if I tear those down, do you?" Garth asked.

"Of course not. It's your room."

The boy didn't move. "Why did you make me come?"

His answer mattered. "Because I want to be part of your life."

His son turned a heated stare on him. "You mean, you want me to be part of *yours*. This isn't *my* life."

There was some truth to that. Enough to make Eric uncomfortable. Was it fair to Garth to haul him across three states every summer and expect him to slide into a new slot as if he fit perfectly? Did Garth really need a father, or was he, Eric, being selfish in putting his son through this?

"It could be," he said quietly. "You used to make it yours."

"You and Mom never gave me a choice."

Pain stabbed his gut. "Are you saying you'd never have come if we had?"

"Maybe." Garth hunched his shoulders. "I don't know. I just don't want to be here now."

"Where do you want to be?" Eric made his tone brutal. "On your mother's honeymoon?"

"I could have stayed home alone," his son said fiercely. "Or with a friend. Mom's not going to be gone that long."

Keeping his voice level, being the adult he theoretically was, took an effort. "As far as I'm concerned," he said, "you're not here because of your mother's remarriage. I love you. I want to spend time with you. This is the only way I can do that. I know it's not perfect. I know it would be a hell of a lot easier on you if your mother and I had stayed married. But we didn't, so it's this or nothing. I would have missed my father if he hadn't been part of my life. I hope that, looking back, you'll feel the same.'' He went to the door. In exactly the same tone, he added, ''Now, I'm going to put dinner on. Why don't you unpack?''

He was just opening the refrigerator when the phone rang. Snatching it up, he snapped, ''Yeah?''

''Dr. Bergstrom?'' The voice belonged to one of two women who ran the extremely efficient message service the veterinary hospital used.

He shoved the refrigerator door shut and leaned against it, rubbing the back of his neck. ''Hi, Beth. What's the bad news?''

''Dr. Hughes is already out on a call and Jed Rice just phoned. His shepherd—you know, that big black one? She got hit by a car. She's in a bad way, he says. He's on his way to the clinic with her right now. Dr. Hughes is up almost to Darrington. She'd be nearly an hour even if she turned around now.''

''Okay,'' Eric said, resigned. As busy as he and Teresa were getting, maybe they needed to hire a young vet as an assistant. ''Tell her to finish up there. If Jed phones in again, let him know I'll meet him at the hospital in ten minutes.''

A moment later he knocked on Garth's door. No answer. He swore under his breath and went in.

The suitcase still sat, untouched, where Eric had

left it. Garth was sprawled on the bed, headphones on, eyes closed. For an instant Eric thought he was asleep, until he saw that Garth's fingers drummed a beat on the bedcovers.

"Garth."

The boy muttered some lyrics under his breath. His eyes remained closed.

Eric shot a glance at his watch, then crossed the room and touched his son's shoulder.

Garth's eyes opened. He yanked off the headphones and glared up at his father. "What?" he asked belligerently.

"Can you get yourself something to eat? One of our clients is on his way into town with a dog that was hit by a car. I don't know how bad it'll be or how long I'll take, but I'm guessing an hour minimum."

Garth jerked his shoulders. "Sure." He settled the headphones back over his ears and added flippantly, "Have fun."

Anger churned in Eric's stomach, but it was depression as heavy as a winter cloud cover that rode his shoulders as he drove to town.

Jed had beaten him there. Eric unlocked the door, and the two men staggered under the weight of the huge shepherd as they carried her from the back of Jed's canopied pickup into the hospital.

She was bleeding and in shock, and one leg was obviously fractured. Eric started an IV, sedated her and took an X ray. The break was clean enough to set.

"You'll have to keep her off it," he warned. "It

won't be easy. Start by planning to carry her up and down any stairs when she has to go outside. Somebody will have to watch her to make sure she doesn't do too much. In a few days she's going to want to put weight on the leg, and she shouldn't.''

The farmer, a brusque man in his early fifties, had his head bent as he stroked the big dog. ''It's okay, girl,'' he murmured. Lifting his head, he said, ''We'll manage. Got the grandkids here for the month. They can take care of her. Bonanza here, she's the wife's baby. Well, hell.'' He ducked his head. ''Mine, too. Nicest dog we ever had. When they were tots, the grandkids climbed all over her. Won't hurt 'em to pay back now. I can handle the trips outside.''

''Then we'll go ahead.'' Eric reached for the razor to shave Bonanza's foreleg.

Two and a half hours had passed by the time he quietly let himself in the front door of his house. Hannah was waiting, and Eric almost tripped over Mannequin, splayed on her back in the middle of the floor.

''Dammit, cat,'' he muttered, ''why can't you find a nice couch like everyone else?'' She blinked at him and didn't move.

No sign of Garth; he was probably still closeted in his bedroom. Trailed by Hannah, Eric went to the kitchen first, to see if Garth had gotten anything to eat. Either he hadn't or else he'd cleaned up after himself. Eric was betting on the first alternative.

He turned to leave the kitchen, then stopped. The house had an open floor plan; separating kitchen and family room was a long wet bar, which he seldom used except to eat breakfast when he was in a rush. He hadn't entertained in a month or more, and he almost never had a drink by himself. But one of the cupboards was slightly ajar. The magnetic latch hadn't quite caught or had bounced back open.

Eric squatted in front of it and swung the door the rest of the way open. Hannah slipped inside to check out the wine rack, empty but for a couple of bottles, and a miscellaneous collection of hard liquor: a good Scotch, half a bottle of vodka, gin for those who partook. He was certain there'd been a bottle of bourbon, as well. But no longer.

He made sure his footsteps were quiet as he went down the hall. He knocked; a moment of silence was followed by a hurried, "Just a minute!"

Eric opened the door. Garth was bent over, hand under the bed. The window was flung open, but even so the unmistakable smell of cigarette smoke lingered.

Garth's head shot up. "Hey!" he exclaimed indignantly.

"So you smoke, too." Eric's voice was hard. Parent, coming down heavy on his kid. Who'd have thought?

"Sometimes." The teenage shrug was sullen. "Big deal."

"Does your mother know?"

"Yeah." But Garth's eyes wouldn't meet his. Translation: Noreen had caught him a few times and forbidden cigarettes.

"Neither of us smoke, and for a good reason. In the long run it kills you. When you're eighteen and have moved away from home, you can make your own decision. Right now you're twelve, and my responsibility. You will not smoke when you're here. Is that clear?''

Garth let loose with an obscenity.

Eric ignored it. "This is your home. You can help yourself to food any time you want. But the booze—'' he leaned over and snatched the bottle of bourbon from under the bed before his son could do any more than jerk in involuntary protest ''—is off-limits. I think you already knew that, didn't you?''

"I just wanted to taste it.''

"Let me repeat—you're twelve years old. Alcohol is illegal for you to 'taste' until you're twenty-one. And by God, you won't drink in my house.''

"Oh, it's *your* house now. And I'm your *responsibility* now. That's all I am, isn't it?'' the boy cried, flinging himself facedown on the bed. When Eric laid a hand on his shoulder, Garth rolled away from it. "Just leave me alone!''

Eric hesitated, feeling inadequate. How was he supposed to handle this? Maybe he should have been more buddy-buddy, talking about how he knew Garth wanted to be a man, but how booze and tobacco weren't the way to be one.

Too late. And the anger simmering in his belly wouldn't have let him, anyway. Garth wasn't stupid. He hadn't been testing his own manhood; he'd been testing his father's control over him.

"Fine,'' Eric said. "I'm going to warm up spaghetti and make a salad. If you want some, you know where to find it. And me.''

In the kitchen he slammed a pan down on the stove too hard, considering its glass surface, and knocked the milk container on its side as he yanked the bowl of leftover spaghetti out of the fridge. Dumping it into the pan, he turned the burner to high, then cursed as he grabbed the dish towel to mop up the pool of milk.

What in hell was he going to do with Garth? In the past year, the boy he'd known had vanished, replaced by a sullen defiant teenager who didn't want to be here. Setting limits was great, but how did a parent enforce them? He couldn't watch Garth day and night; he'd have to leave him alone some of the time. Good God, did he even want the boy with him at the hospital or on farm calls? What would Garth do—sneak out behind the barn for a cigarette while Eric was doing preg checks?

"Noreen," he said softly, "why didn't you send an instruction manual?"

Easy answer: because she didn't have a clue what to do with their son, either. Maybe Garth wasn't too far off in guessing that his mother was dumping him for the summer.

Teresa's daughter, Nicole, had been a pain in the butt when her mother had first moved to White Horse and bought into his practice, he remembered. Maybe Teresa would have some advice.

Anything was worth trying, before he irredeemably blew his relationship with his son. Eric reached for the phone and dialed.

PATRONS AND WAITRESSES bustled around Madeline and Eric's table at the Main Street café. His chili steamed, untouched, in front of him; a toothpick still impaled her turkey-and-swiss-cheese sandwich. Madeline listened to his tale with her elbows on the table and her chin cupped in one hand.

"I locked the alcohol in a cupboard in the garage. Garth conspicuously did *not* throw out his cigarettes. And that was just the first day. In fact, he didn't come out of his room except to use the bathroom, and then he slammed the damn door so hard a picture fell off the wall." Eric leaned back in the booth. His laugh held no amusement. "We're hardly speaking now. He holes up in his bedroom, and I utter dictatorial pronouncements. Parenting at its finest."

Touching had never come easily for Madeline, unless she was reaching for something four-footed and furry. But now instinct had her stretching out her hand and taking Eric's across the table. "It sounds like he's asking for it. What else can you do?"

The tightness with which he returned her clasp belied his wry tone. "Abdicate?"

"Plenty of parents do." Including her father, who had been absent throughout her childhood. He'd sent checks for her birthday and Christmas. She'd seen him twice after he and her mother divorced when Madeline was four. He'd died a few years back, unmourned by her.

"What does he want from me?" Baffled pain filled Eric's eyes. "Or doesn't he want anything?"

"Of course he does!" She squeezed even harder. "He wants love and security and…and…acceptance."

Eric sighed heavily. "God help me, I do love him, and I can't believe he doesn't know that. And, hell, what do I accept? His music? Smoking? The pants bagging around his ankles?"

Feeling a spark of humor for the first time, Madeline tilted her head to one side. "Now wait a minute. You're starting to sound like our parents' generation. Did *your* mother and father like your music and what you wore?"

A reluctant grin lightened his expression. "I seem to remember a few battles."

"Only a few?"

"Okay. More than that." Eric shook his head, still smiling. "I played in a rock band briefly. We practiced in the garage. We were terrible. I bitterly resented being told so. My dad's bellows to 'turn the goddamn amplifiers down' humiliated me."

"But did he quit bellowing?" she asked gently.

"Nah—" Eric broke off. His eyes narrowed. "What are you—a psychologist in your off-hours?"

Reassured, she let go of his hand and reached for her sandwich. "Nope. Just figured a trip down memory lane might not be a bad idea."

"Well, I get your point." He picked up his spoon. "Which still leaves me wondering what the hell I'm going to do with him all summer."

"Do you camp or..." She leveled a look at him. "You don't hunt, do you?"

"Yeah, that's me. I shoot 'em down, then patch 'em up. What do you think?"

"Just asking," she said with dignity. "Take your

son horseback riding. Sailing. Swimming. Whatever.''

He grunted. "I work, remember?"

"Can't you take a few days off here and there?"

His mouth tightened. "Maybe."

"Would he and Mark—"

"Last summer, they were friends," Eric interrupted. "This time Garth has decided they have nothing in common."

Was he really asking for her help? Tentatively Madeline said, "I could take him to the shelter. If he likes animals, that is."

"Yeah," he said slowly. "Yeah, he used to love spending days with me at the hospital, helping me out on farm calls. Circe, one of my cats, is sleeping with him nights, I noticed. He must be inviting her in."

"Well, then?"

"It's worth a try, if you mean it."

She smiled more confidently than she felt. "I mean it. We can always use help. The cats never get enough attention, even if he wants to stay away from the dirty work."

Eric grimaced, the creases in his cheeks emphasized. "Maybe you'd better ask him. I'm afraid anything I suggest he'll refuse on general principle."

"Sure," she said, nervousness fluttering in her stomach. What did *she* know about teenagers? Especially defiant male teenagers? But how could she back out now? Still trying for the blithe "I know what I'm doing" tone, she suggested, "Why don't I come over for a riding lesson this evening and you introduce us?"

"Thank you," he said quietly, his gaze holding hers. "I owe you one."

THIS SUMMER'S GIRLFRIEND was a fox, even if she was almost as old as Mom. She didn't have very big breasts—Dad's girlfriends usually did. But otherwise this one had legs like Julia Roberts's and really pretty thick hair and a neck that was sort of...swanlike. Long and slim and smooth and... Flushing, Garth jerked his gaze away, made uneasy by his descent into poetic images.

In this velvety voice she said, "Your dad talks about you often. It's nice to meet you."

He mumbled something, and even *he* didn't know what. She was too pretty. He didn't know what to say to someone like that.

"Do you ride?" she asked.

What was her name? Madeline. He remembered that part. He stole a glance at her sparkling greeny-brown eyes. "Yeah. I mean, I do summers when I'm here. Not at home."

"Well, you're ahead of me." She wrinkled her nose. "I just started a couple of weeks ago. I've ridden Honey, um, five times. Today is six."

"She never shies."

"Your dad is trying to talk me into going on a trail ride someday. I don't know if I'm ready for that."

This time he looked at his father, who was watching him, not Madeline. *Be nice*, his dad's eyes warned. Like he needed telling. She was talking to him as if he was a human being. Even if it *was* what Dad wanted, he was going to be polite back.

"Honey would never hurt you," Garth said. "Dad and I can borrow horses so you can have her. His partner's family owns a whole bunch."

"So I hear." She turned to Honey, already saddled and bridled. "Well, here goes nothing."

Dad boosted her into the saddle as if she hardly weighed anything. She was actually kind of skinny, but in a good way. Garth couldn't think of a single girl at his school with a bod like hers.

He stayed beside his father, leaning against the fence and watching her take a few turns around the pasture. He hadn't been on horseback yet; his father didn't want him to ride when he was home alone— as if Honey would throw him or something, but that was a parent for you. And *he* hadn't wanted to come out when Dad suggested it. He wasn't about to surrender and do father-son stuff, not when he knew Dad didn't really want him here any more than Mom wanted him at home.

The thought of his mother pierced deep, and he pulled away from it. As if to distract him, Madeline cantered up on Honey just then, her cheeks pink and her eyes more sparkly than ever.

"Your turn," she told Garth, and slid off before he could say no.

So he did ride, a couple of times around the pasture. Once, he really let Honey out, until the wind brought tears to his eyes and the saddle creaked and the mare grunted with the effort. She slid to a spectacular stop in front of Dad and Madeline, who made a face and said, "I would have gone sailing over her head if I'd tried that."

"Honey was trained as a cow horse," Dad said. "You can rope on her or pen. At least you could if you knew what you were doing."

"It looks like Garth does." She smiled admiringly at him. Hopping off the fence, she came to Honey's side. She stroked the mare's neck, still looking up at him. "Did your dad tell you about the cat shelter where I volunteer?"

"He said something about it."

"Any chance you'd like to help out? The cats there love attention, and we just don't have time to give it." The skin on the bridge of her nose crinkled a little as her smile deepened. It made her look cute and young. She lowered her voice. "I figured you might get bored this summer."

Garth's hand jerked on the reins, and Honey danced. Madeline had to back up. "Did Dad tell you to ask me?" he demanded fiercely.

Her eyes met his, her expression open. "It was my idea. I did discuss it with him, though. He said it was okay if I asked you."

Dad was too close to pretend he didn't hear, but although a muscle jumped in his cheek, he didn't say anything.

"Would I be going just when he was there?"

Her eyebrows rose in surprise. "No, your father has to work tomorrow even though it's Saturday. I figured I'd pick you up around twelve-thirty. I'll help clean and medicate for a couple of hours, and you can wander around and check the place out. What d'you say?"

Garth thought about it. But not for long. What did he have to lose? Another day of thrills and chills hanging around the house all by himself?

"Sure," he said, shrugging awkwardly. "Why not?"

CHAPTER SEVEN

MADELINE STOOD in the opening of the sliding glass door, watching Eric's son. He sat cross-legged in the grass, where he'd been for some time. Hand outstretched, almost touching a crouched black cat—his arm must ache, he'd had it out so long—he murmured in a singsong voice words she couldn't make out. His patience and the magic in whatever he was saying were being rewarded. Smudge, who hadn't let anyone touch him since he'd come to the shelter, was inching toward the boy. His rust-colored eyes looked mesmerized, but his sleek black body was coiled tight. Any unexpected noise or movement would send him fleeing.

She waited; Garth continued murmuring. And the amazing happened: Smudge slid forward enough for Garth's fingers to gently stroke his head. The cat quivered, then tilted his chin up for those fingers to reach his jaw and throat. Finally, wonder of wonders, he rubbed the length of his body against that hand, and Garth ruffled the black fur, his hand traveling down Smudge's spine over and over, until even from fifteen feet away Madeline could hear the purr.

Another cat jumped down from a wooden climber. It was Big Yellow, a bully, and now he growled low in his throat. Smudge started, froze for an instant and then flowed away. Garth slowly let his arm drop.

Madeline clapped. "Bravo!"

His head whipped around and, looking disconcerted, he said, "I didn't know you were there."

"I didn't dare move." She smiled. "That was Smudge. He's never let anyone here touch him, not since we turned him loose after he got neutered and vaccinated."

Flushing, Garth said, "Well, probably no one's had the time. I mean, I've been sitting here for a while."

"I know." She sat, too, on a lawn chair just outside the sliding door. Ajax, a snow white elderly cat, jumped onto her lap. Idly stroking him, Madeline continued, "But you seem to have a way with these guys." She laughed, because one was butting his head against Garth's back and another had scrambled onto his legs. "If you come a few more times, you'll have to beat 'em off with a stick."

"I wouldn't mind coming again," Garth mumbled. "It's not like I have anything else to do this summer."

She took that for the face-saving excuse she knew it to be; Ten Lives had had other young volunteers, many of whom lost interest quickly. She'd been scrubbing litter boxes and floors for two straight hours, and not once had Garth looked bored or asked when they were leaving. In fact, she'd seen him only when she glanced out the window.

She couldn't blame him for doing his visiting out here; the day was sunny and cloudless without being hot, late June weather at its best. The grass had recently been cut and raked, and even more cats than usual were outside. Some were sprawling in the grass or napping on the homemade climbers that substituted for trees.

After a long sleepy pause, Madeline asked, "Have you been to the kitten room yet?"

He looked up eagerly. "No, I didn't know there was one."

"I'll show you." But she was too content to leap immediately to her feet.

Garth seemed to feel the same. He shifted to accommodate another cat that slid under his arm and leaned against his knee. Today, she thought, he looked younger than he had the other day, more the boy he really was than the teenager he tried to be. From this side she couldn't see the earring, and the sunlight transformed the fuzz of pale blond hair growing in on his bare skull into a shimmering halo. He looked a good deal like his father: the same narrow intelligent face with sharp cheekbones, the same lanky grace, although less controlled in the boy. His eyes were bright blue, instead of his father's gray-green, but when Garth quit sulking those blue eyes took in everything he saw, processed it, focused on any anomaly as penetratingly as Eric's did. His gaze could be just as unnerving.

Startled at her choice of words, Madeline grimaced. And here she liked to think she'd become completely relaxed around his father.

"Well," she said, letting out a long breath, "shall we?"

The house had four bedrooms, one of which was home to the kittens. Most of the year a couple of huge cages held the litters of younger ones, along with their mothers. Older kittens awaiting placement ran loose in the room. Cushy carpeted hammocks were slung from the windowsills; a bunk bed made a great climber, as well as offering the high perch they loved.

"Cool," Garth breathed the instant she opened the door and he saw two of the older kittens tumbling on the floor in mock battle.

Within minutes he was waving the long wand with feathers attached to the end. Wizard and October raced after it, leaping and growling and snatching it in their teeth when they were quicker than Garth's hand.

Madeline quietly withdrew and left him. In the front office she returned phone calls for half an hour or so, then chatted with Joan, finally returning to the kitten room. Garth had one of the cage doors open and was trying to coax the two little black-and-white guys in the corner to come to him.

"That's Chev and Ron," Madeline said softly. "They were found under a Dumpster at a Chevron station. We called them the Chevron Kids, and somehow that evolved. They're petrified. We really need a foster home for them, somewhere they can get tons of attention for a few weeks. At their age, they ought to come around. If they can just learn to trust people, we could find them a home."

She felt a little guilty. She ought to have talked to Eric before even hinting that Garth take on any project like this. But he was so perfect for it! The idea had come to her when she saw him petting Smudge. Garth had the patience and kindness needed to reassure scared cats and tame the semiferal. Best of all, he had time, something most adult volunteers lacked.

And from what Eric had said and what she'd seen of Garth today, she thought he needed a purpose. Maybe two kittens who desperately needed *him* would be just the ticket. She couldn't imagine that Eric would object.

Well, in for a penny, she decided, and took a deep breath. "I don't suppose..." she began.

At that precise same moment Garth said, "Do you think I...?"

They looked at each other and laughed. "Yes," Madeline said, "I do think you could. *If* it's okay with your dad. You'll have to consult him first."

Garth's shoulders hunched, and in an instant he was the sullen teenager again. "He doesn't trust me to do anything. He'll say no."

"I doubt it." She touched his arm. "He loves animals. I think he'll be pleased you do, too."

Easily read emotions chased across his face: hurt pride, anger, longing, stubbornness. Finally he shrugged. "Yeah, okay. I guess I'll ask him. What can it hurt?"

"Right." Turning, she reached into the cage to pet Ron, the slightly braver of the two kittens. Chev cringed away, tiny white teeth showing as he hissed. She had to be honest. "The one thing that does hurt is when you take these guys home and teach them to love you and then you have to say goodbye."

Frowning thoughtfully, Garth looked even more like his father. "You've done it before?"

"Lots of times." Her smile was crooked. "I still cry every time."

"But are you really sad?"

"No. At least, only partly. I know I can't keep them all. What I'm doing is teaching them how to love and then finding them someone they can love for the rest of their lives. If I hadn't been willing to do that and to cry a little, they'd never have had a chance. So it's worth every tear. Getting to know them and seeing them get braver and then that moment when you know they trust you...there's nothing like it." Memories flooded her, green eyes and rust eyes, long white whiskers and stubby gray ones, the pointed furry faces of a dozen particularly beloved cats and kittens who had passed briefly through her life before she handed them on. For a second her eyes welled with tears. She picked up Chev, who curled into a small ball, and handed him to Garth. "Someday, he'll purr just because you come into the room, and you'll know he's ready."

Garth bent his head as he ran a finger along the bumpy curve of the scrawny kitten's spine. "And then maybe I could take some more."

"That's the spirit!" On impulse she gave the boy a quick hug, retreating before he had a chance to react at all, much less protest. "I'm done here for the day. Shall we go beard your father? Or would you rather ask him alone?"

"You mean, *you'd* ask him?"

She laughed. "No, I mean *we'd* ask him."

"Oh." He thought it over. "If you were with me, he'd probably say yes. He wouldn't want you to think he was a jerk."

Garth might have a point. "Then maybe I shouldn't be there," she said slowly. "I don't want him to agree for no better reason than that."

"Does it matter why he agrees?" Garth asked with impeccable logic. "It's not like Chev and Ron will care. They'll still have the same chance."

"Yeah, but *I* have to keep dealing with your dad when he treats our cats," she reminded him. "I don't want him to feel resentful. Ten Lives needs him."

Garth carefully placed Chev back in the cage, petted Ron, then closed and latched the door. "Okay, then. I'll do it."

"I'll keep my fingers crossed. Give me a call after you talk to him."

Garth promised that he would. She dropped him at home, not going in, although it wouldn't have mattered; Eric wasn't here, anyway. She wished he was so that she could ride, maybe stay for dinner, have him walk her out to her car later for a moment of privacy....

"You," she told her reflection in the rearview mirror, "are behaving like a lovesick teenager!" She pushed in the clutch, shifted into reverse and muttered through clenched teeth, "I can still get through a day without seeing him, thank you very much."

ERIC KNOCKED on Garth's bedroom door. "Dinner's ready!" he called.

Half the time, Garth called back, "I already ate."

Tonight the door swung open immediately, as if he'd been standing by it. "What did you make?" He sniffed. "Eggs?"

"Yup. My world-famous omelets."

Closing the door behind him, Garth started down the hall. "Cool."

Cool? Eric stared after his son. Had Madeline worked a magic spell? He *had* to hear about the visit to Ten Lives.

He made himself wait until he'd dished up the food, they'd sat side by side on stools at the breakfast bar, and Garth had already shoved the first bite of omelet in his mouth.

Then, very casually, Eric asked, "What did you think of the shelter today?"

"It was cool." Garth swallowed, glugged half a glass of milk and wiped his mouth with one hand, then added, "We stayed a couple hours."

"I got Hannah there, you know." Eric smiled ruefully. "Or maybe I should say, she got me. No," he said to the cat, whose upward gaze had become purposeful. "You know you're not allowed on the counter."

Her tail whipped, but she didn't spring upward.

"There're a lot of really scared cats there." His son thrust another bite in his mouth and kept talking around it with an animation Eric hadn't heard since he'd arrived. "I petted this black one named Smudge that Madeline says nobody's touched since he came. I'll bet I could tame him."

"You planning to spend more time there, then?"

"Yeah, I guess." Garth ate in silence for a moment, then shrugged. "Why not?"

"I admire what they're doing," Eric said neutrally. "Did you meet Joan?"

"Kind of. I mean, she buzzed through talking a mile a minute. Then she left for work."

"Yeah, that's one energetic lady."

For the first time Garth looked him straight in the eye. "You don't make them pay when you go there, do you?"

Eric explained the arrangement. "So far it's working out well. They haven't swamped us with sick animals, and I can easily afford the time I give. I neuter right there on the spot, and they bring the females for spaying into the hospital. We've had a couple cats that had viruses and weren't eating that we kept on IVs for a few days. They do a good job there medicating for the minor stuff."

"Oh." Head bent, Garth tore the crust of his toast into shreds. "I was wondering—" He stopped. "I mean, Madeline asked me something…"

"Yeah?" Eric prodded.

"Well, there's these two little kittens," Garth said in a rush. "Chev and Ron. They're black and white, and somebody found them under a Dumpster at a Chevron gas station. See, they're not used to people, and they hiss every time someone tries to touch them, but they don't bite or scratch or anything like that, and Madeline thinks if someone just spent lots of time with them for a few weeks, they'd get friendly and be adoptable."

It didn't take ESP to figure out where this was

going. Eric said dryly, "She has a foster home lined up of course."

"She says they're hard to find," his son told him, his expression earnest, "and she already has a litter of kittens in her extra bedroom. She can't take any more right now, 'cause she has to place these before her mother comes for a visit. Her mother doesn't like cats very much," Garth explained, "and she wouldn't want any in the bedroom where she sleeps."

"I see," Eric said gravely. A kinder father would have ended the suspense and said, *Why don't you do it?* He decided to make the kid carry through, however hard it was for him.

Garth took a deep breath. "The thing is, I thought maybe I could have them in my bedroom. Just for a few weeks." He watched his father anxiously. "I'd change the litter every day, and Madeline said I could bring cat food home so you wouldn't have to buy any, and—"

"Sounds good to me," Eric agreed, taking pity at last.

"They wouldn't be any trouble," the twelve-year-old hurried on. "I won't ask you to do anything. I promise. I—" He blinked. "Did you say yes?"

"You bet." Eric smiled. "I'd foster cats for the shelter myself if I weren't gone such long hours." *Don't push it,* some inner voice warned. *Don't approve so much he starts thinking it was your idea, or it's what you want him to do.* Eric took a sip of the wine he'd poured himself. "Madeline is good at persuading people to do something useful, isn't she?

You'll have to go to an adoption day with her. She charms the socks off people. They go out to shop, come home with a cat. They probably lug that carrier in their front door and wonder what in hell got into 'em.''

"She's pretty," Garth said. A blush flagged his cheeks.

"Yeah, but I don't think that's it." A bite halfway to his mouth, Eric paused to ruminate. "She's... morally uncompromising," he mused aloud. "You find yourself wanting to please her, impress her. Maybe rise to her level. Then she gives you that smile—" He put on the brakes. Good God, he'd just made himself sound like a hopeful puppy dog, wriggling and wagging for attention and a kind word from the nice lady. Where was his dignity?

Garth was regarding him with a disconcertingly adult expression. "You really like her, don't you, Dad?"

Dad. Another first for the summer. A stab of pleasure made Eric realize how much he'd missed such a trivial thing: hearing his son call him Dad.

"I guess I do," he admitted. "But we haven't known each other that long." He shrugged. "We'll see." When Garth didn't comment, Eric asked, "Do *you* like her?"

"She kinda reminds me of this teacher I had last year. For computers. She never had to yell or anything. Nobody wanted to bug her, you know?"

Eric pushed his empty plate away. "Yeah, I've known people like that. This teacher, was she young and pretty?"

"Nah." Garth sounded bewildered that anyone could have that effect on a whole class and *not* be pretty. "Actually she was kind of old. Her hair was getting gray."

The poor woman was probably forty-five. Eric didn't ask whether he fell into the same category.

Garth finished his milk, this time using the hem of his T-shirt to wipe away the mustache. Eric wondered what Chuck Morrison, CEO, thought of such table manners.

The phone rang, startling them both. "I'll get it," Eric said, and slid off the bar stool, taking his dirty dishes to the sink at the same time. "Hello?"

"Hello, Eric." The voice was Noreen's. It sounded as faraway as he knew her to be; the line crackled. "I thought I'd check in and see how things are going."

"Garth's right here. Why don't you talk to him?" Eric said, waving the boy over. Handing him the receiver, he said, "It's your mother."

Garth turned his back and hunched his shoulders. "Mom?" he said, voice low.

Eric interpreted his son's body language as an instinctive plea for privacy. "I'll be back in a minute," he said, and left the room.

Not two minutes had passed when Garth called, "Dad, Mom wants to talk to you."

Surprised, he put down the newspaper he'd barely picked up and went back into the kitchen. "You're already done talking to her?"

Garth shoved the phone at him. Something in the boy had changed in those brief minutes. The sulkiness was back, along with acute unhappiness. "Yeah, like I had so much news," he said rudely, and abruptly left the kitchen.

Frowning after him, Eric said into the receiver, "Noreen?"

"I can tell how much he misses me." Her attempt at lightness failed. "Is he mad at me or just in a generally charming mood?"

Down the hall Garth turned into his bedroom and slammed his door. So much for rapprochement.

"There's a hell of a lot you didn't tell me," Eric said bluntly. "Either that, or he pulled a Cinderella act in reverse in the john of the airplane."

"Oh." She laughed nervously. "You mean the earring and the shaved head? They do look awful, don't they? But they're just the style right now. Kids have to rebel somehow."

Eric's fingers tightened on the phone, and through his teeth he said, "All our son does is shut himself in his bedroom and listen to rap music. He acts like he hates me. Apparently he hates you, too. Not to mention 'Chuckie.'" He mimicked the way Garth said the name. "Is that the style right now, too?"

Her long silence left him feeling like a brute. She never had liked "unpleasantness"—her word for anything that upset her. He heard a ragged breath that might have been a sob. Dammit, why didn't she storm back at him? Remind him that she'd been left to raise their son alone nine months of the year, that she was doing the best she could. Tell him to go to hell. But, no.

"I should have warned you," she said unhappily. "It's just..."

"You thought I wouldn't take him if I knew what a pain he'd be?" Eric didn't like the hardness in his voice any more than she would.

To her credit Noreen sounded surprised and indignant. "Of course not! You have your flaws, Eric, but you wouldn't abandon Garth just because he's going through a rough patch."

Thank you very much.

"That's not what I was going to say at all," she continued. "I thought his problems were with me. Especially with my remarrying. He's always been so close to you. He really looks forward to your calls. I thought everything he said about my dumping him on you was to make me feel bad. Guilty." She sniffed, sighed. "It worked. The thing is, I didn't think he meant it! He loves summers with you!"

"Not this one," Eric said ruefully. He closed his eyes and squeezed the bridge of his nose. "I'm sorry, Noreen. Who the hell am I to criticize the way you raise our son? You're pretty much stuck holding the bag, aren't you?"

"I wouldn't say that." Surprising him again, she sounded bracing. "You've been a good father. I really think this *is* just a rough patch. At heart he's a good kid. I know he loves you, and your opinion means everything."

Eric's mouth twisted. "That's news to me. Although he was warming up to me tonight, until—" Tact stopped him in time; he wasn't about to complete the thought.

But she did. "Until I called." She paused, then admitted, "He's pretty angry at me. I thought by now..."

"That he'd have gotten over it?" Eric turned his back to the counter and leaned against it. "He always was stubborn."

"How true." Her tone was wry now. "Well, I suppose you know why he's mad. He didn't want me to marry. I don't think it's really Chuck—he liked him fine until the subject of marriage came up. I don't know, maybe I've been too wrapped up in the romance. But when you fall in love..."

Whatever she had to say about falling in love was lost on him. He was thinking about the last time he'd seen Madeline. Oh, yeah, he thought, it'd be easy to get so wrapped up in her that he discounted Garth's needs. His instant understanding was a little disconcerting.

He tuned back in to hear his ex-wife saying unhappily, "Probably I haven't handled it very well. But he's been such a brat! The week before the wedding he did a vanishing act one night. It turned out he'd just spent the night at a friend's. The boy's mother thought he had permission. But he did it on purpose to scare me. I don't think I've ever been so angry in my life! I know he wants reassurance, but after that I was so mad I wasn't about to give it!"

"By September he'll be missing you."

"I'm not so sure." She was crying now. "I wish we hadn't parted so bitterly. What if he decides he'd rather live with you? I couldn't say no."

Eric would give anything to have Garth year-round. But under these circumstances... Eric shook his head. "Then I'd say it for you. He shouldn't make that kind of decision when his main motive is punishing you. He needs to go home and work it out with you. And Chuck. Then, down the line, if he and Chuck aren't hitting it off, maybe. You know I'd love to have him. But not like this."

Noreen gave a choked laugh. "Remind me why I divorced you."

"I thought *I* divorced *you,*" he countered in the same spirit, a grin pulling at his mouth. "And I think it was because we didn't have a single damned thing in common. We just didn't notice that when we were twenty-three."

"When you're twenty-three, sex is enough," she said.

Did she have more going for her new marriage than good sex? he wondered.

Her thoughts must have paralleled his, because she asked, "Are you seeing anyone seriously?"

There hadn't been a time since their divorce when he would have answered yes. He enjoyed the company of women; he liked their softness; he liked sex. There was always someone. But "seriously"?

The minute she asked, he had a sudden picture of Madeline. A cat was draped over her shoulder of course, and she was listening with that intense focus that let him know she wasn't just looking attentive, she *was* attentive. Then in a blink, that picture was gone and another took its place. In this one he'd just kissed her, and she was smiling up at him, her eyes dreamy, a smile gently curving her mouth. And God, she was beautiful! His body tightened at no more than the fleeting memory.

"Yeah," he heard himself say slowly. "Yeah, I think I am."

"You *think?*"

"We haven't known each other that long," he said defensively. "I'm too old to jump into things."

"Hah!" Noreen scoffed. "I bet you don't have a gray hair on your head! There's no justice. The only reason *I* don't is because my hairdresser sees to it."

He smiled, even if she couldn't see him. "I probably have 'em, too."

"With hair as blond as yours, you'll just turn white and never notice." She heaved a sigh. "Why am I talking about you when my adoring new husband is no doubt pacing down in the lobby, waiting to take me out for an exotic meal?"

"I don't know. Why are you?" He grinned and, before she could say something tart, added, "Enjoy yourself, Noreen. I mean it. Don't give Garth another thought. He's just throwing a giant temper tantrum. They didn't impress us when he was two and they shouldn't now. You have a right to remarry. He'll come around."

Her voice was thick with tears again. "Yes. Thank you, Eric. I'll...I'll call in a week or two." The line went dead.

He hung up the phone, stood indecisively for a moment, then decided to take the bull by the horns. Something he literally had to do on occasion. He'd rather do the real thing than confront his rebellious son.

Eric strode down the hall and knocked on Garth's door.

"Yeah?" The voice was sullen.

"May I come in?"

"It's your house."

He wouldn't dignify that one with an argument. He opened the door and went in. Garth was stretched out on the bed as usual, holding the headphones he'd obviously just pulled off.

"You should give your mother a break," Eric said mildly.

"What do you know about it?" the boy said with a sneer. "Just 'cause you listened to *her* side..."

"I'd listen to yours if you want to tell it to me." Eric sat down on the bed. "But I don't want you to forget that she's a nice lady. Maybe not perfect, but she tries to do her best. And she loves you."

"*And* Chuckie." Garth said the name with loathing. His face twisted with hate.

"Yeah. And Chuck. But it's not a competition. I know you don't believe me right now, but eventually you'll figure it out. What she feels for him is nothing like what she feels for you."

"Oh, right." Garth turned his face away. His voice was muffled. "Is that all you came for?"

"No." He clapped his son on the shoulder. "Why don't you give Madeline a call? See if she can meet us at the shelter. No reason to leave those poor kittens in a cage when they could be getting used to your room."

Garth shot up onto his elbows. He blinked fiercely

to hide tears, but his face was lit with excitement. "Now? Can we?"

"If she's around."

"Cool!" Garth scrambled off the bed. "I'll go call her."

"You do that."

Eric followed more slowly. He was damned near as excited as Garth, just because their errand meant he'd see Madeline briefly.

A puppy dog. That was all he was. Desperate for a kind word and a pat on the head.

Although a kiss would be better.

CHAPTER EIGHT

A JADE GREEN CHEVROLET was parked in Madeline's driveway. She pulled in beside it, her gaze immediately finding the rental-company sticker in the back window. Her mother had arrived.

Shutting off the engine, Madeline pulled the key out of the ignition but didn't immediately reach to unfasten her seat belt or open the car door. Instead, she leaned her head back and closed her eyes, trying to...what? Marshal some psychic energy, she decided. She wasn't exactly bracing herself—after all, her mother was a perfectly pleasant guest who picked up after herself, had lovely dinners ready most nights when Madeline worked and only got in a dig about the cats every other day or so.

And yet... Madeline sighed so deeply her hair stirred against her forehead. Sometimes she thought her mother's visits would have been less of a strain if they'd yelled at each other nonstop. It was the politeness that got to her, the unspoken words, the...the carefulness with which they conversed. Within twenty-four hours she'd want to scream, by the end of three days she'd be making excuses not to be home, and at the end of the visit she'd kiss her mother's cheek, wish her goodbye and thank God.

Or maybe this year she'd have snapped by then. Especially if Mom stayed as long as she'd hinted she might. Why now? Madeline wondered, rubbing her forehead.

After a moment she grimaced, unsnapped her seat belt, grabbed her purse and got out. On the way up the front steps, she glued a smile on her face.

Good thing, too, because the door was flung open before she reached it. "Madeline!" Mrs. Howard said with apparent pleasure, stepping out to meet her. A cat scooted between her ankles and she started, but—thank goodness—didn't complain, saying only, "You're home earlier than I expected."

"Yes, business was quiet, so I left one of my employees to close up." Madeline submitted to the obligatory hug and kiss that didn't quite touch her cheek.

Stepping back, she studied her mother. Fifty-six years old, she was still a stunning-looking woman. The genes that had blessed and cursed Madeline had come from her, not Madeline's long-absent father. Her hair was darker than Madeline's, and no gray had been allowed to mar the smooth sweep to an elegant French twist. She was still slim to the point of fragility, but she didn't appear to be wasting away. Her brown eyes were serene, not sunken from illness or depression. Her makeup had been flawlessly applied and hadn't dared smear or run. If she was dying of cancer or heart disease, she was doing a damned good job of denying its existence.

So why the insistence on a good long visit when she'd never before spent longer than a week?

"Well. Shall we go in?" Madeline suggested. "Did you have a good trip?"

"Oh, flying is always dull." Gloria Howard crinkled her nose, to Madeline looking uncannily like she did herself with the same expression. "But then," her mother said, "I suppose one wouldn't want a flight *not* to be dull. I prefer my excitement to happen when I have both feet on the ground."

Madeline laughed, some of her tension slipping away. "How true." She put down her purse on the side table in the entryway. "Are you settled in?"

"Yes, but I didn't have a chance to get dinner on," she fussed. "I did notice you've stocked up."

"Of course I did! But I wish you wouldn't feel you had to cook every night."

"I'm sure you don't have a well-rounded diet when I'm not here," her mother said, mouth pursing. "I just like to do what I can to remedy that."

The headache crept back. "Mom, look at me." Madeline held out her arms and rotated. "I'm not horribly skinny, I'm not putting on unwanted weight, and my complexion is good, reflecting my virtuous life." She let her arms drop. "Come on, Mom. Give me a break."

At this point she ought to suggest going to a nice restaurant in Everett. No eatery in White Horse would please her mother. And Madeline always tiptoed around where her mother was concerned. It had never seemed worth provoking more criticism. But she found suddenly that something inside her had changed. She felt...impatient. Freer, somehow, and unwilling to remake herself for several weeks. So what if she shocked her mother? she thought, the impatience becoming more akin to recklessness.

"Let's go out for pizza," she said.

"Pizza?" her mother echoed.

"Why not? It'll be good for you." Madeline headed for her bedroom, where three cats snoozed on her bed. "Just let me get out of this dress and into jeans."

"Jeans?"

Madeline stuck her head back around the door frame. "Why don't you put on jeans, too?"

Her mother was staring at her in astonishment. Madeline ducked back into her bedroom and let her mother think it over. After a moment she heard Mrs. Howard say, "Well, I suppose…"

Two minutes later Madeline came out wearing jeans and a T-shirt depicting a woman who had obviously just been sleeping but who now had a cat sitting on her chest, its nose almost touching hers as he willed her to get up and feed him. Maggie followed Madeline, meowing insistently.

"No, I won't feed you," Madeline told her. "You know I don't open cans till later. It won't do you any good to beg."

Arms raised as she bundled up her hair, she came face-to-face with her mother coming out of the guest room. To Madeline's astonishment, she, too, had changed. Her stylish jeans had a knife-sharp crease down the front, and her peach-colored sleeveless knit top had a matching jacket, so the outfit wasn't exactly ultracasual, but still…

Madeline blinked. "That was quick."

"I never waste a great deal of time on makeup or clothes," Mrs. Howard said primly. "You know that."

Startled, Madeline thought back. Her mother was always so impeccably turned out Madeline had come to think of her as obsessed with appearance, but it was true that she couldn't ever remember waiting for her or seeing her spend more than five minutes in front of a mirror. She'd just assumed... And she hated people who assumed something and didn't bother to find out the truth.

She gave her head a shake. The knot held. "I'm hungry. Shall we go? I'll drive."

"Yes, fine."

"Uh...I wouldn't leave that door open if you don't want cats in there."

Her mother hastily closed the bedroom door. "It's not very...restful, having so many of them. Wouldn't you be happy with just one or two?"

"Nope." Madeline strove to sound cheerful. "I enjoy every one of them. To each her own."

"I suppose so," Mrs. Howard agreed grudgingly.

White Horse Pizza Parlor was on the main street. The tables were metal with Formica tops, the booths vinyl-upholstered. But the pizzas were divine, the breadlike crusts thick and chewy, the sauce spicy, the cheese subtly flavored without being greasy. And there were no video games, which meant no beeps or crashes or rat-a-tat of mock gunfire overpowered the murmur of voices. This was one of Madeline's favorite restaurants. She had never brought her mother here before.

But Mrs. Howard looked cautiously around, sniffed and said, "I hope the pizza is as good as it smells."

"Better," Madeline told her.

They agreed on plain cheese—it needed no embellishment—and ordered salads, then settled at a booth to wait for their food. It was these moments Madeline dreaded; they had nothing meaningful to say to each other. Either they sat in stiff silence, or Mrs. Howard criticized under the guise of concern.

But the recklessness persisted; her mother had insisted on coming and making her stay longer than a week, so she might as well be inculcated into real life, á la Madeline.

"On Saturday I'm doing an adoption day for the shelter," she said without preamble. "Why don't you come?"

It was her mother's turn to look startled. "Why... that would be interesting," she said, her tone holding only a hint that she was dubious. "What do you *do* at one of these?"

"I put the cats in cages, if the store has them, or sometimes in a temporary kennel that we can set up at the front of the store. And then I sit there." At her mother's expression, she laughed. "I rarely do much sitting. I talk. Even people who aren't interested in adopting like to stop and chat, tell me stories about their cats. And ones who are vaguely thinking about getting a cat want to hear all about each one. If you like people, it's actually kind of fun."

"*Do* you like people?" Mrs. Howard asked.

What an odd question for a mother to ask her

grown daughter. But then, Madeline and her mother didn't know each other very well anymore, if indeed they ever had.

"Actually I do," she replied. "People, cats and horses, I'm discovering."

Her mother arched one perfect brow, disapproval coloring her tone. "Horses? You haven't gone into a new kind of rescue work, have you?"

"No, but I've been taking riding lessons." She hesitated to tell her mother about Eric. But how could she avoid it, unless she made him stay away for the next few weeks? "Actually," she admitted, "I'm seeing a man who's giving me the lessons on his horse."

"A man?" Mrs. Howard was obviously trying to sound only mildly interested. But her whole body quivered, like a pointer seeing a flock of ducks. "You never mention dating."

"Don't I?" Madeline left it at that. She was reluctant to admit she rarely dated. It sounded like a weakness, and she never exposed her weaknesses to her mother.

With a friendly smile but no finesse, the waitress arrived and plopped their salads in front of them. "Pizza'll be along in a minute," she assured them.

"Thank you," Madeline said, picking up her fork.

Her mother did the same, but wasn't about to be sidetracked. "Will I meet this man?"

"Probably." What was that saying again? In for a penny, in for a pound? "His name is Eric Bergstrom. He's a veterinarian here in town. He takes care of the cats at the shelter. He has a teenage son who's kind of a problem. Garth is here for the summer, but actually he and I are getting along fine. He's volunteering at Ten Lives."

Her mother bore an expression of stunned fascination. "Garth is volunteering? Or Eric?"

"Garth. Well, both actually. Eric isn't charging us for his veterinary services. But Garth—who's twelve, by the way—visits cats at the shelter, and he took two scared kittens home to get them used to people."

"How nice." Plainly Garth wasn't the one who interested Mom. "This veterinarian must make a good living. Is he handsome?"

"Yes he—" Madeline broke off when the waitress appeared with the pizza.

Her mother waited only long enough for Madeline to dish up two slices and push her half-eaten salad aside.

"What does he look like?" she prodded. "If he has a son who's twelve, he must be older than you are. Unless he and his wife had him while they were still in college?"

"Eric's thirty-eight," Madeline said patiently. "He's tall and very blond, with…oh, kind of grayish-green eyes."

Her mother continued her inquiries. Madeline found herself answering without the irritation she'd expected to feel. These were *motherly* questions, not those of the business manager she'd once been for Madeline or the critic she'd become.

And therein, Madeline realized, was the problem: somewhere along the way, her mother had quit being her mother and become her manager; Madeline in turn became a property, not a beloved child.

Maybe, Madeline thought as she drove home, there was still hope. It could be that her mother had awakened one morning and wondered what had happened to the little girl she'd sewed Halloween costumes for and walked to the first day of kindergarten. Maybe she'd even missed her.

Or maybe not. By the time they stepped in the front door, Mrs. Howard was already saying peevishly, "By morning I suppose my nose will be running. It always does when I stay here. Keeping all those cats out of my bedroom doesn't do much good when they've been shedding in there year-round."

Madeline had never—not once—seen her mother blow her nose during a visit. She gritted her teeth and said nothing.

"I'm terribly afraid my stomach will be upset, too," Mrs. Howard continued. "The pizza tasted good, but it's so greasy! I hope you don't eat it often."

"I never get an upset stomach."

"But the cholesterol!"

"Mine's 148."

Her mother sat, knees properly together and back straight, on the living-room couch. When Benjamin, the flame-point Siamese, strolled up, she shooed him away with her foot, shrinking back into the sofa cushions as though he might attack any moment. Poor Benjamin gave her an indignant look and stalked out of the room even though Madeline extended her hand and murmured his name.

As soon as he was gone, her mother straightened and took up where she'd left off. "A low figure like that can be deceptive, you know. Besides, you have to think about the future."

The recklessness had worn off, like a drug that could buoy her only so long. "I'm sure you're right," Madeline said expressionlessly, hoping that agreement would be enough.

But no. "I can recommend some good books on nutrition." Tiny frown lines formed on her mother's brow. "Perhaps I ought to buy a low-fat cookbook or two while I'm here. That way you wouldn't have to hunt for them." Or, her tone implied, ignore her advice and not buy them at all. "If I show you how delicious healthy eating can be, you might stick to it."

A familiar weariness swept over Madeline. "Mom, I do eat well most of the time. I have a salad almost every day for lunch. One of my favorite restaurants is a vegetarian place just down the street from my shop. You really don't need—"

"But what do you put on your salad?" her mother interrupted. "Just because you start with lettuce doesn't mean you won't end up with a higher fat content than a cheeseburger has."

Madeline nodded with increasing desperation as Mrs. Howard went on and on. Maternal concern? Or was Madeline's figure and complexion still all her mother gave a damn about? Sometimes Madeline was tempted to ask. But neither recklessness nor anger had yet carried her to that point, because there might be no going back. Without sisters or brothers, without a father, she *needed* her mother.

Or rather, she thought wryly, she needed to know that her mother was there *if* she needed her—"there" preferably being her mother's home in Southern California. *Not* Madeline's spare bedroom.

She snapped to attention, suddenly realizing that her mother had fallen silent. Apparently Mrs. Howard had worn out this particular topic.

Now what could they talk about? Madeline had a familiar sinking feeling. Visits were fraught with these moments. The past was forbidden, they knew little about the other's day-to-day life, and their basic philosophies were worlds apart.

She and her mother looked at each other with mutual awareness that neither had a thing to say. The silence wasn't a comfortable one. It stretched and thinned like a taut rubber band until Madeline could feel tiny cracks weakening it. She groped frantically for something to say. Anything.

"Tea?" It was the only thing she could think of. "Would you like a cup?"

Her mother leaped to her feet, exclaiming, "Why, yes! That sounds nice. You do have herbal, don't you? I was just reading a study about caffeine..."

Going ahead to the kitchen, Madeline made a horrible face. Three weeks. She could survive anything, if it only lasted three weeks.

"THANK YOU for inviting my mother, too," Madeline said in a low voice.

Eric lounged beside her on the leather sofa in his

living room. A moment before, he'd announced his intention to go stir the spaghetti sauce simmering on the stove, but Mrs. Howard had volunteered to do it.

Now he reached out, tangled his fingers in Madeline's hair and tugged gently. She slid toward him. He smiled, eyes heavy-lidded. His expression was enough to awaken warm shivery feelings in her belly.

"Are my manners so bad you think I'd invite you to dinner and leave your mother sitting at home?" His lips brushed her cheek.

"No, of course not." Madeline turned her head, seeking his mouth.

"Besides, she seems nice." He kissed her lightly, then nipped her lower lip.

Madeline heard the tap-tap of her mother's returning footsteps. She hurriedly sat up and scooted away from him. Eric lifted a brow, but didn't comment.

Mrs. Howard hadn't missed her daughter's hurried retreat. She offered them a benign smile. "Your sauce looks and smells divine. How wonderful that you're a cook, too."

Mercifully he didn't ask what his other attributes were alleged to be. Madeline was grateful, as well, that her mother was too well bred to tell him the truth, which from her point of view would have been looks and money. His respect for animals, his kindness and generosity toward them, wouldn't rank on her list of important attributes in a potential husband.

Madeline's body jerked, and she covered up by shifting position. Eric gave her a curious glance, but went back to making polite conversation with her mother.

Husband? The word echoed in Madeline's head. No, it did more than that; it ricocheted.

Disturbed, she slipped into denial. *She* didn't see Eric that way; marriage was the last thing on her mind. But of course that was the way her mother would think. A woman of her mother's generation would naturally assume a trip down the aisle was the logical culmination to dating.

With a surreptitious glance at Eric, Madeline smoothed away her frown before it fully formed. Even so, she was perturbed enough to admit to a false note in this easy assumption: if marriage was a woman's goal, why hadn't her mother remarried? She must have had chances—probably still had them—but she'd never dated seriously in the many years since her husband had left. Or had she? As stilted as their conversations were, would she have told her?

A timid voice in her head whispered, *You could ask her why she didn't remarry.*

How simple. How obvious. So why *hadn't* she ever asked?

Because they never talked about the past. The facile answer came quickly. Because it hadn't occurred to her to wonder about her mother's life beyond the superficialities. Because her own anger didn't allow her to feel any empathy, much less sympathy, for her mother.

She stared straight ahead, momentarily unaware of her mother and Eric. Was she really that self-centered?

"Madeline."

She whipped her head around. "What?"

Eric raised an eyebrow, but said only, "I just heard Garth come in. If you want to check on the kittens before dinner..."

"What a good idea!" Grateful for an excuse to escape, she jumped to her feet. "Did he go to his room?"

"I'm afraid so." To Mrs. Howard, Eric said ruefully, "My son seems to be at a difficult age. He's gone from a friendly boy to a rebellious teenager since last summer. I don't know if he's forgotten his manners or is just ignoring them."

Madeline winced. His remark might have been aimed at her. She paused in the doorway. "Mom, if you want to see the kittens..."

Her mother visibly shuddered. But she smiled sweetly. "Didn't you say they're frightened? One visitor is probably enough."

Eric smiled with approval, and Madeline whirled and stomped down the hall, her brief contrition squelched. He'd actually bought her mother's act! He probably thought *she* was the one who wasn't behaving well! Well, maybe she wasn't, but too bad!

She raised her hand to knock on his son's door. Maybe Garth would let her hide out in his bedroom. They could console each other for the world's unfairness.

The image of herself slumped on Garth's bed, headphones shutting out the world, a snarl on her lips, restored her sense of humor. She ought to be relieved Mom had made a polite excuse. Imagine if she'd said, "Heavens, no! I hate cats!" Considering

Eric's vocation and avocation, that would have been a social blunder souring the rest of the evening.

She rapped.

Garth's muffled voice said, "Yeah?"

"It's Madeline. May I come in?"

"Yeah! Yeah, sure!"

She opened the door cautiously. No kitten hurled itself at the gap, so she slipped inside and pushed the door shut behind her.

Garth was sprawled on his stomach on the bed, almost nose to nose with the two kittens, curled in the shelf of the bookcase headboard.

"Hi," she said softly. "How're they doing?"

"Great!" He smiled at her over his shoulder, his face impish and charming without its usual sullenness. "Come and pet 'em."

As she crossed the room to his bed, she glanced around. The walls were bare, nail holes showing where posters and pictures had previously hung. Books were piled and CDs scattered atop a plain maple desk. Unclosed closet doors revealed an open suitcase on the floor, clothes jumbled inside it.

"Chev and Ron have been playing in there," Garth said. "I, uh, usually kinda fold my stuff."

"Ah." She smiled back at him. "Don't you love having kitty litter in your bedroom?"

"I change it, like, twice a day, but it's still pretty stinky," he agreed. "But that's OK. They're worth it."

"I'm glad you think so."

He scooted over on the bed. She felt as if they'd become friends, and without self-consciousness, she lay on her stomach beside him. Two sets of gold eyes regarded her warily, but when she reached over and ruffled silky backs, first one, then the other, began to purr.

"Ron really likes to play," Garth told her. "He especially likes that feather thing. You oughtta see him jump!"

"Chev still hide?"

"Yeah, mostly, but he's getting braver. He didn't purr at first, but now he does. And when I hold him, sometimes he seems to like it for a few minutes. If I flick the toy by him, he'll snatch at it, then scuttle back under the desk or in here. I bet in another week or two, he'll come out."

"I bet so, too." When she quit petting, Garth's hand took the place of hers. Out of the corner of her eye, she watched him. His eyes were soft, the curve of his mouth tender. She could see the boy Eric had described before this seeming stranger had showed up. Obviously that boy hadn't disappeared—he was just hiding. She suspected that, like Chev, he'd get braver and appear more and more often, too.

Turning her attention back to the kittens, she said, "Chev's finally putting on weight. Actually Ron's filling out, too, isn't he?"

Garth cleared his throat. "Yeah."

She glanced at him, only to find that he'd been watching her. The moment their eyes met, a fiery blush leaped from his neck and up his cheeks. He turned his head and pretended to be concentrating on his four-legged boarders.

What was going on? Puzzled, she waited.

"Dad thinks you're really pretty," he said, voice stifled. "I mean, he always dated pretty women, but you're even prettier."

Uneasiness balled in her stomach at the reminder of how Eric himself had answered when she'd wondered why he'd asked her out. *Because you're beautiful and I'm attracted to you.* Maybe she'd been kidding herself that their relationship had deepened.

"Did he say that?"

Garth still wouldn't look at her. "Sort of." Even more awkwardly he added, "But, like, you *are* pretty."

Lightning bolt. What an idiot she was. Poor kid, no wonder he was uncomfortable! He was telling her *he* thought she was pretty, and here she was stretched out on the bed beside him! At twelve years old, any boy was becoming aware of girls and women.

She laughed and said, "Thanks. You ought to see me first thing in the morning." Pretending to sigh, she sat up. "I have a feeling dinner is about ready. Shall we?"

He didn't move. "I'll probably just eat in here."

"Oh, no, you won't." Only half kidding, Madeline gave him a stern look. "My mother is here. I need rescuing."

Garth finally rolled onto his side, open surprise on his face. "But you're a grown-up!"

"I'm still a daughter. She's still my mother. Habits and, oh, tensions from when you're a kid don't necessarily go away, you know." Madeline grimaced. "There's a lot of stuff we've never talked about."

He frowned. "Why not?"

Good question. "Would you believe I'm a coward?"

He stared. "It's not like you're scared of her." More uncertainly he added, "Are you?"

"No." She smiled reassurance. "Nothing like that. I guess I'm just…still angry inside. I'll tell you about it sometime, okay? But we really ought to go eat or our parents will come looking for us."

He hopped up. "That sounds really weird. You're, like, my dad's age."

"He has parents, too, you know."

"Well, yeah, but—" Garth's brow crinkled "—they're my grandparents!"

She held open the door for him. "But they're Mom and Dad to him."

"Yeah. I mean, I know, but…"

Madeline grinned at him. "I can't imagine my mother as a little girl, either. Wait'll you meet her."

Garth was a model of politeness during the introductions. In turn, Mrs. Howard only gave his earring and shaven head one startled glance, then smiled graciously.

During dinner Madeline was secretly amused by the boy's frequent intense scrutinies of her mother. Eric, if he noticed, didn't comment, and had enough sensitivity not to remark on Garth's unexpected display of manners. Mrs. Howard went out of her way to include him in the conversation. Madeline gradually relaxed.

Maybe that was why her mother succeeded in taking her by surprise.

"You remember Elizabeth," she said to Madeline,

"my friend from high school? She's still here in Seattle, and we were talking yesterday. She suggested she and I take a little trip. She called Lake Quinault Lodge, they still had rooms available midweek, so we're off on Monday! I hope you don't mind, Madeline." She smiled conspiratorially at the others. "I thought my daughter could use a little break."

Truer words had never been spoken. Madeline refrained from agreeing aloud.

"And a little adventure sounded like fun," her mother continued. She gazed around with satisfaction. "I've never been there, but I understand the lodge is very nice, and the woods worth seeing."

"Dad says it's a rain forest," Garth piped up. "We went over there last summer. It's really cool! You won't believe how big some of the trees are."

He went on, enthusing about the moss that hung from branches and carpeted the ground, and the huge rotting trees that lay on the forest floor. Madeline didn't really listen. Clearly neither did Eric. His meaningful gaze had captured hers, and the faintest of smiles flickered at the corners of his mouth.

A shiver of half-apprehension half-excitement feathered down Madeline's spine. He was thinking, as she couldn't help doing, as well, of how long it had been since they'd been alone. Really alone. Since Garth's arrival, they'd seen each other a dozen times, but either Garth was with them or they were meeting for lunch in a crowded restaurant. The one afternoon they were at the shelter at the same time, the housekeeper and Joan had also been there, and two other volunteers had come to round up the cats that needed attention. Not exactly intimate. And then her mother had arrived.

But now his eyes promised they'd find a way to be alone. She knew he didn't have only a quiet dinner or a kiss on her doorstep in mind. Nor could she blame him. She thought about the same thing every time she watched his loose-limbed walk, melted at his smile, shivered at his touch.

She even thought she was ready. Sort of. She had a sudden image of swimming lessons when she was a kid: to pass advanced beginner's, she'd had to jump from the high dive. Once up there, she'd looked down and panicked. But the other kids crowded the ladder behind her, and rows of parents sat watching in the stands. Her own mother was there. She couldn't chicken out! And so she closed her eyes and jumped.

This was a little like that. Everyone else had already jumped. Her friends were married, or divorced and dating. The volunteers at the shelter all casually mentioned their husbands or the soccer or basketball games their children had played in. Before she hadn't envied them. Recently she'd been shocked to realize she did.

So here was the moment. If she wanted a solitary life, she could keep standing up on that high dive all by herself. If she wanted what everyone else had— a husband, children, a *family*—then she had to jump sooner or later.

Just like then, she didn't know if it would hurt when she hit the water. But maybe she'd be lucky. Maybe it wouldn't.

Maybe Eric wasn't dating her, wasn't looking at her now with molten eyes, only because she was "even prettier." Maybe he was falling in love with her.

As, she thought with shock, she was with him.

CHAPTER NINE

"DESSERT?" THEIR WAITRESS at the small seafood restaurant smiled. In the background, conversation hummed.

Eric raised a brow at Madeline. She considered trying to stuff in a piece of cheesecake as a delaying tactic, but decided that might backfire. Chickening out was one thing; getting sick all over her date was another. She shook her head.

"Just coffee," he said, never taking his eyes from hers. The waitress departed.

During dinner Madeline had—almost—been able to forget the unspoken ending to this evening. Eric had been affable, relaxed, willing to discuss anything, his sexual intensity banked. But now...

Madeline swallowed hard. Conversation. That was what they needed. If they talked, she wouldn't think. Imagine. Discover that anticipation could teeter like a seesaw between excitement and terror.

"Do you know," she said chattily, "we've gotten through an entire dinner without talking about your son or my mother?"

"Uh-huh." A smile played at the corners of his mouth without altogether taking shape. He saw right through her. He must. "That was the general idea, wasn't it?" he said lazily.

"I suppose..." Seizing gratefully on the arrival of the coffee, she thanked the waitress too profusely and took an immediate sip. And burned her mouth, at which Eric's smile grew.

Dammit, no matter how amused he looked, that glow in his eyes remained, and she felt his sexual awareness like a space heater set too close.

"Garth is doing wonders with the kittens," she said, trying to appear unruffled.

"The kittens are doing wonders with Garth." Eric appeared momentarily distracted. "He still spends most of his time in his bedroom, but he doesn't have those damn headphones on all the time. And he tells me about the kittens' progress with reasonable civility. Even invites me in to visit them once in a while."

"He'll come around."

Eric grunted. "I worry about what'll happen when the kittens get adopted."

She worried about that, too. The first time was the hardest. Eric's son was younger, tenderer, than she'd been when she said goodbye to her first foster babies. "Do you want me to hold off? He could keep them all summer."

"Then he'd be even more attached." A twisted smile replaced the frown. "And *I* would have two more cats."

"There are worse fates."

"I think I have enough. Especially considering..." He clamped down on that one.

Thank God. What if he'd been about to say, *Especially considering how many* you *have?* If they got as far as combining households—

Don't think about it, she told herself.

She lifted her coffee cup and discovered it was empty. A leisurely second cup was unlikely to be on Eric's agenda. Fed by a burst of adrenaline, her heart took an uncomfortable leap.

Eric smiled and lifted one hand. The waitress appeared like magic. Of course. "We'll take the check now," he said.

Madeline had never felt so many complicated emotions, had so many unprovoked physical responses, all at once. She wanted nothing more than to have Eric kiss her until she couldn't think at all; at the same time she was praying he'd drop her off at her door without even a hint that he come in. She wanted to stay the friends she'd come to think they were; but she also wanted him to say, *I love you.*

The truth was, she conceded ruefully, she couldn't make up her mind. Or perhaps she wanted everything and was afraid to go after it.

But does it have to be tonight? that insidious cowardly voice whispered.

She drew in a ragged breath, squeezed her hands together—and saw in alarm that he was laying some bills in the open leather folder and rising to his feet.

"Ready?"

No, she was not ready. Far from it! But she managed to smile and get to her feet. "I need to stop in the ladies' room."

"Sure."

He steered her out with a hand at the small of her back. So little, that touch, but it sizzled through her silk blouse, made her every nerve quiver. The door to the rest room looked like a rabbit's hole did to a rabbit when the shadow of an eagle floated near.

There was, of course, a limit to how long she could linger. She couldn't even brush her hair, because she'd twirled it into a French roll. She didn't carry her makeup, so she couldn't touch that up. She simply washed her hands and stared at herself in the wall of mirrors.

She looked like her normal self. Maybe a little paler than usual, maybe her eyes were larger, darker, her breaths shallow. But no one who didn't know her well would notice a thing. Her linen slacks were elegant; her amber silk blouse draped her breasts seductively. Too seductively, she thought, suddenly anxious. She turned this way and that, studying herself from different angles. Anxiety clogged her throat. Oh, no. She'd given the very signals she'd hoped to avoid. She'd thought to look businesslike. Reasonably attractive. Friendly.

All *he'd* been able to see across the table no doubt was the plunging neckline, the fabric clinging to her breasts, the shimmer of amber.

Yes, that nasty little voice in her head murmured, *and you don't really mind him looking, do you?*

"Oh, shut up!" she snapped, and stalked out of the room.

Eric was waiting, his pose relaxed, patient; he leaned back against a railing, feet crossed at the ankle, arms braced to each side. The way his jacket hung emphasized his broad shoulders; the fabric of his slacks was pulled tight over the long muscles in his thighs.

Though the rest-room door closed silently behind her, his head turned as though he'd felt her body heat. He watched her come toward him, and he was no longer smiling. His eyes were narrowed, intent. Hungry.

He still didn't move. "Ready?" he said again, his voice low, husky.

Her uncertain nod apparently satisfied him, because he straightened, took her arm and propelled her toward the exit.

The drive home from the hilly seaside town of Edmonds was mostly silent. Her chatter had dried up. Eric pushed a CD into the player, and the clear piercing tones of a jazz trumpet filled the car. The music seemed to speak aloud her fear, her hope, her shimmering excitement and welling sense of inadequacy.

Letting the notes seep into her, Madeline closed her eyes.

What was so frightening about making love with this man? She wasn't a virgin; she'd had a couple of relationships in the reckless period after she left home, full of anger. She hadn't had time to date before; besides, late nights might leave bags under her eyes. Her attachment to a man, she'd thought bitterly then, might loosen her mother's grip on her. So it had been inevitable, when she'd broken free, that she would plunge into all the experiences other girls had had in high school.

It was probably also inevitable that they would be

unsatisfactory. She was like a girl let free from a convent, a girl who knew nothing about the real world. The knight in shining armor didn't ride up on his white steed; true love eluded her. And sex was thoroughly disappointing.

Worse yet, sometimes it seemed she'd escaped nothing. Her looks were still all that mattered. Her two lovers had told her she was beautiful. They'd let her hair cascade through their hands as though they were adventurers who had found gold. Her breasts were perfect, her skin porcelain, they said. They stared as they undressed her, and she could feel their greed.

Each relationship had lasted a year. She hadn't had one since. She'd told herself she didn't want another. All men cared about was a woman's beauty. *She* was more than her hair and skin and legs. Underneath she was different, unrelated to the face she saw on television and in magazine advertisements. *She* had nothing to do with the veneer that was all any man saw.

She sneaked a glance at Eric's profile, unreadable in the dark interior of the car. Passing headlights reflected glints in his pale hair, shadowed his eyes, made him somehow mysterious, a stranger.

She felt a tremor, resisted it. He wasn't a stranger. He was different from other men. He did see beyond the surface to *her;* he cared about the same things she cared about.

Didn't he?

By the time he parked in her driveway, she was light-headed from imagining the best and the worst ten times over. Even so, her heartbeat sprinted when he turned off the ignition, abruptly silencing the trumpet. All she could hear was her pounding heart.

He turned to her, laid his arm along the back of the seat behind her. This much was familiar; now was when she always turned to him and lifted her mouth to meet his. She loved kissing him, being kissed by him. But other nights he'd walked her to her door, kissed her again, slowly, then murmured good-night and left. Tonight she knew he wouldn't.

Unless she refused him. *You can,* she thought, to give herself courage. But she knew she wouldn't.

His lips came down on hers, hard, hungrily. Her mind blurred. His hand stroked her throat, angled her head so his mouth could claim hers more completely. She gave a small whimper, and he groaned.

"May I come in?" he asked roughly.

Trembling, she whispered, "Yes." Of course he could.

She'd been living for this moment. Doubts were gone, swept away by passion and a sense of inevitability.

"You know I want you."

"Yes."

A jolt ran through him, and his grip on her arms tightened for an instant. "I wasn't sure..."

She wished she could see his face better. "Sure you want me?"

He made a sound in his throat. "I've always wanted you. I wasn't sure you wanted me. You've been...skittish."

She was still skittish. If only he'd kiss her again.

Talking gave her the space to think, to replay all of her "should I or shouldn't I" debates. She couldn't tell him that.

"I'm not one of your patients."

He pulled back a few inches. "My patients?" His mouth quirked. "Oh. Can't 'skittish' refer to people, too? Don't worry. I didn't mistake you for a horse."

Laughter helped. So did the next kiss. They parted only long enough to stumble out of the car and meet around by the front bumper. He'd never before done more than brush the sides of her breasts. Now he did, molding them with his palms, stroking them, kneading gently. Her hands, in turn, found their way under his shirt to his bare hot skin. Muscles rippled under her touch, and the sense of power was a marvelous aphrodisiac. He groaned, low and harsh, and yanked her to him for another deep kiss.

Every now and again they took a step—she was dimly aware of that much—but she was still befuddled when he prodded, "Key?"

She gave a dazed look around. They'd reached her doorstep and she hadn't noticed. Thank God she'd had the presence of mind not to leave her purse in his car; she dug blindly through its contents. Keys. They had to be in here somewhere. Eric's mouth on her neck didn't help, but her hand at last closed on their jagged edges.

"Here," she whispered.

He had to back up while she fumbled for the house key and inserted it into the lock. She turned the knob, and they nearly fell in, staggering and then regaining their footing.

Humor threaded the ragged sensuality in his voice. "If we'd gone down on the floor, we wouldn't have gotten back up."

Even as she chuckled, her breath caught. "I wouldn't have cared."

"Good." His hands gripped her buttocks and he pressed her tightly to him.

The feel of his erection against her belly awakened long-buried desire. Her hips lifted, sought a natural resting place.

"If we don't make it to your bedroom in the next thirty seconds, it'll be too late," he growled. "Last door?"

She murmured wordless agreement.

He didn't give her a chance to lead the way. With startling abruptness, he lifted her off the floor. She gave a squeak, wrapping her legs around his waist and her arms around his neck.

"I don't want to let go of you," he told her, his eyes glittering with pale green fire.

She touched his mouth, which slanted into a purely male smile that did nothing to lessen the impact of that gaze. Her fingers trailed to his jaw, shaven but rough, then to the long grooves carved in his lean cheeks.

"Don't let go of me," she said as he shouldered open her bedroom door, sending cats scattering from her bed and out of the room.

Eric lowered her onto the comforter. In a voice that had the texture of corduroy, rough and velvety at the same time, he said, "Never."

A thrill quivered through her.

And then his gaze swept over her with the possessiveness of a man claiming something as his own. "God, you're beautiful."

She wanted to hear, "I love you." But she had to admit he was beautiful, too. As he unbuttoned her blouse and pushed it aside, she did the same to his shirt, fumbling with the last few buttons. He gave a sound of satisfaction at the same moment she did. His fingers felt callused against the tender skin of her breasts. That texture, like the grittiness of his jaw and the roughness in his voice, only heightened her excitement.

Oh, his shoulders were wonderful, broad and smoothly muscled under tanned skin. No mat of hair disguised the contours of his chest; he was sleek and brown and warm under her exploring hands, and his heartbeat drummed as frantically as her own.

"Your breasts are perfect," he murmured, and bent to kiss first one nipple, then the other, before drawing one into his mouth. The vibrations of his voice played on her skin as he freed his mouth enough to nuzzle her. "I knew they would be."

She chilled a little, but the pull of his mouth had an electric effect on her body. Her hips lifted and pushed against his thigh, braced between her legs, and he gave a soft laugh of triumph before suckling her other breast. This time she felt his teeth, and she cried out from the intense pleasure of it.

But then, oh God, then, he reared up to gaze at her, a fierce grin of male satisfaction on his face. With the air of a connoisseur, he stroked circles on her belly with his fingertips. "Your skin is incredibly soft. How the hell do you stay so white, so silky?"

She said nothing, only stared up at him.

He reached behind her head and deftly pulled the pins from her hair, tossing them to the carpet, sifting her curls through his fingers. "Your hair is glorious."

Still she gazed up at his face, so taut and male, but his face had become *their* faces, and his words, his compliments, bled together with *their* words, *their* paeans to her beauty, never to *her*.

He wasn't different. She'd been fooling herself.

Madeline was suddenly cold. Her muscles tightened and her hands curled into fists.

Above her Eric noticed and he stiffened; his gaze sharpened. Her hair slipped unnoticed from his fingers.

"Is something wrong?"

"Yes." The word was bald, as icy as she felt. "I can't do this."

"You *what?*"

"Would you please get up?"

He swore and rolled to one side. "What the hell...?"

"Nothing's changed, has it?" Madeline said bitterly, scrambling from the bed. "I should have listened to my instincts in the first place."

"Instincts? Goddammit!" he roared. "Tell me what's going on!"

Feeling naked in a way she hadn't two minutes ago, Madeline turned away from Eric as she shrugged into her blouse. "Only one thing counts, doesn't it?" she said. "You want a beautiful woman to show off, a beautiful woman under you in bed. You're just like all the other men I've ever met!"

Eric uttered a sharp profanity and jackknifed to his feet. "You *are* beautiful! What do you want me to do—poke your hipbones and tell you you're bony but I'll have you, anyway?"

Facing him, she cried, "I want you to see something besides my 'perfect' breasts! What if they *weren't* perfect? What if they were drooping or covered in stretch marks? Would I qualify as a potential bed partner next time? Oh!" Infuriated and sick, she spun around again, shutting out the sight of him. "Garth was right!"

"What?" Teeth set, Eric caught her arm and pulled her to face him. "What in God's name are you talking about?"

"He said you dated me because I was pretty," she said, wrenching herself free. "Fool that I am, I told myself it wasn't true."

"You *are* pretty!" His voice rose to a bellow. "That doesn't mean I don't admire your soul, or whatever the hell I'm supposed to be commenting on when I have a hard-on for you!"

Hot and cold at the same time, she clutched her blouse together. "You never did answer my question. What if my breasts weren't perfect?"

He grabbed his shirt from the bed and, with quick angry movements, yanked it on. "I wouldn't have wanted you of course! I'm so goddamned perfect myself I won't settle for anything less in a woman. You know me—I have to have the best of everything.'' He stopped after having shoved three buttons through random buttonholes. Slinging his tie around his neck, he went on with icy contempt, ''Yeah, I drive a Rolls, buy my clothes at Brooks Brothers. Nothing but show-quality purebred pets for me. Hell, I may make my living treating other people's mangy animals, but I wouldn't have one in my house! I admit it. You've got me pegged.''

She pressed a hand to her stomach to quell her nausea. ''You know I don't mean—''

''No?'' He stopped in her bedroom doorway and gave her a look so scathing, she had to close her eyes. ''Then just what *do* you mean?''

Even if she could have answered, he didn't give her a chance. When she opened her eyes, he was gone. The front door slammed so hard pictures on the wall vibrated. Eyes saucer-wide, Maggie shot into the room and dove under the bed.

The car engine gunned in the driveway, roared as he backed out. A moment later the sound receded as he drove away. Out of her life, in every way that counted.

Starkly she wondered which was worse—to think she'd been right, or to think she'd misjudged him totally?

She began to cry, standing there in the middle of her bedroom, the sobs shaking her, the tears streaming unchecked down her face.

Dear God, what if he *had* loved her?

DAD HAD CABLE TV. If you could call it that, Garth thought incredulously, flicking through the choices with the remote. It took him about ten seconds. There were only fifteen channels, instead of the fifty or so he was used to. He settled on a Jackie Chan movie he'd seen before, but it was still kind of cool to watch him whirling and just levelling all these bad guys by kicking them in the chops. The fact that the movie was half over didn't matter; it wasn't like the plot mattered. Or the dialogue.

He turned his head at the scrape of a key in the front-door lock. A second later Dad came in.

Garth opened his mouth to say hi, but the word never came out. Dad's expression was terrible, as if somebody had just died or something. His eyes stared zombielike, like he hadn't even noticed the TV was on, or his own son was sitting there. Every line on his face was deeper, harsher.

"Dad?" Garth said uncertainly.

His father's head turned, but still blindly. "Yeah?" he said in this dead voice.

"Are you all right?"

"Me? Yeah. I'm okay." He came around the couch and sank down heavily, then didn't say anything else, just stared at the screen. A commercial for beer had replaced Jackie. Dad didn't even drink beer that Garth had ever seen.

"You...you look kinda weird." He was scared now. Had something happened to Mom?

Dad bent his head suddenly and squeezed the bridge of his nose between his fingers. Garth had a feeling he was squeezing really hard.

"Madeline and I seem to have parted ways." His father gave a ragged sound that he maybe meant to be a laugh. "That's like saying the vet at the county animal shelter is 'putting animals to sleep.' I seem to have made a major misstep, and I still don't know where I put my foot wrong."

Garth sat silent, shocked. His father was always so *solid,* like he never made mistakes and things never went wrong. Now he looked as if he'd been clobbered, only not in a way Garth understood.

Dad kept talking, but not to Garth. Maybe he'd forgotten he was there. Or hadn't really noticed in the first place.

"She despised me all along," he muttered. "Am I such a scumbag?" He gave his hair a yank that must have hurt. It seemed to remind him of something, because for the first time he turned his head and his eyes zeroed in on Garth. The look in them was angry and confused. "Did you tell her I was dating her only because she's pretty?"

"No! Why would I say that?" Garth answered in bewilderment. "I mean, she *is* pretty. Really pretty." He swallowed. "But she's cool, too. I mean, she's nice. And the stuff she does for cats is—" he struggled for the right word "—well, it's special."

His dad groaned a word he'd never said around Garth before. And then he just sagged into the couch cushions, head back, eyes closed. "I, uh, I really liked her," he said thickly.

Dad wouldn't cry, would he? The idea horrified Garth. "But can't you fix things?" he asked hastily. "Tell her you're sorry for...well, for whatever you did?" What *had* his father done?

"I don't think it's that simple." Dad gave him this twisted smile. "But who knows?"

Garth's thoughts jumped forward. "What about Chev and Ron?" he asked anxiously. "She won't want to come and see them, will she."

"Probably not." A sigh seemed torn out of Dad's chest. "No. But she'll call you. Just don't tell her she's beautiful."

"Why not?" A memory flashed, and Garth's eyes widened. "I...I think I already did."

His dad gave him this strange look. "What'd she say?"

He frowned, trying to remember exactly. "I guess she said thanks."

"I should be so lucky." Dad shook himself. "Oh, hell, let's go to bed. Unless you're really watching that."

Now Jackie Chan was hanging out of a helicopter. Garth shook his head and picked up the remote.

After brushing his teeth and medicating and feeding the kittens, Garth turned out his light and climbed into bed. He rolled onto his stomach, reached one hand into the shelf of the headboard and found Ron. No, Chev—the fur was downy, instead of silky. He scratched gently, undemandingly, until a soft comforting purr began.

A spurt of anxiety brought his eyes wide open, staring into the darkness. Madeline wouldn't take the kittens back, would she?

But she'd said she didn't have any other foster homes right now. Even if she was mad at Dad, she wouldn't take it out on these guys, he decided. He couldn't imagine she would. The fear receded.

But like the tide leaving shells, a few lumps of unhappiness stayed in his stomach. Even if she let him keep Chev and Ron, probably she wouldn't take him to the shelter anymore. He'd been a whole bunch of times now. He looked forward to going! Probably Dad would drop him off once in a while, but it wouldn't be the same when Madeline wasn't taking him. She wouldn't even be there!

Garth still glowed with pride, remembering the way she'd applauded when he petted Smudge. And the way she smiled when she noticed him cuddling this really sweet cat named Peanut, who was also ugly and skinny and losing hair and kind of smelly. He guessed some people didn't like the stink he left on your clothes. And when she saw how great Chev and Ron were doing, her face just lit up.

He'd never wanted to please anyone as much as he did her. He could see why Dad liked her so much.

Garth wanted to see her. But the idea of Dad marrying her scared him. Look what had happened with Mom. All she could think about or talk about was Chuckie. Garth didn't matter that much anymore to her. Chuck had been nicer to him at first, too, probably because he was trying to impress Mom.

He frowned. Was that why Madeline had been so friendly?

"No," he whispered. "She likes me. I know she does."

But what if she and Dad really fell in love? If his

own mother had quit paying any attention to him, he bet Madeline would, too. And Dad.

Mom kept saying she wasn't dumping him. But she was. Dad kept saying he wanted him. Maybe he really did. But if he had Madeline, he wouldn't. Garth couldn't begin to compete with her.

Along with the purr, his anxiety quieted and his eyes grew heavy. Now he wouldn't have to compete. Now Dad wouldn't be too busy to want to have him here. So maybe this way was better, even if he *couldn't* go to the shelter.

Chev stirred under his hand, and he heard the soft crunch of Ron eating dried food.

"I've got you guys, anyway," he whispered, and let sleep take him.

CHAPTER TEN

MADELINE SAT on the board of Ten Lives, which sounded more formal than it was. Jean and the four volunteers met once a month at the shelter, ordered a pizza and discussed successes, failures and the direction they were going.

Today's meeting was held in Joan's kitchen; everyone munched on veggie pizza, talked in quick bursts between bites and laughed frequently.

Madeline finished a slice while listening to another volunteer talk about a conflict with the manager of a store where they'd been holding adoption days. They agreed on a possible solution. In the lull afterward she said, "Joan, I don't know that I even told you about a promising conversation I had this week."

Heads turned her way. "A woman who'd called to see if we could take an older cat—Sophy, the beautiful white short-hair who came yesterday—turns out to head a hospice organization. They provide nursing care and meals to terminally ill patients who are still in their homes. Sophy belonged to a young man with AIDS who recently died and had no one willing to take the cat. This woman—Maria Garcia—says that pretty regularly they're left having to place pets. But the interesting part is that they have

patients who would love to have a cat but don't feel
they can adopt one because they worry about what
would happen to the animals when they die. I told
her I'd get back to her, but—'' Madeline glanced
around at the other members ''—what do you think
about the possibility of our placing cats temporarily
through her? She thinks that in most cases the cat
could be indoor only, so that ones who are leukemia
or FIV-positive could go. They'd have a home for a
while, get lots of affection, and the fact that *they're*
terminally ill, too, wouldn't matter.''

"Essentially, these would be foster homes," Carla
said.

"Right."

They discussed the idea, excitement generating the
electricity that kept all of them going through times
of discouragement and frustration. In the end the vote
was to give it a try. Cats that were currently unplace-
able could enjoy homes, even if for a short time; the
patients would have someone to cuddle and love,
without worrying about what would happen to their
new pet when they died.

"Just so we check them out," Joan said. "If we
place a leukemia-positive, we have to be sure the
person is trustworthy. It might be best to visit, make
sure the windows are screened and the setup is such
that the cat can't wander out."

"We'll emphasize the fact that these cats are con-
tagious," Madeline agreed. "I don't mind doing the
visiting."

"Good." Joan closed the lid of the empty pizza
box. "Any more business?"

There seemed to be none. Amid a chorus of good-byes and some personal gossip, the women departed, Joan for work and the others for home. Only Madeline stayed. Garth was in the main part of the house—she'd picked him up after making sure Eric wouldn't be home—and now she tracked him down to see whether he was ready to leave.

She found Eric's son patiently visiting with a couple of shy depressed newcomers whose owners were in the midst of a divorce and had decided neither could take care of the cats. Curiously the big gray male was also the more timid and frightened of the two. His sister, a smaller gray-and-cream tortoise-shell, was somewhat more willing to peek out of the cage or to hop down from the upper shelf when someone visited.

In response to Madeline's hi, Garth said, "They're really nice cats. How come they're here?"

She explained.

He frowned. "Well, why couldn't either the man or the woman take the cats? I mean, did they ditch their kids, too?"

"God knows." She'd had the same thought. "In this case, the woman said they were selling the house, both were renting places that either wouldn't allow pets at all or demanded huge deposits, and she couldn't cope."

"Yeah, but look at these guys." After having tried to stay aloof, the male pushed suddenly against Garth's hand, then tilted his head for those wonderful fingers to find the right spot. His eyes were so huge and anxious and he was so grateful for the attention that Madeline's heart ached. Garth's, too, apparently, because he sounded distressed. "How could someone just *leave* them?"

"I couldn't," she said quietly. "Too many pet owners just don't see animals the same way we do. To them, their cats are like, I don't know, nice furniture or favorite sweaters. To be enjoyed, maybe even indulged, but not mourned when they wear out or become inconvenient. Trouble is, the cats mourn."

"Yeah." He was silent for a moment. "You'll find a new home for these guys, won't you?"

"I hope so." She blinked so he wouldn't see the tears that stung her eyes. "They're eleven years old, though, so they'll be hard to place. Especially since they really ought to stay together if we can possibly manage it."

"Yeah." Garth's voice was subdued. He slowly closed the cage. "Did you want to leave?"

"I'm ready." Madeline worked up a smile for him. "How about you?"

"I guess. Can I get some more litter for Chev and Ron?"

He threw a couple of bags in the trunk of her car while she collected a sack of canned cat food to replace what he'd already used.

Today was the first time they'd seen each other since her breakup with Eric. She'd run into Teresa at the post office and delicately worked the conversation to find out which days Eric would cover at the clinic. She'd waited this morning until she was sure he'd left, then phoned Garth.

Now in the car, she gave him a sidelong glance,

wondering how much Eric had told him. And oh, it was pathetic, but she needed badly to know whether Eric was any happier than she was. Maybe she'd been no more than another woman he'd dated. Probably she'd be better off not knowing, but she wasn't strong enough to resist.

"How are you and your dad getting along?" she asked casually.

Garth shrugged. "Okay."

Well, *that* was informative. "He, um, told you we aren't seeing each other anymore?"

"Yeah." Garth stole a glance at her. "He didn't say why."

Because he told me my breasts were perfect. "I guess he thought the things we said should stay private."

"Yeah." Garth sounded disappointed.

"I'm afraid it was mostly my fault."

"Yours?" he said incredulously.

She drove half a mile in silence. What finally came out wasn't exactly what she'd meant to say. "Sometimes I wish I didn't look the way I do."

His eyebrows shot up so high they nearly touched his hairline. "But...but you're a babe!" Crimson flooded his cheeks. "I mean...that is..." His Adam's apple bobbed. "I'm sorry."

"No, don't be." She took one hand off the wheel to touch his arm lightly. "You see, that's the problem. All anyone ever sees is my face or my figure. They don't see *me*. I realized your dad didn't, either."

Now deep furrows appeared in the boy's forehead. "But he really liked you."

Are you sure? How do you know? she wanted to ask. *What did he say about me?* But she had some dignity remaining.

Not much.

After the tiniest of pauses, she asked, "Is he upset?" Pray God her voice didn't betray that this one question was the entire point of the conversation.

"Yeah, I think so." Garth was still frowning. "He looked awful that night. Since then...I don't know, I guess he's kind of quiet."

Did *quiet* translate to *suffering?* Maybe he just didn't have anything to say. The black hole inside her expanded. She wanted to know that he *hurt,* that he felt empty, angry, lost. She wanted to know that she'd been more than a pleasant diversion.

"Do you miss him?" Garth asked in a small voice.

Madeline was silent again. "Yes," she admitted at last. "And you. I've had fun with you guys. I'm glad you could come today."

He mumbled something that she understood to be, "I like going."

"I do, too," she said, giving him a crooked smile. "You know, there has to be a shelter like Ten Lives in San Francisco. You could volunteer there. Maybe foster cats."

"Chuckie probably hates them," Garth said gloomily.

"Or maybe not." Her smile became more natural. "Ask him, and your mom. Think of the cats. Not your pride."

"It's not pride—" He stopped. Emotions chased each other across his face. "Maybe it is. Kinda. But I have good reason..."

She turned into his driveway. "I bet having your mom remarry is a real shock. Especially if you don't like your stepfather."

Garth bowed his head. With only that peach fuzz of hair covering his scalp, he looked so vulnerable, the ripple of vertebrae exposed on the nape of his neck. "Chuck's not that bad," Garth said haltingly. "But he's all Mom pays attention to anymore! We were okay without him! Why did she have to get married?"

Lonely decisions and empty nights. The answer came without hesitation, which worried Madeline. What happened to being happy with her own life?

Probably Garth's mother used to tell herself—and her son—the same thing: they were happy; nothing ever had to change.

In front of Eric's house Madeline put the car in park. Facing Garth, she said, "I don't know your mother, but...sometimes it's hard for a woman to be on her own." She raised her hand to forestall an explosion. "I know she wasn't exactly on her own, but even if you were a help and you two are good friends, it's not the same as having another adult. It's a different kind of relationship. Your mom has this fierce need to protect you and make sure you don't have to worry about things like money or safety or her health or her own past or future." Now how did she know that? Madeline wondered. "She needs someone she can talk to about stuff like that. And—"

she flashed a wicked smile "—we are, after all, biologically programmed to want sex. You've probably begun to notice."

He blushed again.

"Scoot," she said. *Before your dad comes out.* "Before I say something even worse."

His smile was a youthful version of his father's charm. "Okay. If you want to get rid of me."

"Garth."

"Just kidding." He opened the car door and hopped out, then hesitated. "I wish you were staying for dinner."

She did, too. "Thanks," she said. "Maybe I'll take you out one of these nights."

"Cool!" He slammed the door and waved goodbye as she drove away—hoping she didn't meet Eric's pickup in the driveway.

Or maybe Eric was already home, standing back from a window watching his son race toward the house. Eric probably wanted to run into her no more than she wanted to run into him.

Unexpectedly the thought stung. Her vision suddenly blurred, and she had to brake at the foot of the driveway and rest her head against the steering wheel for a moment. Most nights the tears didn't come until she was in bed, alone but for the comforting presence of the cats curled the length of her body like pearls on a string.

"Dammit," she whispered, lifting her head and drying her tears with the back of her hand. "He didn't love you. Live with it."

With a deliberate effort, she wrenched the picture

of Eric off her mental bulletin board and replaced it
with one of her mother. Waiting in Madeline's small
house, probably already dishing up dinner. Preparing
a few tactful critiques like tiny barbs to insert in her
daughter's flesh. Apparently *not* preparing to go
home in the near future.

Turning onto the road, Madeline wondered if her
mother had ever had a fierce need to protect her. If
so, how had maternal devotion twisted into a deter-
mination to use her daughter? And did her mother
even know the difference?

"GOOD DAY?" Eric asked casually as he set an onion
on the cutting board.

"Yeah, it was okay." Though somewhat bland,
this was a step up from three weeks ago, when Garth
would have said with blistering sarcasm, "Yeah,
right."

"I saw Madeline drop you off." He'd hidden behind the curtains like an old busybody.

"We went to the shelter." Garth was making the
salad. He shook wet lettuce leaves, soaking everything within three feet with a fine spray. Including
his father. The boy appeared not to notice. "These
two cats just came in. They're eleven, and they're
really nice, but they're scared, and Madeline says
they'll be hard to place 'cause nobody wants ones
that old."

"Why are they there?"

"Their owners are getting divorced and don't want
them anymore." Garth studied him, and Eric could
feel what was coming. He continued chopping the

onion. "Don't you know somebody who'd take them?" Garth asked. "I mean, you know practically everybody in town, right?"

"Well, I wouldn't put it that strongly."

"I really like those cats." Garth ripped the lettuce into huge chunks, which he dropped into a bowl.

Having Garth care about something again was worth any price. Eric vowed he'd find a home for that pair if it killed him.

Resignedly he asked, "Do you know if they were indoor only or if they're used to dogs?"

"No." His son frowned. "I guess you'd have to ask Madeline."

"Or you can ask her."

He gave his father a sidelong glance. "Yeah. I guess." He reached for a carrot. Peelings flew. "She says she misses you."

The knife slipped and blood beaded on Eric's finger. He swore. What the hell was wrong with him? Of course she'd said that—when his twelve-year-old son asked her! If she really missed him, she'd call, say she was sorry, ask if they could talk. She'd give him a chance to say, "I like the heart that's underneath your perfect breasts, too."

He ran cold water over his finger, remembering her breasts, ivory and rose, just big enough to fill his palms. And he remembered her face, mouth puffy from his kisses, her eyes huge and dark, the color running across her perfect cheekbones....

He swore again. Something base and male in him refused to rise to sublime heights. He wanted her body. He couldn't help it. God, he wanted her right now, this minute, and he was standing in the kitchen with his son.

She'd wanted him, too, he'd have sworn it. But he'd said the wrong words, or else she'd flat out panicked, in which case nothing he'd said would have been right. Either way, how was it fixable? He couldn't watch everything he said forever; if she had more confidence in her inner self, she wouldn't care so much what people thought about her outer.

"I suppose," he said, drying his finger on a paper towel, "you told her I missed her."

"I might have. Just to be polite, you know. I mean, I couldn't say, 'Nah, Dad doesn't mind.'" Garth shot him an inscrutable look. "But it wasn't like you wanted to marry her or anything, did you?"

"No. I wasn't ready to walk down the aisle." He frowned at his reflected image in the dark window above the kitchen sink. A heaviness in the pit of his stomach made him wonder. *Had* he been ready to say, "I do"? "I thought you liked Madeline," he said.

Garth turned a pair of round innocent blue eyes on him. "I do."

Those damned words again.

"She's cool," his son continued. "She said maybe she'd take me out to dinner some night."

Oh, that'd be fun, sitting at home thinking of his own son out with the woman he— Whoa! He didn't love her. They'd only known each other for six weeks or so. He had the hots for her. He liked her. Teeth clenched so hard the enamel must be cracking, Eric made himself recite silently, *I do not love her.*

He just couldn't quit thinking about her, which was different.

These days it seemed as if every damn thing he did at work made him think about Madeline. The very next day, for example, he got to be the lucky one to explain to a man old enough to know better that, yes, a cat *could* get pregnant as early as six months. In fact, a female cat invariably *did* get pregnant that early unless spayed first.

The fellow chewed that over. "I just figured she was getting kind of plump."

Through the wall of the kitten's abdomen, Eric felt the shifting of several other lives. "Kittens rarely get obese."

"I guess it's, um, too late to spay her, huh?"

Eric stroked her soft black head. "I'd say she's due any day."

The man hoisted his jeans. "My girlfriend's real fond of her, see." He shifted uneasily. "Well, I guess I am, too. Pixie's a nice cat. She sits on my lap when I watch TV. Pays closer attention to Mariner games than my boy used to. But what do I do with the kittens?"

Eric handed him a Ten Lives business card and ushered man and pregnant cat out. Madeline would not find this story amusing.

On Eric's way back in, he met Teresa coming out of one of the other examining rooms.

"Why do I bother speaking in the schools," he asked rhetorically, "when the kids' parents don't seem to understand the birds and the bees? Hell, maybe I should go speak at the seniors center. Or the Rotary luncheon.''

"You *are* speaking at the Rotary luncheon,'' she pointed out. "Last week of July. Tell them all to neuter their pets.''

"Yeah, yeah.'' He shook his head and started to pass her. "Maybe I'd better take my pointer and a chart that shows female anatomy.''

Teresa snagged his arm. "Got a minute? I have somebody I'd like you to meet.''

Without the slightest curiosity he followed her. In the examining room a Dalmatian puppy—the latest fad—stood on a stainless-steel table. The pup's owner was a pretty brunette in tight chinos and a knit top that nicely outlined her breasts—breasts that would have done a hell of a lot more than fill his palms.

He tore his eyes away. Teresa was introducing the woman, who apparently owned a local window-glass business.

"Nice to meet you, Rhonda,'' he said, shaking her hand. She wasn't in any hurry to take it back. He shouldn't have been in any hurry to *give* it back. Mildly surprised at himself, he let her hand go and leaned against the door. "Puppy have a problem?''

"No, she's just here for shots.'' She gave him a smile that might have been a come-on, but was the kind he liked: direct and friendly.

He felt no stirring of interest.

"Rhonda's a friend of mine,'' Teresa told him. "Just figured you two might as well meet.''

It finally penetrated: Teresa knew he and Madeline

weren't seeing each other anymore and she was trying to set him up with her buddy.

"Well, good to meet you, Rhonda." He ruffled the
puppy's fur. The skinny tail whipped. "Enjoy this
little guy. Make sure you take him to an obedience
class."

A hint of wryness in Rhonda's smile told him she
understood he wasn't interested.

"Teresa has been giving me the same lecture. It's
okay—I grew up with Dalmatians."

"Ah." He opened the door. "Well. I'm sure we'll
see each other again."

The next patient was already waiting in the examining room he was using today. This one was the
fattest little terrier he'd ever seen. Not pregnant; just
three or four inches of fat wrapped around the poor
thing's rib cage so that she could barely waddle.
He'd been giving the dog's elderly owner lectures on
not feeding her table scraps, measuring out the dog
food, encouraging a little more exercise. So far, no
cigar.

The old lady looked up eagerly when he came in.
"I think she's lost weight, Dr. Bergstrom. She cries
at night, she's so hungry, but I've been strong." Her
face crinkled into a sheepish smile. "Mostly."

"Well, let's take a look." Eric bent down and
hoisted the solid chunk of terrier onto the scale. She
didn't try to take a piece out of him, which was
something. Maybe, he thought, amused, she was
weak with hunger. Now *that*, Madeline would think
was funny.

The sense of loss slammed into him afresh. He

fiddled with the scales to cover the moment during which he couldn't have spoken to save his life. The pain subsided. He glanced at the chart, then raised an eyebrow at today's weight.

"Congratulations, Mrs. Rodenas! You're right. She's lost a pound."

She clapped her hands and chortled. "I knew it! Can I give her just a little treat to celebrate when we get home?"

"Now you know better than that," he said sternly. "You don't want to lose Julitta at an early age, do you? She's barely begun her diet. Let's shoot for another pound by next time."

Mrs. Rodenas, pleasantly padded herself, shuffled as slowly as her dog. He escorted them out, one patient step at a time, then—speaking of waddling—turned back to find Teresa lying in wait again.

"What was wrong with Rhonda?" she demanded.

Eric played dumb. "Wrong? What do you mean?"

His partner splayed her hands on her belly—over which the lab coat no longer fit. Voice dry, she said, "You know exactly what I mean! Where was the playful smile? The bedroom eyes? The husky tones?"

He snapped. "What? Did you promise I'd perform like a goddamn toy poodle? Flirt on command? Well, let me tell you a secret. I don't circle pretty women as if they were in heat and I were a mindless male dog, whatever the hell you think!"

Damn Teresa, what did she do but smile with blatant satisfaction. "You're in love with Madeline."

He let out a bellow and tugged at his hair. "Don't

even try to explain your convoluted female thinking! I don't want to hear it!'' He stalked down the hall to his office and slammed the door. Residents of the kennel responded with a chorus of unhappy howls and yaps.

Eric flung himself into his chair and stared moodily at the wall. He should be getting ready for surgery. He needed steady hands and concentration. This was not the moment to feel his gut churning.

Damn her! he thought again, and then realized that he saw not Teresa, but Madeline, clutching her shirt to her breasts.

He muttered a colorful profanity and shot back to his feet. Teresa met him in the surgery room. Thank God, she said nothing, only smiled. He gritted his teeth and began scrubbing.

A couple of hours later he stripped off his lab coat and wished his partner a terse good-night. He supposed he could go home, but he'd been putting off a visit to Ten Lives. Madeline had spent most of yesterday there; she wouldn't have any reason to come back today, would she? It ought to be safe.

He let the staff know where he was going, then checked the supply of basic meds in his truck. A short five-minute drive, and he pulled into the lane leading up to the shelter. He parked, collected a bag of supplies he knew he needed and started toward the house. He was almost to the doorstep when he saw her car.

So she *was* here. He swore softly. He wasn't in the mood to get their inevitable meeting over with.

As he retreated, a boy's laugh rang out. Oh, hell,

his son was here, too. He'd look a damned fool if they saw him skulking away.

Eric strapped his bag back into place in the truck, then walked silently to the corner of the garage, where the chain-link-fence runs began. He stood in the shadow of the woodpile and glanced into the yard. His heart almost stopped.

Madeline wasn't ten feet away with Garth, who sat cross-legged in the grass. Wearing snug jeans and a sleeveless shirt that exposed slender creamy shoulders, Madeline squatted on her heels beside Garth, her head cocked as she looked down at the cat in his lap. The bundle of hair at her nape was even cruder than usual; thick fiery tendrils tumbled over her cheek and down her neck. Her profile was flawless, with that straight little nose, high curved forehead and delicate chin.

Eric reached out and grabbed the chain-link fence until it bit into the pads of his fingers. God, she was beautiful! More than beautiful. She laughed then, and his chest cramped. A moment later, as he stared hungrily, her laughter stilled, and small crinkles appeared on her forehead as she listened to something Garth was saying. Eric could hear the words; they just didn't fit together into anything meaningful. All he felt, heard, saw, was her. As she listened, she idly stroked several cats who tangled their sinuous bodies around her legs. Nerves shivered under Eric's skin as he felt the tenderness of her touch. It was *his* heart that felt the gentleness of the hand she laid on Garth's shoulder.

Apparently his son qualified as one of the shy

frightened wild creatures she let herself love. Too bad *he* didn't.

If she knew how he hurt...

On a spasm of wrenching pain Eric closed his eyes, pried his fingers loose and backed silently away. He had to leave. Now. Before they saw him. Before he had to do any more pretending.

He got into his pickup and drove until he came to a packed dirt turnoff beside the road. There he put on the emergency break, turned off the ignition and pounded the wheel with his fists.

Why, why, why couldn't he have some of that bottomless love she handed out so freely to the lost and angry?

Maybe, an inner voice suggested, *because all you can think about is how beautiful she is. Admit it: she's right.*

No. Goddammit, no! She was wrong. It wasn't just her looks that got to him. It was...everything. Her incredible compassion. Her smile. Even her prickles. She reminded him of some of the cats, the ones that craved human affection but feared it, too. He wanted to know why she was that way. He wanted to know why she disliked her mother. Why she was willing to keep extending herself for his son.

He made himself picture other beautiful women he'd known. Deliberately he thumbed through mental files, remembering Noreen on their wedding day, his college girlfriend lying atop him laughing, several other women he'd dated, one he hadn't. Perfect cheekbones, soft mouths, shimmering hair. And he felt...nothing.

Panic grabbed him then. He stared blindly ahead through the windshield. Dear God, he *was* in love with her. He didn't just want her, he needed her.

And he had absolutely no idea whether she'd give him a second chance.

CHAPTER ELEVEN

OH, LORD. Eric was here.

Madeline lifted her foot from the accelerator, stalling her car halfway up the driveway to the shelter. Muttering under her breath, she restarted the car and threw it into reverse. Too late. Joan appeared in the parking area and waved.

With all the courage of an ant scuttling from an ominous shadow, Madeline thought maybe she could somehow avoid him. If he was in the surgery room, she could slip into the house. He wasn't likely to come looking for her.

She shifted into first, drove forward and parked in her usual spot. Getting out of the car, she glanced at Eric's pickup. "I see Dr. Bergstrom's here."

Duh.

Joan, too, glanced at the pickup. "He came about an hour ago. He's already neutered Whitey and Friendly, and all the male kittens. Now he's doing some blood draws and checking Nefertiti's skin."

"Oh, good." Madeline edged toward the main house. "I just stopped by to clear up some paperwork."

Joan didn't budge, making it hard for her to keep

sidling toward the front door. Arms crossed, Joan asked, "What paperwork?"

Madeline stole a glance at the feral building. Eric didn't burst out. "I'm organizing all the old release forms, trying to match them to the adoption contracts."

Joan gave her a frankly astonished stare.

"Okay. I'm avoiding my mother."

"She's still here?"

"I think she's moved in with me and just hasn't thought to mention it."

"She might mention it if you were ever home," Joan suggested.

"Maybe I'll go home and weed, instead."

At last her friend moved, firmly taking Madeline's elbow and ushering her toward the house. "As long as you're here, why don't you give me your opinion on something? Since we're finally going to be tiling the garage with that grant money, I was thinking of having the old cages torn out and new ones built. They could sit on top of some catproof cabinets. You know, with locks and the whole shebang."

Once inside the house, Madeline felt reasonably secure. The garage had no windows looking out toward the front, so she couldn't watch for Eric, but it wasn't as though he'd hunt her down. He probably despised her, she thought, which lowered her mood another notch.

She and Joan briefly discussed where they'd put the new cages and how they'd manage while the tile was laid and the grout cured and sealed.

Finally Joan glanced at her watch. "Listen, I've

got to run. Can you take Sassafras out to the feral building before Eric goes and have him check her ears? She's been scratching, and the drops for mites don't seem to have helped.''

"Joan—"

Already bustling out, the older woman gave her a starchy look. Joan had once been a third-grade teacher and it showed. "I'm going to be late to work if I don't go. Caroline is the only other one here, and she's out giving him a hand."

"I don't want—"

"Don't whine. You've got to see him sooner or later. Today is as good a time as any. See you."

"Joan…"

She was gone. Madeline muttered a word she rarely used. Then reluctantly she grabbed a carrier and went in hunt of the elderly black-and-white cat. Maybe she'd get lucky and Caroline would meet her at the door of the feral building. She might not have to set eyes on Eric.

Sassafras proved elusive. Mudhen, the homely shelter "manager" strolled importantly ahead of Madeline through the house, growling at cats who dared attempt to distract her from her mission. Warier ones scattered once they saw the carrier. Caroline, a volunteer in her fifties, came in once and released two cats.

From down the hall Madeline called, "Tell Dr. Bergstrom I have one last cat for him to look at."

"Will do!" Caroline said. The front door closed a moment later.

Having failed on the first pass through the house,

Madeline started all over. This time she found her quarry tucked in a fleece bed on top of a cage. The old cat grumbled but didn't struggle as Madeline popped her into the carrier.

Fastening the carrier door, Madeline peered inside. "He's not going to hurt you, Sassafras, my sweet." All the *S*'s hissed soothingly off her tongue.

Carrier in hand, she stepped out the front door but stopped on the doorstep, her heart sinking. The parking lot had emptied; not only was Joan's station wagon gone, so was Caroline's small blue Honda. The only two vehicles left were Eric's pickup and Madeline's car. Why hadn't Caroline said she was leaving?

Feeling light-headed, Madeline kept going. The gravel crunched underfoot. The door to the feral building opened easily. Inside was the admitting area, well organized and spotless. She carefully closed the door behind her. It was either very quiet in here, or her heartbeat was drowning out all other sound. Did Eric hear her coming? Did he know it was her?

Did he *care* if it was her?

She turned down the hall. The door to the surgery room stood ajar. Now his voice, low and husky, came to her.

"Are you waking up there, guy? Come on, take deep breaths. You'll feel better before you know it. And just think, Madeline can find you a home now." Pause, then another, "It's okay. Don't worry."

To hell with Joan. Panic rising, Madeline stood

stock-still a few feet from the door. She couldn't do this.

She eased one foot back. Sassafras let out a piercing meow.

Even bigger and broader-shouldered than she remembered, Eric filled the doorway. To her hungry eyes, he looked wonderful, face lean, lines carved deep from nose to mouth, lab coat rumpled. Pure male, with those big hands that she knew were so gentle with the animals—and with her.

"Come on in," he said quietly.

She drew a shaky breath. "Hello, Eric."

"Caroline said you were coming." His voice was like one of those touches: calluses just a little scratchy, banked strength, incredible restraint.

Her own came out in a squeak. "I thought she'd still be here."

"I told her not to wait."

"Oh." She stood there, everything she should say to him crowding her tongue, tangling it so nothing got said. "I...I have Sassafras here."

"Let's take a look." He backed into the surgery room.

She followed. The stainless-steel table gleamed; in cages along one wall, two older kittens were lifting groggy heads.

Eric's hand brushed hers as he took the carrier. "Madeline..."

"Eric..." she said at the same exact moment.

His clear light eyes took in her face with the intensity of a surgical laser. "You first."

She squeezed her fingers together. What if he

planned to say, *I'm dating someone else now.* Or, *Let's not let the fact that we dated for a while get in the way of our working together here.* What if he was just trying to smooth the awkwardness? "No. You, please."

"All right." Eric backed away from the table where he'd set the cat carrier, then leaned against the windowsill and rubbed his hands over his thighs. "I, uh...I wanted to apologize." He grimaced. "I knew you were sensitive about your looks—you've made that plain enough—and what do I do but ignore your feelings. The truth is, it's easy to compliment someone. It's a hell of a lot harder to tell someone how you feel. Madeline—"

"No!" The word burst out. "Please! I'm the one who should apologize! I...I led you on and then I turned coward at the last minute. Nothing I can say is adequate, but...I'm sorry." Tears burned in her eyes.

Eric made a guttural sound and crossed the tiny room in two long strides.

"No!" she cried again, backing away. "Let me explain. Please."

He stopped abruptly right in front of her and held up his hands. "All right," he said roughly. "Explain."

Poor Sassafras was blessedly quiet. Madeline bowed her head. "The thing is, I started acting and modeling when I was only five. Well, my mother entered me in a beauty pageant first. I won. An agent approached her..." She didn't even remember her first assignment. Those early years were a blur: hot lights, adults giving overly simple orders in saccharine tones, dumb clothes. "It must have been too tempting for her. My dad was nowhere around, and Mom was an LPN—a licensed practicing nurse. Surviving financially had to have been a struggle. Here people started offering all this money if I'd just work for a day, a week..." She let out a long breath.

"But you kept working."

She peeked upward and saw anger darkening his eyes. "Constantly. I never went to public school. My mother tutored me for the first five or six years, then I attended a performing-arts school in L.A. Of course, I was hardly ever actually there."

"Didn't you tell your mother you hated it?"

"Not until I was a teenager." She made a face. "Before I got rebellious at about fifteen, it was just...life."

"And your money?"

"As my manager, Mom took a cut. That's what we lived on. The rest she invested. I used some to start my business. I still have quite a bit. My mother wouldn't steal from me. She has too many... principles." Oh, how dry that sounded!

He searched her face. "You hate her, don't you?"

"No." Although there'd been times she wondered. "I wanted her to love me for myself, not for my face and what it could earn." There. She'd said what she hardly acknowledged even to herself.

She still wanted her mother to love her. How pathetic, she thought, disgusted at herself. Did nobody ever completely grow up? Or was she the only one still mired in childhood?

Eric lifted his hands as though to grip her shoulders, but stopped short of touching her. Instead, his fingers flexed, then curled into fists before he shoved them into his pockets.

"And now," he said emotionlessly, "you want someone else to love you for yourself. Not your face. Or your breasts."

"Is that so unreasonable?" she begged.

He uttered a raw profanity. "No. God almighty, no!" His head went back, and he rubbed his neck. "I'm a cretin."

"You didn't know."

"I knew."

"Eric, I'm the one apologizing, remember?" Inexplicably she felt steadier. "I'm the one with the problem. It's...okay to think I'm beautiful. I guess," she admitted, "I want you to."

He focused on her face again, his eyes glittering, his mouth a taut line. "Are you telling me it's not too late?"

"If—" she had to clear her throat "—if you haven't decided I'm a flake."

"Oh, God." Voice pure grit, he closed his eyes. "Do you know how jealous I've been of my own son?"

"No," Madeline whispered.

"I saw you talking to him. You laughed, and touched his shoulder."

"I thought...you wouldn't mind if I kept bringing him here."

"I was glad. For him. But for myself—" now at last he gripped her shoulders, and she felt a tremor in his hands "—I wanted it to be me, even if we were nothing more than friends."

She'd flattened her hands on his chest, but at that she pulled back in alarm. "Is that...what you want? To be friends?"

"What do you think?" he asked, and then he kissed her.

She *couldn't* think. Her mind was incapable of any activity beyond simple dizzy awareness that his mouth was heaven. Hard, sensuous, skillful. And more—this kiss had a desperate edge that shook her as deliberate seduction never could. She whimpered, and her arms slid up around his neck. His hands moved to her back, her hips, lifting her, pressing her against his length. His teeth closed on her lip.

And, oh, the magic words he murmured as he strung kisses along her jaw, down her throat, over her T-shirt to the swell of her breasts.

"You're not just beautiful on the outside, you know. You talk to those damn cats, in that husky little voice, as though you've got enough love to make up for the rest of their wretched lives, and I want some of it. When you laugh, it makes me smile the rest of the day. And you listen to me. God! do you know how long it's been since anybody really listened?"

Her bones dissolved and she arched her back as his hands slid up under her shirt. "No," she croaked.

"No?" His head lifted, and sudden sharp awareness returned to his eyes. "Oh, my God," he said, straightening. His fingers clenched on her shirt, and then he released her, spreading his hands wide as he

backed away. "Here I go again. You give me a re-
prieve, and I'm on you like those poor lonely damn
cats in the house. Madeline, I'm sorry."

"Sorry?" She felt stupid. And bereft.

"No. I don't want to be friends." A muscle
jumped in his cheek. "But I have *some* self-control,
believe it or not. Let's start over. You weren't ready
for sex. Fine. I want you, but not until you're sure,
really sure, I'm not just lusting over your body."

"I'm sure." Was she?

"No." He gave a wry smile. "This isn't exactly
the time and place, anyway."

Sassafras chose that moment to utter a plaintive
meow.

"I guess not," Madeline said. Although it would
be easy not to care where they were.

"Can we go to dinner?"

"My mother has probably already got ours in the
oven."

He swore. "Lunch tomorrow?"

Madeline nodded.

A smile twitched at the corner of his mouth and
then failed. "I missed you."

She swallowed and blinked to forestall tears. "I
missed you, too."

"Good." Eric gave her a quick hard kiss. "Okay,
let's take a look at this cat."

COMING IN THE DOOR from work on Friday, Eric
scooped up Hannah, who, as always, was waiting to
meet him. Early or late, she never missed. At first
he'd worried that she sat there all day staring pa-

tiently at the closed door. But Garth swore she didn't; apparently she just had good hearing.

"Hey, Dad." Garth lounged on the living-room couch with a black kitten on his shoulder. "Look, Ron's checking out the house. I don't think he's scared at all."

Mannequin slept on an ottoman only a few feet away, no more interested in this kitten than she was in anything else. Eric couldn't decide if she was brain-dead or just placid. As long as she didn't need life support to keep breathing, he supposed it didn't matter. Lord knew she wasn't any trouble.

"Good," Eric said. He ran his fingernails down the little guy's spine. "Now why don't you put him back. Teresa invited you over for dinner. Says Mark would be happy to have you spend the night, too, if you'd like."

A scowl immediately clouded the boy's open expression. "I won't spend the night. And I don't want to have dinner there."

"Tough," Eric said unsympathetically. "I'm going out, and I don't want to leave you alone all evening."

Garth didn't move. "I don't need a baby-sitter. I'll just stay here."

"No, you'll go to Teresa's." Eric tried hard to keep his voice level and pleasant. No point in letting this escalate to a major confrontation. Nonetheless, he wasn't caving in. He and Garth got along better these days, but his son was spending entirely too much time alone. They still had half the summer to go; it was time he hung out with some other boys.

And, dammit, he and Mark had been friends in the past!

"Why?" Garth burst out. "Where are you going, anyway?"

"Dinner with Madeline." He hadn't told Garth about yesterday's lunch; somehow his renewed relationship with Madeline still felt insubstantial, unreal. He needed to know they were going somewhere with this before he put up with anyone else's scrutiny.

If he expected any emotion from Garth, it was delight. He didn't get it.

His son's face flushed. "But you're not seeing her anymore!"

"We had a talk and decided to give it another shot," Eric said mildly. "That okay?"

"No, it's not okay!" Garth shot to his feet and had to grab Ron, who tried to leap to safety. For once, the boy didn't think about the kitten first. "I don't want you to date her!"

Eric shook his head in hopes of clearing it. This couldn't be happening. But no. His son still stood there, bristling.

"You like her!" Eric exclaimed. "I don't get it."

"She's my friend! Not yours anymore!"

"But she was your friend before..."

"She hasn't called in days and days!" Garth spit out. "Now I know why! All she can think about is you! She was probably just friendly so I'd talk about *you*."

"Madeline isn't like that."

"Oh, right." His son sneered. "If Mom can be like that, so can she!"

"Your mother loves you," Eric said wearily. "She's on her honeymoon, for God's sake."

"Who're you going to dump me on when *you* get married?" Garth spun on his heel and half ran to his bedroom.

"Garth!" Eric bellowed.

Slam.

Now what? Eric gently deposited Hannah on the back of the couch and went to stare out the window. Should he cancel with Madeline? Leave the boy here alone? Insist Garth get ready to go to Teresa's? Try for another father-son talk?

He rubbed a hand over his jaw. Was Garth really afraid that Madeline didn't like him for himself? Did he think his father wouldn't have time for him if he was dating? Or did Garth even know himself why he was upset?

Eric moved restlessly. Damned if he'd let a twelve-year-old's temper tantrum keep him from seeing Madeline tonight. Garth couldn't be allowed to win. Manipulating parents by sullenness and threats had to be discouraged.

Frowning, he went down the hall. He stopped and rapped on Garth's door, raising his voice. "I'm going to take a shower. You get ready to go to Teresa's."

"I'm not going!" his son yelled.

"You don't have to spend the night, but you *are* going for dinner." Eric didn't wait to hear further protests. He just hoped like hell Garth didn't flat out refuse to step foot out of his bedroom. Eric couldn't quite see himself slinging a struggling teenager over his shoulder and throwing him in the car.

Half an hour later, dressed in suit and tie, hair still damp, Eric rapped on Garth's door again. "Let's go," he called, and kept moving down the hall.

After a pause that had his neck muscles locking, he heard the bedroom door open and close behind him. Garth followed him out, got into the car, slammed the door and slouched low in his seat. He didn't say a word during the two-mile drive to Teresa and Joe Hughes's big modern house. When there, Eric pulled into the driveway and turned off the ignition.

Into the silence he said, "We're going to need to talk."

Without looking at him, Garth reached for the door handle.

"Okay," Eric said. "Maybe I should have let you stay home tonight. I don't know. But I do know one thing. Now that you're here, I expect you to be civil. They're a nice family. They like you. Mark's been disappointed that you weren't interested in coming over. Just because you're mad at me, don't take it out on them. Got it?"

Of course Garth didn't answer. Eric hadn't really expected him to. He walked his son to the door and said hi to Joe, who raised his eyebrows as Garth barely mumbled hello and went in, still without saying a word to his father.

As soon as he was out of earshot, Eric said, "We had a fight. He wanted to sulk in his room. I made him come."

"He'll have a good time." Joe's voice was, as usual, calm and amiable. "Mark has a new game on CD-ROM that he thinks is better than eating, which is saying a hell of a lot."

Eric laughed ruefully. "I felt so smug when Teresa was having trouble with Nicole. *My* kid would never act like that."

"Pride goeth and all that." Joe nodded toward the living room. "Want to come in?"

"No, Madeline is expecting me. Teresa has the number of the restaurant."

"Why don't you bring her over here for dinner some night?" A smile touched Joe's blue eyes. "I hear so much about her and we've never met."

"Sounds good." Eric slapped him on the shoulder. "Better make it soon. Once the baby's born, you won't be doing much entertaining for a while."

"I don't know," Joe drawled. "At least we have a homegrown baby-sitter."

"True." Eric lifted a hand in farewell. "I should be back before midnight."

Anticipation was singing in his blood by the time he parked in Madeline's driveway. Too bad her mother was still here. Knowing how she'd used Madeline made it harder to be friendly—not to mention that her presence precluded anything more intimate than a handshake between Madeline and him.

He'd hardly taken his finger off the doorbell when the door swung open. He liked that Madeline never kept him waiting so she could make some kind of grand entrance.

But it was her mother who stood smiling in the

doorway. "Eric, how nice to see you again. Come on in. Madeline's not quite ready." She bustled ahead. "Have a seat. Can I get you something to drink?"

"No, thanks."

Madeline's mother must have been damn near as beautiful as Madeline when she was younger. Her expertly styled hair was darker, but the bone structure was much the same; only the fine lines beside her eyes and mouth and the air of fragility showed the additional years. Sometimes her expression was disconcertingly similar to Madeline's. What she lacked was her daughter's warmth.

He asked about her trip to Lake Quinault Lodge. She raved about the scenery, the service, the rustic rooms. Eric stole a surreptitious glance at his watch. Was he early? No, it was now ten minutes after the time they'd set. Well, Madeline might have gotten held up at work. What was ten minutes?

Another five minutes passed before he heard a door down the hall open. Heels clicked on the hardwood floor. Midsentence, he lost track of whatever he'd been saying and rose to his feet. A second later the sight of Madeline hit him like a fist to the solar plexus.

A shimmering green sheath fit her tall impossibly slender body like a second skin. If she wore a bra or underwear, he didn't know where they were hiding. No, of course she wasn't wearing a bra—the spaghetti straps of the dress couldn't hide one. Heels added a couple of inches to her height. Covered only with the faintest sheen of silk, her legs went on forever. Her gleaming auburn hair was swept back into a French roll. Freshwater-pearl earrings dangled nearly as long as her neck. And even her face—by God, he couldn't actually see the makeup, but she glowed, her cheekbones subtly accentuated, her eyes huge and mysterious, her mouth an incredibly sexy pout.

This was the Madeline Howard whose face and figure had been worth a fortune.

Her thick dark lashes batted flirtatiously. "Aren't you going to say anything?"

"You're magnificent," he said, then cursed himself. Was this some kind of test? Was he supposed to prove he could keep his eye fixed on her inner beauty no matter how she gilded herself?

But she was smiling. "Thank you," she murmured. "I don't think I need a wrap. Shall we go?"

As she passed, her scented warmth brushed him. If he'd still been breathing, he would have quit then.

Her mother, hands clasped, smiled her approval. "Have a good time!"

In a dream he escorted Madeline out to his car and held open the door for her. As she swung her legs in, her dress rode up, exposing a sleek expanse of thigh. Dazed, he circled the car to the driver's side.

It had barely begun, and already this was the most bizarre evening he could recall. Garth, who adored Madeline, didn't want his father dating her. Meanwhile, Madeline, who hated being judged for her outer beauty, had dressed as seductively as a Victoria's Secret model.

Eric stole another glance at her. She smiled and

deliberately crossed one long slim leg over the other. He shook his head again, although it hadn't clarified anything the first time, and tried to get the key into the ignition despite his acute awareness of her thigh, only inches from his hand.

Damn, how he wanted to touch her. His fingers itched to wrap around her leg and slide up into the shadow beneath the hemline of that skimpy dress. He was hard already, and he still hadn't gotten the damned car started!

"Where are we going?" she purred. Oh, hell, she probably just asked, but his nerves were so on edge now everything she did had provocative overtones. If this was a test, he was going to fail.

He named a classy Italian restaurant on Fifth Avenue in downtown Seattle. He got the car started at last, the clutch in, but saw her when he had to turn to look over his shoulder to back out.

"Oh, I love that place!" Madeline said in a voice that was just a little huskier than usual.

They talked during the drive; Eric hoped he wasn't making a complete fool of himself. By the time he parked half a block from the restaurant, he couldn't remember a thing he'd said. Or she'd said. All he knew was that her voice was like a velvet coverlet pulled over his head, so his whole world was darkness and texture, incredibly sensuous but also smothering.

Even in a restaurant where beautiful people dined regularly, she got a reaction. As they were shown to their table, a pool of silence spread ahead, murmurs behind. Her usual brisk stride had been replaced by a sexy sashay that increased his discomfort, along with his arousal. Who *was* this woman?

Who cares? an appreciative side of him asked. He got to spend the evening with this sexy creature, and he was wasting a thought on the Madeline Howard who wore baggy olive green T-shirts and jeans? What, was he crazy?

They perused the menu and ordered, then gazed at each other across the candlelit table. A smile played around her mouth, as though she knew how he felt and was secretly amused.

"Garth took Ron out to explore the house today," he said almost at random.

"Really? Ron and Chev ought to be neutered pretty soon. In fact—"

"They're ready for a home. I know." Eric grimaced. "I don't know if Garth does."

She reached out and took his hand. "Will you let him take on some more? If he's saying hello the minute he's said goodbye, I think he'll take it better."

Even her hand felt different tonight; he knew it was strong, but right now it felt silky smooth, fragile, utterly feminine. She'd painted her nails, he saw, a deep rose that somehow looked just right with the emerald green dress.

What had she said? The teasing scent of lavender that gently wafted across the table seemed to fog his mind. He lifted her hand and pressed a kiss into the palm. She gazed at him with those huge eyes and smiled faintly.

Garth. That was it. Could he take some more kittens.

"Sure," Eric said. "Of course. Do you have any more that'll make him feel as needed?"

"We always have more." The hint of dryness in her tone sounded like her normal self. "We just got in a mom and litter. Five kittens. He'll enjoy them."

Six cats in the bedroom. Oh, hell, Garth wouldn't care.

Wine and salads came. They talked about politics, business and cats. She admitted to having missed her riding lessons; they planned a trail ride the next weekend, her first.

"Can you find another horse so Garth can come?"

He'd imagined the two of them ambling along in the sunshine, maybe taking a break beside the stream, stretching out in the tall grass while the horses grazed nearby. But she was right. "Why not?" he said. "Maybe your mother would like to ride, too."

She rolled her eyes, and he had the satisfaction of having pierced her armor, however briefly.

Over dinner they moved on to movies they'd seen, concerts and theater they'd attended. She'd just been to the touring production of *The Phantom of the Opera*, having missed it the first time it came to Seattle. Jealousy burned in his gut as he wondered who she'd seen it with. She was careful to avoid saying, and he was damned if he'd ask. Rage rose, swift and unexpected. *He'd* had the chance to date and hadn't taken it! But she went to the Fifth Avenue Theater? For all he knew, she'd been out every night the past two weeks! Maybe she hadn't been dating him exclusively in the first place. He'd assumed——

"Why are you frowning so fiercely?" she asked in that velvety voice.

He grabbed the first excuse that came to him. "Worrying about a dog I did abdominal surgery on today. Sorry."

Her eyes were magnificent, bottomless wells of femininity and understanding. He could drown and not care.

"You don't have to be sorry," Madeline murmured. "Tell me about it."

He did, though he kept wondering who'd sat next to her at *The Phantom of the Opera*. Had he discreetly held her hand? Where had they gone to dinner? Had she minded him telling her she was beautiful?

Maybe not; maybe that was why she'd blossomed in confidence enough to be willing to quit hiding behind ugly clothes and messy hairstyles.

By the time they finished their coffee and left the restaurant, Eric was a churning mass of confusion, frustration and hunger. He wanted her, but he also, for reasons he didn't understand, resented her manipulation of him. She was trying to drive him to the edge; she *had* to be!

But he'd vowed to be patient; he had self-control, he reminded himself grimly. She wasn't ready for sex. He was prepared to wait until she was damned sure it was what she wanted to do.

He seriously doubted that she'd become certain of anything since Wednesday.

The drive home was mostly silent. Romantic music poured out of the speakers. Every streetlight and passing headlight shimmered over her long legs and the slippery green fabric of her dress. He couldn't think about anything but her. His palms were sweating.

He found himself remembering the first date he'd ever been on. His parents had a 1971 Chevy that stalled easily. It happened twice that evening, both times in the middle of intersections with oncoming traffic. Ellen Marie Fitzgerald—good God, he not only recalled her name, he saw her plain as day!— had squealed. She had also not only opened her mouth for his kiss at the end of the evening, she'd let him touch her breast.

More than he was going to get tonight.

They were entering the city limits, and he put on the turn signal for Madeline's street.

Her voice came to him, clear as his memories. "Is Garth home?"

Desire lanced through him, a painful stab. "No." The one word was so rough he cleared his throat. "He's at Teresa's."

Her hand touched his thigh. "I'm sure," she whispered.

"Thank God," he said, and accelerated past the turn to her house.

CHAPTER TWELVE

ALL HE WANTED was to pull that dress up around her waist, yank off her silk stockings and bury himself in her. Guaranteed to send her running.

Patience, Eric thought tensely. Finesse. Their love-making had to be good for Madeline. He knew in his bones that this was his one chance.

He didn't pull over to the side of the road to kiss her, much as he wanted to. He wasn't sure they'd have gotten any farther if he had, and she deserved better than a quickie in the back seat.

When he parked the car in the garage, shutting the rolling door with a push of the button, he turned to her, still not letting himself touch. "Are you sure?" he asked hoarsely.

Madeline nodded, almost but not quite smiling. "How many times do I have to say it?"

"A hundred." He put his hand to her throat, pausing where her pulse beat frantically, then slid it upward to her jaw. "A thousand." He bent his head, mouth poised just above hers. "A million."

This kiss was deep and slow and left him feeling drugged. He grazed her lips with his teeth, traced the curve of her cheek, nibbled on her earlobe. Then he lifted his head and for a moment just gazed at the

perfection of her face. A blush ran across her cheekbones, her lashes formed a thick fan against ivory
skin, and her mouth was soft. When she opened her
eyes, he saw the dark dreaminess that he'd imagined
nights when he couldn't sleep.

"We'd better get in the house," he said roughly.

She stared at him with clouded eyes, then blushed
again and gave a small nod.

Her dress rode up as she swung her legs out. Then
she dropped her purse and had to bend over to pick
it up from the concrete floor. Finally she was on her
feet, far less gracefully than usual. Maybe she felt a
little foggy, too.

He kissed her and wrapped his hands around her
hips, lifting her against him. She felt so good there
he hurt. If she quit on him this time, he was going
to sink to his knees and bellow like a wounded bull.

Still kissing her, Eric maneuvered them through
the door into the kitchen. He stumbled over something, staggered, regained his footing. Looking down,
he realized it was Hannah, waiting just inside. The
cat gave her speciality, a silent meow, and gazed up
hopefully.

"Oh!" Madeline tugged away from him and
scooped up the small gray tortoiseshell. "Did we almost trample you? Sweetie, you're getting plump."

Eric groaned and sagged back against the wall.

Madeline lifted her head. A smile quivered on her
sexy mouth. "I suppose we could talk later about
how she's doing."

"Much later," he said from low in his throat. He

watched her deposit Hannah on the floor. "Come here."

"Ooh, how macho," she teased, but took a step, anyway, and melted into his arms.

Hannah didn't follow them down the hall. Eric did have to evict Mannequin from his bed and plop her out in the hall, shutting the door in her sweet vacant face.

Madeline's breath was warm on his neck. "It's just like my house."

They wouldn't have room on the bed if they combined their households. The thought wasn't such a jolt this time. They'd manage. They could keep their bedroom door shut. Like now.

He framed Madeline's face with his hands, his fingers slipping into her smooth hair. "I'll ruin it."

She smiled, lifted both arms like a ballerina pirouetting and pulled out pins that dropped to the carpet in a brief shower. Her glorious mane fell free, tumbling over his hands and her silken shoulders.

He heard an animal sound that shouldn't have come from a man. Her mouth opened willingly for his; he ravaged it, his tongue thrusting. At the same time he shimmied up her dress and drove his hands inside her panties, gripping her high firm buttocks.

He was going to embarrass himself if he didn't get inside her.

Finesse. She wasn't ready. She couldn't be.

He wrenched his mouth away and squeezed his eyes shut, breathing hard through his nose. When he opened his eyes, he looked down into hers.

They were misty and wondering. "I'm sure," she

whispered, for the third or fourth or hundredth time just over the thunder of his heartbeat.

Hands trembling, he very slowly peeled off her panties and stockings, kneeling at the last to slip the silk off each foot as she lifted it. There she stood above him, naked from the waist down, gloriously slim and pale, with a V of silky dark curls holding a hint of the same fire as the auburn hair that now swung down over her breasts.

His hands went back up, from her ankles to her calves, stroking the backs of her knees, up, up her thighs. God, her skin was smooth! She took little sobbing breaths. When he reached those curls, he didn't dip his fingers in. Instead, he bent down and rubbed his cheek against them. And then he turned his face and kissed her there.

The breath that escaped her was closer to a sob than a sigh. He kissed her again, then rose to his feet, lifting her with him, wrapping her legs around his waist, tumbling them both onto the bed.

Not ready. Finesse.

But she squirmed as though she was, adjusted her hips to cradle him and ran her fingernails over his back. Only his pants were between them. He thought he might go crazy. He sought her mouth again, willing himself not to rip down his zipper and take her.

Not yet.

Instead, he wormed his hand under her back and found the zipper of her dress, working it down even as he kissed her. Once it tangled with the bedcovers and he swore. Madeline giggled and arched her back to give him better access. When her dress loosened, he made another guttural sound and tugged it down.

He'd been right. No bra.

"You're—" He stopped.

"You can say it." Madeline was working on his last shirt button. "I'll say it." She pushed his shirt off his shoulders. "You're beautiful. Sexy." Her hands searched the contours of muscle and bone. "Will you take your pants off?"

"In a minute." Now her searching fingers were driving away what little sanity he still possessed. "They're the only thing keeping me from having you."

Madeline said simply, "I know," and kissed his nipple.

He'd never removed an article of clothing as fast as he did those slacks. Then he put on a condom damn near as quickly.

Just for one second he reared above her, looking, savoring, not quite believing. He'd been afraid they would never get here. He didn't know how they had. Why she'd changed her mind. Why the evening had been one long seduction, why her thighs were parted to welcome him, why she was saying again, "I'm sure. Eric, please."

And then he lowered himself over her, found the damp hot entrance to her body and thrust. Every muscle in his neck and back was rigid as he fought to go slowly. Madeline's arms came up around his neck and she let out a long, sighing, "Ooooh."

Heaven. Sheathed so tightly in her, he paused long

enough to brush her mouth with his and murmur, "You feel incredible. *I* feel incredible."

"Yes." Her eyes didn't seem quite able to focus. "Me, too. I didn't know…"

Gasoline to the fire. Eric pulled out, buried himself again. Again. And again. Desire roared over him like a sonic boom rumbling from the sky. Madeline cried out and clung, hips lifting to meet every driving thrust.

When he didn't think he could hold on for another second, shivers started deep in her belly and spread, ripples of exquisite tightening that had her stiffening, digging her fingers into his shoulders and gasping. The rhythmic squeeze of her muscles carried him over the edge.

Heaven.

SHE'D NEVER FELT more gloriously feminine and fulfilled in her life than she did when Eric kissed her on her doorstep and left her that night.

After slipping inside, Madeline turned the dead bolt, did a twirl and laughed out loud.

"Madeline? Is that you?"

Oh, Lord. Her mother was sitting up waiting for her.

Reluctant to ruin her mood, she ran her fingers through her hair, hoped the end of her evening wasn't too obvious and moved to the open archway. "Yes, I'm home."

Mrs. Howard sat primly at one end of the couch, the lamplight pooled on a book open in her lap. "Did you have a nice time?"

"Yes, very nice." Even more reluctantly Madeline stepped into the living room, where she couldn't avoid the light.

Her mother's eyebrows rose. After a pause she said, "You looked lovely tonight."

The slight emphasis on the *looked* made obvious that it was past tense. In other words, now Madeline's appearance was tawdry, past its bloom. The first compliment she remembered hearing from her mother in years, and it was delivered with a sting.

"That's all you've ever cared about, isn't it, Mom?" Appalled, she heard herself say the unspeakable. Couldn't stop herself now that she'd begun. Had she shed all her inhibitions tonight? "I should apologize for letting you down. How dare I live without taking care that my face and clothes are flawless!"

Her mother stared at her in shock. "What on earth are you talking about?"

"Oh, you know exactly what I'm talking about." A part of Madeline gloried in the freedom to say everything, to let the bitterness she'd nourished so long leach from every word. Another part of her stood back, horrified. She didn't have to do this. It wasn't necessary for her accusations to escalate. All those years she and her mother had been so careful not to destroy their fragile relationship. Why blow it now?

Too late, because she'd already launched her attack. "All you ever wanted was the money and the glamor and the glory of my success! Forget having a daughter who might get pimples or skin her knee or be too busy with school or friends or a boy to play her part. I could never be fallible.'' Hopelessly she threw up her hands. ''Fallible? I couldn't be a kid! Do you know what I felt like by the time I was a teenager?''

Mrs. Howard rose to her feet and stood extraordinarily still. ''No.''

''Like I was for sale.'' Bile rose in her throat. ''And you were the seller.''

Under bright spots of makeup, her mother's face had gone pale. ''What a dreadful thing to say!''

''Wasn't I?'' Madeline challenged.

''No!'' Ghostly white stood out on the knuckles of her mother's hands as she clasped them together. ''I did my best for you.''

Something close to hatred laced Madeline's voice. Contempt, perhaps. ''That was your best?''

For a moment Mrs. Howard's gaze faltered and her mouth trembled, but then she lifted her chin and looked Madeline straight in the eye. ''I suppose,'' she said with dignity, ''I did want the money and the glamor. Once we'd stumbled into it, it was tempting. But what you've forgotten is that you wanted that life, too. From the time you were a tiny girl, you came alive on the stage or in front of photographers. You begged to go to auditions.''

''We fought constantly!''

''When you were a teenager. Other parents fought with their teenagers, too. Underneath, I thought you loved the life. If nothing else, I hope you'll believe that much.''

''How can I?'' Madeline's voice rose and she

whirled away. "I begged you to let me spend the night with friends or date or play sports! I wanted so badly to be like everyone else."

She felt her mother's tentative touch on her arm, and she flinched.

"I'll say only one more thing." Now Mrs. Howard sounded completely composed and inexpressibly sad. "After your father left, we were desperately poor. You were too young to know. We lost our house right away, and the places I could afford to rent got worse and worse. Your day care ate up half of what I earned. I had absolutely no skills that would give us a chance. When I read about the beauty pageant, it seemed like—" her voice quivered "—a bright spot in our lives. Something fun. Exciting. You were so pretty. I suppose I was channeling my own longing for chances I'd never had. I don't know. But when you won and the agent took you on, and then they offered money for you to spend a few hours modeling…" She was begging now. "It had to be better than the way we were living."

Madeline couldn't have spoken if her life depended on it. Her eyes were dry, burning, and her stomach churned with pain. She couldn't even bring herself to face her mother.

For the longest time neither moved or said a word. At last Mrs. Howard said quietly, "I always loved you. I'd have loved you even if you weren't pretty. I was…proud of you, I admit it. I let you be our financial salvation. Maybe that was wrong. But it had nothing to do with how I loved you. Or how I love you now."

"Then why," Madeline whispered, "didn't you ever say that?"

"I don't know."

Madeline felt as much as heard her mother leave the room, a whisper of footsteps receding, the soft closing of the guest-room door. And now the hot tears poured down her cheeks.

GARTH DIDN'T TALK on the way home. Eric had studied himself carefully in the mirror after dressing to be sure he didn't have a smear of lipstick on his neck or some other dead giveaway. Except for a stupid grin he couldn't seem to wipe off his face, he saw nothing unusual. And what kid really looked at his father, anyway?

Not his. Garth stalked past him to the car, slumped down in his seat and, when they reached home, hurried into the house and slammed his bedroom door.

"Good night!" Eric shouted.

No rejoinder came from his son.

Tiredness replaced some of his earlier buoyancy. He opened canned food for the cats and made his usual nighttime rounds, locking up and checking windows, then took a quick shower and turned out the lights. By that time, only darkness showed beneath Garth's bedroom door.

Eric's bedcovers held a wisp of Madeline's perfume—and a muskier scent. Sex. Restless, he kicked off the covers and lay sprawled on his back, wearing nothing but boxer shorts, staring up into nothingness.

He wanted her here again, warm and substantial, her voice drifting softly from the darkness beside him: "I'm sure." He wanted to feel again as if he could walk on water, as if she loved him.

Instead, uneasiness stole over him, settling heavily in his stomach, keeping his eyes open, shoehorning his thoughts into an inescapable maze.

Why, tonight, had Madeline defied everything she believed, everything she feared? Why had she flaunted her beauty? Seduced him?

Why was she suddenly "sure"?

He flung an arm over his face and clenched his teeth. Had he really made love to *her?* Or to a total stranger?

And how could he ever ask her?

Worse yet, why—despite his uneasiness—had he gotten so sexually excited? She was a beautiful woman. Was that all it took to push his buttons?

Hell. Maybe he was as shallow as Madeline had accused him of being.

By the time the sun rose and his alarm clock buzzed, he hadn't found any answers to his questions. He wasn't sure he liked himself any too well this morning, either.

To Eric's surprise, Garth emerged for breakfast, even though it was a Saturday.

"I have to work today," Eric said, probably unnecessarily.

His son nodded. "You always work on Saturdays."

"Teresa and I switch sometimes."

Garth picked up the empty milk carton and shook it. "Do we have any more?"

"Hmm?" Eric set down his coffee cup. "Oh.

Yeah. Sure. In the fridge.'' He watched the boy opening cupboard doors. ''Last night okay?''

Garth's shoulders hunched, but after a moment he gave a jerky shrug. ''Yeah. Mark and I played computer games and just talked and stuff.''

''Good,'' Eric said without expression. He didn't dare say anything that might be construed as ''I told you so.''

''He wants to see Ron and Chev.''

''He's welcome any time.''

''Yeah, he might come over today.'' Garth poured milk on his cereal, then dumped several spoonfuls of sugar on for good measure.

Eric raised an eyebrow, but didn't comment. Instead, he said, surprising himself, ''You've met some of the women I've dated. Were they all beautiful?''

Garth stared. Milk sloshed out of the bowl. ''Yeah, pretty much,'' he said, after apparently giving it some thought. ''I mean, weren't they?''

''It's not the only reason I dated them.'' And who the hell was he arguing with?

Garth gave him an odd look and set the bowl down on the table. He turned the chair around and straddled it. ''Sure, Dad,'' he agreed with the air of a nursing-home attendant pacifying a senile resident.

''You don't believe me.''

''I didn't really *know* them,'' Garth said reasonably. ''Except Madeline.''

''And?'' Eric found himself leaning forward.

''Well?'' His son looked at him with eyes too shrewd for a kid his age. ''*You* oughtta know why you like her. How should I?''

Good point. One that stuck with Eric all day. It was his turn to make farm calls, primarily pregnancy checks on dairy cows. While he stood ankle-deep in liquid manure, hand squeezed in a big bony Guernsey's rectum as he felt for the pealike growth in the ovary, his thoughts continued stumbling through the maze he'd become lost in last night.

Had he chosen women for their beauty rather than their character?

This was a hell of a moment for a memory to come to him. Danielle...something. Her last name eluded him. She was short, a little plump, mousey-haired; not homely, exactly, but no beauty, either. They'd been in 4-H together, and he'd really liked her, but now he cringed at how dismissively he'd rated her. "Nice" hadn't cut it. They'd become friends, and eventually he'd become aware that she expected him to ask her out. She'd been watching him when she hadn't thought he'd noticed. He'd become aware of her as a girl, too. She'd had nice breasts; he'd done his own share of staring. But she hadn't been pretty enough to be seen with. He started being busier with other friends. He'd dropped her flat.

Shortly afterward, he'd begun dating Cindy Hawcroft, a cheerleader and, ultimately, a homecoming queen. Dumb as an Irish setter, but as pretty as one, with hair the same shade of red. The two of them hadn't had a damned thing in common. Apparently that hadn't mattered to him then.

Shamed, he left the Eide farm and headed for the next. During the drive, he ran through all the girls he could remember dating in college. Pretty, every one. There'd been others, but friends only. He didn't date a girl who wouldn't excite the envy of his friends, however much he liked her.

He still didn't. Beautiful women awakened his hunting instincts like a weak calf did a wolf's. Had he ever seriously considered asking out a woman who was merely pleasant-looking?

He couldn't remember a one.

Eric parked his truck in the next farmyard, got out and automatically began suiting up in rubber overalls and vest and a new plastic sleeve.

His first reaction to his self-analysis had been to decide he was scum, but now he decided it was worse than that. He was pitiful. So concerned about what other people saw when they looked at him, he'd married a woman he had nothing to say to. And he hadn't even learned from that mistake!

The farmer came up behind him and slapped him on the back. "How's Dr. Hughes?"

Eric accepted the greeting as it was meant. Selecting vials of drugs he might need, he inserted them into slots on a tray. "Fine. Another month to go."

"Irene is knitting some little thing for her. Hat and booties, I think."

"I'll tell Teresa." Preparations complete, Eric said, "Well, I'm all set."

When he got home at five-thirty, he phoned Madeline. She sounded subdued, reticent.

"You okay?" he asked, leaning against the kitchen counter.

"Me?" Her voice held a false note of surprise. "Just tired. You must be, too."

"Long day," he agreed.

"And a late night."

"An incredible night," Eric said warmly.

"Yes." The note of constraint sounded again. "Yes, it was."

He gripped the receiver more tightly. "You're not sorry?"

The pause chilled his soul. "No, of course not."

"You're free tomorrow?"

"What did you have in mind?" she asked cautiously.

"Remember that trail ride we planned? Garth's counting on it."

"Oh, no! I'd completely forgotten! Let me think." He heard a muffled conversation. She came back on the line. "What time?"

"We'd better not make it too long a ride if you want to still be walking Monday. Say, we leave here about ten?"

"Sounds good. I'll be at your place by then." She drew an audible breath. "I'd better go. See you tomorrow, Eric."

Frowning, he hung up. No *I love you. I can hardly wait to see you. Did you dream about me?* Just, "See you tomorrow."

Great. Not only did he have to doubt his own motives, now he had to wonder about hers, as well.

Had she gotten cold feet? Or had the real Madeline Howard come to, looked around and recoiled from what her alter ego had done in bed with him last night?

THAT MORNING, Madeline had been waiting for the hot water to boil when her mother came into the kitchen. Their eyes met for one stark pain-filled moment before Madeline looked away.

"I shouldn't have said what I did last night."

"Maybe you should have said it years ago."

"Why?" Madeline blindly poured boiling water over the tea bag in her cup. "What's the point? It doesn't help to whine about the past. All I did was hurt you."

"As I apparently did you."

Madeline faced her again and was shocked by how much older her mother looked this morning. Wearing a bathrobe, she had yet to put on her "face," as she called it. The real face was carved with lines of exhaustion and age. Her pale lips were pinched, and traces of gray showed at the roots of her hair. She must have stayed here longer than she'd intended, or she would have had her hair done right before she'd come. Madeline had never seen her mother show her vulnerability as she was right this minute, in the kitchen at nine in the morning.

On a rush of remorse, Madeline said, "Can I pour you some coffee or tea?"

"Coffee, please." Mrs. Howard sat down heavily, as though her legs had given way. She said nothing about the detrimental effects of caffeine.

"Mom…"

"Madeline…"

They both stopped. After a defenseless moment Mrs. Howard said quietly, "I think I ought to go home."

Yesterday her mother's announcement would have been welcome. Now, the idea of her mother going—and with things left like this between them—upset Madeline.

"You don't have to," she said, and then realized how graceless that sounded. She took a breath. "I've been wondering about this visit. Something has been different about you."

How delicately put! Not quite a question, but begging for an answer nonetheless.

"Yes." Mrs. Howard concentrated on stirring nonfat creamer into her coffee. After a long pause she said, "Lately I seem to have been thinking a lot about my life. Something to do with my age, I suppose." Still she stirred the coffee, the action meaningless, something to fix on. "No, that's not quite true." She looked up at last and visibly braced herself. "I'm getting married. At least I'm considering it. I haven't decided."

Getting married? Her mother? Not so long ago, Madeline had wondered why she never had. So why was the idea so shocking now?

She sank into a chair. "Why didn't you say?"

"There's a good deal we haven't said to each other, isn't there?" Mrs. Howard's smile wasn't very successful. "In this case...well, I suppose I'm so undecided I felt I ought to keep it to myself. Or perhaps I was just waiting for the right moment."

Instinct had Madeline reaching across the table to cover her mother's thin hand with her own. Gazing at the sight—women's hands both, now—she realized how seldom they touched. She gave a gentle

self-conscious squeeze and let go. "Why are you undecided? Don't you love him?"

A soft smile transformed her mother's face. For an
instant she looked thirty years younger. "Yes, I think
I do." She sounded almost surprised. "It's not that.
It's me." The creases and sags of age reappeared on
her face. "I haven't exactly been a success at relationships. Your father of course. And...I wasn't
much of a mother apparently."

Madeline closed her eyes, guilt stabbing deep.
How many times had she hinted that visits remain
short or begged off completely? Made excuses to
herself for not calling? "I...haven't been much of a
daughter, either."

"Parents bear the responsibility."

"Do they? I'm an adult, too." In theory. Maybe
children never did become adults where their parents
were concerned.

"You weren't during the years that counted."

"Mom..." Madeline wasn't ready to let go of her
bitterness altogether; perhaps it didn't happen that
way, like a floodgate opening, but rather in a slow
trickle, like a crack in a dam. Maybe a little of her
stored anger had leaked out already. "Mom," Madeline said again, "if you did the best you could,
what's to regret? I was a child—I didn't understand
what you faced. I promise I'll think about what you
said last night. But you shouldn't let any...coolness
between us keep you from making a commitment to
a man."

Her mother lifted elegant brows. "Haven't *you?*"

"All I've asked for is a man to see beneath the surface. It has nothing to do with you!"

"I'm not so sure," her mother murmured.

Madeline let it pass. Not certain she wouldn't regret this, she said, "I wish you'd stay a little longer, Mom. Maybe, now that we're talking, we should do some more of it. You'll have to tell me about my future stepfather."

She was shocked to see tears spring into her mother's eyes. Madeline had never seen her cry. But Mrs. Howard dabbed them with a napkin and said with quiet dignity, "Thank you. I'd like that very much."

Madeline couldn't be sorry she'd suggested it. Tomorrow she might be, but not today.

Who knew? She and her mother might even become friends. Miracles happened.

CHAPTER THIRTEEN

MADELINE GRABBED the saddle horn and held on for dear life as Honey's powerful hindquarters bunched. With a lurch, the horse propelled herself up a steep four-foot bank.

"You can open your eyes now," Eric said, amusement a husky undertone in his voice.

Madeline did, cautiously. He waited on top of his borrowed gray Arabian, arms crossed as he leaned negligently against the saddle horn. Boots scuffed and dusty, denim shirt rolled up to show lean brown forearms, he looked at home on a horse. Behind her, leather creaked and the bay mare Garth rode let out a grunt of effort as she, too, mounted the bank.

Acres of grassy land planted with tiny seedling Douglas firs stretched out ahead. Right now, the grass and wildflowers dominated, daisies and tall purple spires of fireweed and a few delicate bright blue blooms that looked like flax. The well-beaten trail they'd been following widened to the width of a logging road here and wound in long swoops between the rows of seedlings.

"Oh, this is wonderful!" Madeline said with pleasure. The sun felt gloriously warm on her face and bare arms; she found she even liked the smell of leather and horse sweat mixed with the tang of the deep forest from which they'd just emerged.

According to the sign at the entrance, this enormous tree farm was open to walkers, cyclists and horseback riders, but closed to motorized vehicles. Half-a-dozen horse trailers had been parked outside the gates when Eric had backed his own trailer into one of the few remaining slots. The drive from White Horse hadn't taken more than half an hour. Garth had told Madeline that last summer he and Garth had trailered up here every week or two, usually with Teresa and her kids. The place was so big—stands of fifty-year-old trees alternating with those the size of Christmas trees—they had yet to see any of the other riders.

Now, eyes bright, Garth announced, "We can gallop here. It's really cool! We just go and go."

"Gallop?" she echoed nervously.

"Garth can gallop," Eric corrected. "You can go any speed you want."

The disappointment on the twelve-year-old's face made her feel like a killjoy. "I'll try cantering," she decided.

Eric grinned, teeth flashing in his lean tanned face. "You can always close your eyes and just hold on tight."

"Well!" She pretended to take offense. "Is that how you think I handle stress?"

He didn't answer immediately, although his gaze didn't leave hers. He said at last, slowly, "Plenty of people do."

Much as she'd like to, Madeline couldn't deny she

might be one of them. The other night, for example. She'd been standing in front of her closet thinking about what to wear for their dinner date when this impulse seized control of her. She'd put on a dress that had been untouched in her closet for years, used makeup with all the skill she possessed, reached for the highest heels she owned. Not even a moment of revulsion when she looked at herself in the mirror had stopped her. No, she'd spent the evening being someone different—someone flirtatious, at ease with her sexuality, bold.

The really creepy thing about it was that she hadn't once stopped to wonder *why* she was doing this. Maybe she'd just closed her eyes—to her motives, to how Eric would respond, to whether she wanted even for one evening to be this other woman.

Now she opened her eyes. And she knew.

She'd been afraid. Afraid she'd lose him or never have him to start with. Deep inside, she'd reverted to believing that only her looks made her lovable. She had to enhance what she had, use it for all she it worth, or he wouldn't want her. After all, it was her "perfect" breasts he admired, her eyes, her waist, her legs.

Still she sat staring at him, the horse moving restively under her. Was that what falling in love did to a woman? Eroded her confidence to the point where she'd do anything to have and keep a man?

Her trance was broken by Garth. "Can we go?" he asked, his horse prancing and tossing its head.

Eric's eyes held a challenge now. Madeline raised her chin. "You bet."

Garth let out a whoop, leaned forward and loosened his reins. The half-Arab bay he rode exploded forward, dust puffing behind her in the hot summer air. Not wanting to be left behind, Honey did a small dance. Palms suddenly sweating, Madeline took hold of the saddle horn again, said, "Okay, Honey," and eased back on the reins.

From a standstill, the quarter horse leaped into a lope. Unprepared, Madeline snapped back in the saddle, but her death grip on the horn held, and a moment later her body was moving in an easy rocking motion with the big gelding's. Eyes watering, she turned her head to see that Eric was right beside her.

"You okay?" he asked.

"Yeah," she called back, and then laughed. "It's fun! Garth's right. Hey, race you!"

She gave Honey a timid boot with her heels. The horse responded with a burst of speed that made Madeline's vision blur. Ahead, Garth was still yelling. Hair streaming down her back, exhilaration like champagne in her blood, Madeline let out one modest whoop.

Even over the thunder of hooves behind her, she heard Eric's laugh of sheer pleasure.

Now *this* was life!

This, and making love with Eric.

The scary part was the wondering whether he'd have wanted her nearly as much if she'd just been herself.

GARTH HATED the way his dad looked at Madeline. It was too much like the way Chuck looked at his mother, and his mother at Chuck. They'd lock eyes and get this stupid expression on their faces, and nobody else would exist.

He liked being with Madeline, too. Like today was mostly cool. She didn't ignore him or anything. But his dad spent most of his time watching her when she didn't know. It was like she was all he could think about.

Right now they were riding along together, talking in low voices, as if he was nobody up here, maybe a dog that all they had to do was call every once in a while.

He yanked too hard on the reins, and Kineta ducked her head and danced in protest.

"I'm sorry," he murmured, stroking her sweaty dusty neck, but he reined her in until Dad and Madeline came even with her.

Madeline flashed him an absent smile, but Dad didn't even seem to notice he was there.

"Grandma called yesterday," Garth said loudly.

His father turned this distracted look on him that became a frown. "You didn't say anything. Did she want to talk to me?"

"Not especially." Actually she *had* asked if Dad was there, but she hadn't left a message or anything like that.

"This is your mother?" Madeline asked Dad.

"Yeah, he calls his other grandmother Nanna. My parents live in Denver."

"She said they might fly out in August so they could see me," Garth interjected.

"Oh? Good." But Dad didn't sound very interested. He was looking at Madeline again.

"Grandma is really pretty," Garth said before Madeline's attention wandered, too. "I mean, she is in pictures. When she was young, you know." Dumb! he told himself. Like Madeline was going to care about what his grandmother looked like.

But she actually did cock her head and say, "Really? Is she blond like you and your dad?"

"Yeah, she has blue eyes like me. She's—" he tried to think of the right word "—like a princess or something."

"Regal?"

"Yeah." That was it. "Her back's always really straight, and she's never silly and she never laughs so you can see food in her mouth, and she's... graceful, you know? And when she tells you to do something, you do it, even though she never yells."

This weird expression crossed Madeline's face. "She sounds like my mother. I hope she's more of a hugger than mine. I was thinking the other day that we hardly ever touch."

Garth didn't exactly mind that Grandma wasn't a hugger; Nanna wasn't, either. His friend Dave had this grandmother who always squished him to her huge bosom and kissed his cheeks and cooed at him, and she didn't care if his friends were standing there or not. It made Dave major, mass embarrassed. Secretly Garth thought it might be nice to be hugged like that.

But now his dad said in a funny voice, "No, she

isn't very physically demonstrative, either. Maybe it's their generation. She and my father never kissed or held hands in front of us kids, much less in public.''

"Mom doesn't like it when Chuck kisses her in front of anyone," Garth said, the words just popping out and surprising him. "She's kind of regal, too."

Nobody said anything. Dad stared straight ahead, his face getting this dazed look that reminded Garth of the time he'd finally gotten mad enough to punch Tim Bancroft, and then Tim had just stared at him with that same stunned expression before he'd toppled over like a tree going down. Only, nobody had hit Dad.

Madeline was watching his father, too. "Are you okay?" she asked in a voice so soft and sweet it tightened something in Garth. For a second he wished that she was his mother and talked to him like that. But she wasn't, and no stepmother was going to think he was anything but a nuisance.

Dad gave his head a shake. "What? Of course I'm okay. Just...had a thought. Sorry." He gave this fake grin. "Want to gallop again?"

Garth didn't know how Madeline could look even prettier with her hair falling down and windblown and her nose starting to get sunburned and her T-shirt and jeans dusty, but she did. She lit up, and he wondered if that was what actors and models did when the camera came on.

"Race you!" she said really fast, and gave Honey a kick. Honey had been trained for cow-penning, so she could turn on the back burners. Madeline barely grabbed hold in time, and the last sight he had of her face, her mouth was open in a big O.

Dad's smile looked more natural. "Shall we let her win?"

"Heck, no!" Garth loosened the reins and whacked Kineta's rump with the flat of his hand. As the mare rocketed forward, leaving Dad in the dust, Garth thought, *now* this *was cool. He'd kick Dad's butt.*

If only it was just him and Dad riding, like it used to be. With Madeline around, his father would forget all about him by the time they caught up to her.

OUT OF THE MOUTHS of babes. God, what a moment for a revelation!

Two days later Eric still reeled from the insight Garth had hit him over the head with.

He was getting in a short run before work, taking a circle that was about three miles. Even this early in the morning the day was hot; it was going to be a scorcher for the Pacific Northwest, which might mean the thermometer would reach ninety. Sweat dripped from his face and soaked his T-shirt. He hardly noticed. He was too busy reliving that moment Garth had pointed out the obvious.

Noreen had a hell of a lot in common with his mother. They were both blond, slender, elegant, untouchable. The untouchable part had been the challenge; he remembered how Noreen had intrigued him with that cool classy air, how determined he'd been to shatter it and see her flushed and panting with passion.

Well, passion had been easy. He never had penetrated the shell in any other meaningful way. She didn't get angry or laugh until she fell out of her seat; her eyes didn't fill with tears or outrage or excitement. She loved Garth. He had no doubt she was an affectionate mother—up to a point.

She was probably rather like his own. Which was undoubtedly why he'd married her.

Not that Eric thought he had an Oedipus complex. But he had an uncomfortable feeling that he had wanted something from his mother—still did—that he hadn't gotten, that she wasn't capable of giving. And that Noreen had been the stand-in. Noreen, and possibly all the other women he'd dated.

His father was a brilliant man, a professor of mathematics. Physically he was large, blockish, even a little clumsy. Inept socially, as well, he must have been a source of constant irritation to his wife, who loved to entertain, dress well, be seen at the right events. She'd worked, too, in public relations and fund-raising for a private prep school in Denver, and very successfully—her aristocratic style had undoubtedly made potential donors feel inadequate and therefore eager to rise to her standards by writing huge checks.

Even as a kid, he'd wondered why his parents had chosen each other. They didn't *fit*. Their ambitions were different. His mother had a way of belittling his father, just tiny jabs, but constant. She still did it, and they were still married. Eric sometimes wondered if his father even noticed.

She hadn't been all that warm and accepting with

Eric and his sister, either. Madeline's remark on Sunday had sent a jab of shocked recognition through him. Hell, he didn't remember ever being held or hugged or patted. His mother didn't offer back rubs after a tough football game, didn't straighten his shirt collar or brush back his hair. She didn't touch.

He was a fool not to have understood years ago that he was subconsciously trying to recreate his relationship with her, to have the warmth and complete acceptance of a woman who measured up to his mother's standards. In other words, an equally beautiful woman.

So Madeline had been right that her looks were what had drawn him, although not for the reasons she probably suspected.

The big question was, what if Madeline was no longer beautiful? What if they got married and she put on sixty pounds? What if she was in a car accident and her face was damaged? What if she had a mastectomy?

How would he feel about her?

He knew one thing: he had to decide before their relationship went any further.

"AUDITION: *The Man Who Came to Dinner,* female and male roles, July 30, 7:30 p.m., Everett Historic Theater.

The newspaper open on the counter before her, Madeline read the brief notice again and again. She hardly ever even glanced at the Billboard section. This time, as she'd idly thumbed past it, the casting call had jumped out from the newsprint as though it glowed.

Madeline had stopped by the newspaper office to drop off a photograph for the Pet of the Week feature sponsored by local veterinarians—including Eric. Behind head-high partitions, she heard voices and the hum of computers and printers. Since she had to wait for Carmen, the young Chicana woman who always put the feature together, she'd opened the newspaper.

She was still looking at that darn audition notice.

She *had* loved to act. The day she left behind her modeling career, she'd pulled a mental curtain closed, resolving never to peek behind it again. A good deal of her past was behind that curtain, gathering dust, like old props left behind when a theater shut down for good.

Lying awake last night, she'd decided it was as if she'd opted for selective amnesia, only it hadn't been as selective as she'd thought. She'd come to detest a couple of the props; but because she'd chosen not to remember any of them, her emotions had become diffused, until all she knew was that the curtain hid something she'd hated, something that had made her feel dreadful about herself.

Her mother had shaken the dust from the velvet and dragged her over, insisting she peek through a crack. Most of what she saw was still shrouded, indistinct, but some small bits of her youth were clearly visible, and they weren't the bogeys she'd imagined them.

Her mother had probably figured she was a natural for the beauty pageant after seeing her ham it up in school plays. Oh, how she'd adored being the center of attention, even if the audience was just her classmates! At some point she'd done community theater. Thinking back, she realized her mother must still have been working two jobs; how she'd managed to get Madeline to rehearsals and performances, she couldn't imagine. But the experience had been unalloyed joy. Her singing voice was none too great, but she'd played Annie, anyway, fake freckles on her nose. Later she was Heidi, and one of the daughters in *The Sound of Music* and...oh, half a dozen other roles.

Eventually she'd been too busy modeling to waste time on unpaid theater. She'd done commercials, but they weren't fun the way stage acting had been, and she'd been too successful at what she did to audition for movies or television. She ought to have done it, anyway; she'd always blamed her mother for making that sweeping decision for her. But now she wondered whether she'd ever even told her mother how she felt or what she wanted. Or had she assumed that Mom would magically know?

Truthfully Madeline was far from certain she'd had the talent to make it as an actress, anyway. She'd never know.

Still, it might be fun to be on stage again. The thought crept insidiously into her mind as she read the audition notice yet again. Why not try?

Wearing a tight short black skirt, hair a wild mass of permed curls, Carmen popped around the partition. "Hi, Madeline. I thought that man would never quit talking. Do you have this week's picture?"

She shook off her self-absorption. "Yep. Right here."

"Terrific. Come on back."

They wound their way through the maze of cubicles where the newspaper sales force had their offices. Carmen pulled up an extra chair for Madeline and settled in her own. Within minutes she'd run the photograph of Meow, a big homely orange cat, through her scanner and begun sharpening it up on her computer screen. Once Carmen was satisfied with the clarity and the horizontal form the ad would take, Madeline dictated a short description of this issue's Pet of the Week—Meow wasn't handsome, but he was as sweet and gentle as they came—which Carmen typed in. Some brief editing, the insertion of the sponsor's name and the Ten Lives logo, and she printed off a copy of the weekly feature.

Madeline looked it over once more. "Bless you, Carmen! It looks great, as always. Did I tell you we got two calls in response to last week's picture of Coco, the elderly Siamese? She went to a great home."

"I'm just talented." Carmen winked. "Give me a call when you find me that silver Abyssinian."

Carmen thought it was a joke. Madeline figured that one of these days Carmen would be in for a surprise. Just about every color and shape of cat showed up at Ten Lives sooner or later.

Still thoughtful, Madeline went back to the shelter where she'd left Garth. Chev and Ron would be neutered this week. Unspoken was the corollary: they would be going to next week's adoption day. Garth had been unusually quiet when she left him at Ten Lives, disappearing immediately in the direction of the kitten room.

She found him, instead, with Mittens and Dusky, the eleven-year-old brother and sister, suffering now from colds. The cage door stood open; Dusky was huddled up on the shelf behind the flap that gave the cats some privacy. Garth held long bony Mittens, who was pressing his cheek to the boy's and rumbling in pleasure.

"He's gotten so skinny," Garth said, anxiety in his voice. "He eats, doesn't he?"

"Not the past few days, and not a great deal before that. He's got an ulcer on his tongue, and his nose is so plugged up he can't smell the food. He'll look interested if we open a can, but then he puts his nose down to it, and you can see that it might as well be Styrofoam. If cats can't smell, they won't eat."

Garth listened with stricken eyes. "But what's going to happen to him?"

"Well, we've been hydrating him—using a syringe to inject fluids beneath his skin. If he doesn't start eating pretty soon, we'll have to force-feed him, and that's tough. Cats hate it, and it's hard to get enough down, especially at the shelter, considering our limited amount of time." As she spoke, she stroked the top of Mittens's smooth gray head. Gently Madeline added, "We'll do our best."

"Can I take them home?" Garth blurted. "I mean, once Chev and Ron are gone? Or maybe before if Dad'll let me?"

She knew a moment of relief that he had accepted

the inevitability of the kittens' departure from his life, but then it was supplanted by disquiet.

"Are you sure you wouldn't rather foster that mother and her litter? They'll be fun, and they need someone, too."

"You don't think I can take care of Mittens," he accused.

She tilted her head to one side and contemplated his stormy mulish expression. On a sudden impulse she hugged both him and the cat. He was darn near as skinny as Mittens. "Actually I have no doubt that you can make him fat and happy! But he and Dusky won't be as entertaining as the little guys have been."

For a moment Garth buried his face against the big gray cat's fur. "I don't care," he said in a muffled voice. "I want them. They don't deserve this."

Looking at Garth's bent head, covered by its pale stubble, Madeline felt an odd almost painful squeeze of something powerful. It was more complex than simple pride in his compassion. It was almost possessive, as though she were personally responsible for his fine character. As though he were hers. In astonishment she recognized the truth: what she felt was indeed proprietary. If she had to label it, she'd call it maternal pride and affection.

How very odd to have such emotions for the first time not for a tiny vulnerable infant, but for a sometimes sullen preadolescent.

Eric's son.

But she was pretty sure her feelings didn't have anything to do with Eric. Garth was the one who was special, with a depth of compassion extraordinary for a boy his age.

"No, you're right" she said, "they don't deserve it. Talk to your dad tonight. Maybe he has a spare bedroom where they could go until we place Chev and Ron. Let's warm up some of the AD cat food—it's high in protein, and it's softer than the usual canned cat food, so we can use a big plastic syringe to squirt it into his mouth." She grinned. "We'll give him a meal right now, whether he likes it or not."

"Sure!" Boy and cat rubbed noses, and then Garth disentangled Mittens's claws from his shirt and gently set the big guy in the cage, closing the door and latching it. "That way I'll know how to do it."

Mittens wasn't crazy about the experience. Half the food ended up on Garth's shirt, but enough went down the cat's throat to give him more nutrition than he'd had in days. With a damp cloth Garth tenderly wiped away the spills that stained Mittens's white chest.

That small gesture brought her another surge of pride. She masked it by saying lightly, "You're a good kid."

He gave a mischievous grin. "Mom and Dad might not agree with that."

Madeline smiled back. "Oh, they might get mad once in a while, but I bet that deep down they agree with me."

On the short drive home she and Garth chatted about how other cats at the shelter were doing, which ones she'd take to that week's adoption, why a perfectly nice cat had proved hard to place, how Ten Lives raised enough money to pay for food and litter.

She was turning into his driveway when Garth said, too casually, "We're going somewhere to dinner. So I guess you should just drop me."

Don't come in was the unspoken but clear message. Perhaps it was childish to feel hurt, but she did.

She hid that, too. "Sure. Going somewhere fun?"

"Dr. Hughes's. She and Dad are friends, too. And I guess Mark and I are kinda friends." He spoke dubiously.

She had no right to feel hurt afresh that she hadn't been invited, too. Teresa and Eric *were* friends. It was okay if they hadn't wanted to include her, she told herself sternly.

Garth hopped out of the car almost before she'd stopped. Was he that eager to get away from her?

"I'll talk to Dad about Mittens and Dusky," he said quickly. "See ya. Okay?"

"Sure."

Just then Eric came out the front door and walked toward the car. He was limping again, Madeline noticed, and exhaustion had drawn fine lines beside his eyes and mouth.

"Dad must be ready to go," Garth said. "Bye." He slammed the car door.

She couldn't just drive off, even if Garth *was* dying to get rid of her. Eric came around to her side of the car, his son hovering behind him. Madeline rolled down her window.

"Hi," Eric said, bending down to give her a brief

but oddly convincing kiss. "You can come in, you know."

"Garth said—" The agonized look Garth was giving her registered, and Madeline stopped. Aha! So hurrying her off was only Garth's idea. Still, she wouldn't give him away. "I don't have to loiter every time I come by, you know."

"I like it when you loiter." Eric waggled his eyebrows, making "loiter" sound mildly risqué.

"Aren't you two—" Another horrible grimace on his son's face killed her question. Okay, what was going on here?

Eric had straightened and was looking down the driveway. "Here's your ride, Garth. Shouldn't you change? I'll hold them off, but you'd better make it snappy."

One more desperate look her way, and then Garth took off for the house.

"His ride?" Madeline queried.

"Yeah, the Hugheses are taking him out for pizza and a movie. He and Mark had a pretty good time the other night."

"Really." Why, that little brat! She couldn't quite sustain simple indignation, however; *why* was Garth trying to get rid of her?

"Will you stay for dinner?" Eric asked.

Her mother intended to spend the evening glued to a television miniseries, so the decision wasn't a tough one. Madeline got out of the car and joined Eric in greeting the Hugheses, sans Nicole, who was doing something more to the liking of a seventeen-year-old. Teresa wrinkled her nose when she said that.

This was the first time Madeline had met Joe Hughes. If she weren't already in love, it would have been easy to envy Teresa. Her husband was strikingly handsome in a roughhewn way, with broad shoulders, very blue eyes and a slow warm smile. Madeline had always liked Teresa. She was pretty sure she could be friends with Joe, too.

Garth reappeared, gave his father and Madeline one last gloomy look and hopped into Joe's car.

In the house Madeline phoned her mother, who didn't sound as though she felt deserted when she told Madeline to have a good time. Madeline shook her head at Eric's offer of a drink.

"You starved?" he asked.

Something in his tone snagged her attention. Like his son, he sounded just a little too casual.

She shook her head. "Not especially. Don't slave in the kitchen."

"I wanted to talk to you."

Her heartbeat accelerated. "That sounds serious."

His eyes met hers. "It is."

No red roses or candlelight. She doubted he was going to ask her to marry him. Did he want to tell her that making love had been a mistake? Had he kissed her in greeting only because it would have looked odd if he hadn't?

By now she felt light-headed, apprehension fueling her with adrenaline. "Okay," she said.

"Let's sit down."

He waited until she chose one end of the couch

and curled her legs under her—more to huddle in self-defense than for comfort.

He sat a few feet from her, but not close enough to touch. "I've done a lot of thinking this past week."

"I have, too." If he didn't want to continue seeing her, was she cowardly enough to agree that she'd decided the same thing? Pride seemed so absurdly important.

"The other night was wonderful." So why wasn't he smiling? Why were his eyes intent, grave? "But I've been wondering. I've never seen you in a dress like that. Or so much makeup. I had the feeling all evening that I wasn't really with *you*."

She huddled deeper. "Who did you think you were with?" It came out snappish, offended.

"I couldn't quite figure that one out." The small lines between his brows deepened. "I thought we'd agreed there wasn't any hurry, that you had to be sure I wanted more than your perfect body." He emphasized "perfect." "Then what happens, the next time I see you, it's like you're shoving it in my face. 'See? This is who I am.' And, dammit, you're seducing me."

"You, of course, fought me, kicking and screaming." She heard her disdainful tone in disbelief. He wanted to talk about something that had really happened, and she was putting him off with sneers.

"You know I want you." He rubbed the back of his neck. "I want you right now. I don't give a damn what you're wearing." His gaze lowered meaningfully.

Madeline looked down at herself. Her jeans were loose, faded and a little grungy. Ditto for the T-shirt that had been a muted teal early in its lifetime and now was closer to gray. She'd washed her hands before she left the shelter, but her nails were unpainted. Her hair...well, she wouldn't think about what her hair was doing. She knew her face was bare of makeup.

"Is that so? Friday you could hardly keep your hands off me," she said. "You're not having any trouble tonight."

His eyes pinned hers. "How do you know?"

Her breath snagged in her throat. "Garth says everyone you've dated was pretty. Your wife was pretty."

"Yeah." His mouth twisted. "I told you I've been doing some thinking."

"And?" Nothing in the world had ever seemed more important.

"My mother was beautiful but cold. I, uh, concluded that I've been trying to find a woman who looked as good, but gave me the warmth she didn't." He grimaced. "Pretty pathetic at my age, to realize."

Madeline began to breathe again, but painfully. "No woman can stay beautiful all her life, no matter how hard she tries."

He seemed not to hear her. "I realized that Noreen has the same air as my mother. Touch me not." His eyes sharpened. "You don't."

She blinked. "What air do I have? Take me?"

"You know," Eric said obliquely, "I've been jealous of Garth. Even of the cats. I wanted you to touch me as tenderly, smile at me the way you do at them. I wanted you to give a damn about me."

"I do," she whispered, and knew it was the truth. She would do anything, give up anything, for him. She'd tried to give up herself the other night. "But I don't understand."

Still he didn't touch her, yet she felt him physically, felt the tension radiating from him. "What don't you understand?"

"Are you saying that I'm fulfilling some childhood fantasy?" Her effort to sound flippant failed.

"I'm saying I don't care what you look like. Whatever I wanted from women in the past was so shallow it has nothing to do with what I feel for you."

Her heart began to drum.

"You're the woman of my dreams, not my fantasies."

Tears filled her eyes. "Then make love to me the way I am. Please."

"I thought you'd never ask," Eric said roughly, and hauled her into his arms.

CHAPTER FOURTEEN

NOTHING HAD EVER FELT sweeter than Madeline's head resting trustingly on his bare shoulder, her fingers idly tracing muscles and ribs as he lay sprawled on his back on the bed.

"I wish you could spend the night," he said huskily.

"Mmm." He felt her smile as she kissed his salty skin. Dreamily she said, "Then we could make love again and again, and maybe again in the morning."

Eric ran his hand down her back, slender and utterly relaxed. "You like it, huh?" he asked in amusement and gratification.

"Mmm." Her fingers went still then, and she was quiet for a long moment.

"What are you thinking?" he asked.

"I never did before." It came out in a small burst. "After I left home—I told you about that—I met a man. We had a relationship. He used to like to look at me and tell me how beautiful I was. How perfect."

Eric winced at his unfortunate choice of compliments.

"It was like somebody running their hands over a work of art. I hated it."

He couldn't see her face, but he was reassured by

the fact that her voice held vehemence but no passion. She was telling him about something she'd put behind her, not a source of current anger.

"Later there was another man." Her fingers resumed their exploration, circling his nipple. "He wasn't quite so blatant, but it was the same. I don't know if it was their attitudes that put me off sex, or whether it just wasn't right with them." With a rich throaty chuckle she rolled on top of him. "Not like this."

"You tempt me."

"Enough?" she asked archly.

"Oh, I think so." He wrapped her fingers around the evidence of his sincerity.

Madeline seemed pleased. Her enthusiasm was a hell of an aphrodisiac, he found. Their conversation didn't resume for nearly half an hour.

"Fun?" he asked.

This time she lay sprawled under him, sweat-dampened curls sticking to her temples and forehead. Her flushed cheeks and glowing eyes made unnecessary the shy smile and breathy, "Yes, I thought it was fun. How about you?"

"Hell, yes." He rolled onto his side, taking her with him. "We have another hour and a half. Who knows? Maybe we can try it again before zero hour."

She chuckled, but tiredly. How easy it would be to fall asleep with her in his arms! Considering Garth's current attitude about their relationship, however, having him walk in on them in bed together would *not* be wise.

Her thoughts must have been paralleling his, because she said suddenly, "I had the feeling tonight that Garth didn't want me to stay here with you. Is he mad at me or something?"

Eric lifted his head. "Mad at you? Lord, no. He thinks you're the sun and the moon. If I was a lesser man, I wouldn't appreciate the constant barrage of 'Madeline says' and 'Madeline thinks'—as though your words were gospel."

"I'm sorry."

"But I'm not a lesser man." He kissed her forehead. "I like hearing your name."

"Oh." She stirred. "But then why didn't he want me here?"

Truth or subterfuge? It was no contest.

"I don't think it has anything to do with you personally," he said. "He's afraid of losing me if I get too interested in you. He's convinced his mother doesn't have time for him now that she's remarried. He figures neither of us will want him if we have new relationships."

"Oh, no! Poor Garth." To his surprise she tugged away from him and sat up, hair falling Lady Godiva-like over her breasts. "He *has* spent a number of evenings alone when we've gone out. I can understand why he'd think that."

Eric reached for her. "Don't take him too seriously. He'll come around."

She scooted back a few inches. "Will he?" Her gaze seemed to search for anything less than total honesty from him. "His mom probably does have less time for him. He *needs* you right now."

Alarmed, Eric braced himself up on an elbow. "Dammit, he's *got* me!"

"But he's obviously not confident that he does." Worry lines formed on her forehead. "Have you talked to him?"

"Yeah, and gotten nowhere."

Hesitantly she said, "We could take it easy for a while. I mean, he'll be going home again in September."

He stared incredulously at her. "You're not suggesting that we don't see each other."

"Well..." Incomprehensible feminine wheels were turning in her pretty head. "We could casually. It's only six weeks or so."

He'd just made love to her, and by God he wasn't going to wait six weeks to do it again! Or to talk, he realized a split second later; he called her almost every day just to hear her voice, to know what she was thinking and doing, to feel her sympathy and interest in the happenings of his day.

"No," he said uncompromisingly. "Garth can adjust."

Eyes grave, Madeline contemplated him for a disquieting moment. "I've grown very fond of your son. I don't want to hurt him."

"You won't hurt him."

"I'm not so sure." Her teeth closed on her lower lip, and then she rose from the bed in one fluid movement.

If he hadn't been so apprehensive, he could have lain there for hours watching her bend to recover her various bits of clothes from the floor where they'd been discarded. As it was...

He swung his feet to the floor. "You don't have to go yet." Panic tightened his chest.

She cast him a single distracted glance. "We both need to think. Garth deserves that much."

"I *have* thought!" he snapped. "What the hell kind of father do you imagine I am?"

"A good one." She favored him with a gentle smile as she reached behind to fasten her delicate wisp of a bra. The movement made her breasts thrust forward. "Too good not to put him first right now."

He argued; she listened, nodded, repeated that she liked his son too much to hurt him and continued getting dressed. To Eric's shock, twenty minutes after the subject had come up, she was gone.

He had no idea whether she intended to come back.

Eric swore, long and viciously. He yanked on the rest of his own clothes—he'd been shirtless when he walked her to her car—and went to stare broodingly out the front window.

Time for another little talk with Garth—who by God was old enough to show some maturity and give his blessing to his father's romance.

Because hell on earth would be having to choose between the woman he loved and his son.

DAD WAS ENSCONCED on the living-room couch when Garth came in at eleven. He tossed aside his book when he saw him.

"Come on in. Sit down."

Garth plopped down on a leather ottoman and spun in a circle. "The movie was really cool! They had these lasers that—"

"Spare me," his father said dryly. "I don't think it's my kind of entertainment."

"You like subtitles," his son said scornfully.

"Five minutes into the movie you quit noticing them."

"Yeah, right."

Dad straightened from his sprawling position and rested his elbows on his knees. He suddenly sounded serious. "Garth, about Madeline—"

On a spurt of alarm, Garth demanded, "What did she tell you?" He'd thought they were friends!

His dad's brows rose. "What makes you think she told me anything?"

Garth scrambled to cover his slip. "I just thought... I mean, why do you want to talk to me about her if she didn't complain or something?"

"Because I suspect you still don't want me seeing her, and she's important to me. But neither of us want to hurt you."

Garth spun in a couple more circles, not sure what to say. Whenever he thought about Madeline and his dad, he felt tangled inside, scared and angry and guilty. Finally he muttered, "What do you want me to say? It's okay?"

"That'd be a good start."

"Well, it's not okay!" Garth burst out, lifting his head. "I mean, I don't care. If you can figure out someplace to dump me, I guess I don't have anything to say about it, do I?"

"Nobody is dumping you," his father said quickly. "Your mother expects you back in September, just like always."

"Oh, and you believe that," he said sarcastically.

"Yeah." Dad's voice was level. "I know your mom. I know how much she loves you."

"Easy to say," Garth mumbled.

Dad ignored that. "Do you just not want me to remarry? Or do you object to Madeline in particular?"

How was he supposed to know? No, that was kind of a lie to himself. "What, are you just going to pick someone else out if I don't like her?" he asked rudely.

Dad's eyes narrowed. "You know better than that."

"Well, what difference does it make, then?"

His father lost it. "Goddammit, talk to me!" he roared. "How can you not like Madeline?"

Garth glared at him. "I do like her!"

"Then what?" As he always did when he was agitated, Dad tugged at his hair until it stood up in clumps. "What's the problem?"

"You want to know?" Garth shot to his feet. "I'll tell you! She's too cool! You won't want me around if you've got her!"

Dad rose to his feet, too. "Garth, I love you. You're my son. This isn't a competition!"

"No?" Garth asked belligerently, his fingernails biting into his palms. "I heard you and Mom talking when you left. It was all about who I'd live with. It was like I had to choose!"

"We never asked you to choose!" Dad had a satisfyingly shocked expression. "We wanted the best for you. We weren't arguing over you."

"And Mom," Garth raged on, "she picked Chuckie, didn't she? It was me or him, and he won!" The knowledge was a flesh-eating acid in his stomach.

"Her relationship with him has nothing to do with her feelings for you." Dad gripped Garth by the shoulders and looked deep into his eyes, as though to convince him with this fake-sincere gaze. "She loves you. *I* love you. Dammit, even Madeline loves you! She'd be your stepmother. Wouldn't you like that?"

Garth ducked his head and shrugged.

"What?" his father asked.

Garth hated being a crybaby, but tears filled his eyes. He wouldn't look up. "Why would you love me when you can love her?" The question was raw.

"Because you're my son. Because I love you no matter what else is going on in my life." Dad went on and on, saying all the same stuff Garth had heard from his mother. So he just tuned it out and nodded every once in a while. No adult was going to say, *Yeah, you're right, I won't really want you around once I have her.* They didn't want to admit it was true even to themselves. But he could see through their phony baloney.

Dad finally let him go. Garth went into his room and cast himself onto his bed. In a second Ron had hopped up and was walking on his head, peering down at his face. Garth rolled over, squeezed Ron in a hug that had the kitten struggling and began to sob in huge silent gulps.

Ron and Chev were the only ones who really loved him, and he was going to betray them.

"YOU'RE WELCOME to come with me to the cat-adoption today," Madeline said as she stuck a can of cold juice in her tote bag. "What I do for Ten Lives is important to me."

"Yes, I see that." Her mother set down her coffee cup with a decisive click. "I'd like to come."

"You would?" She had to be hearing things, Madeline thought.

"Certainly." Mrs. Howard stood. "Do I need anything?"

"A book maybe, in case you get bored. I always bring a drink. Sometimes a bag lunch."

On the drive to the shelter Madeline kept sneaking glances at her mother. Yes, she really was here. Especially amazing, since she had yet to visit Ten Lives, despite knowing Madeline's involvement.

"It may not be very clean yet," Madeline warned. "Volunteers will barely be getting started changing litters and feeding the cats."

Serenely her mother said, "Well, I hardly expect it to look like my living room."

Right.

Mrs. Howard hovered in the entry while Madeline and Joan stuffed cats and kittens into carriers. To her credit, she helped carry them out to the car and stack them on the back seat and in the rear of the station wagon. Nor did she say a word on the drive to Lynnwood about the chorus of yowls that filled the car, although a pained expression occasionally crossed her face. And, bless her heart, she carried cats into the big pet store, giving Madeline time to set up the sign, lay out materials on a card table and put cats that were likely to get along with one another in the large wire cage with shelves that the store had provided.

"No, these'll stay in their carriers," she told her mother, gesturing at several to her left. "They're not crazy about other cats." Glancing past the older woman, Madeline felt her heart lurch. "Oh, here's Eric and Garth."

"Dr. Bergstrom!" Mrs. Howard gushed. "How lovely to see you again."

Wordlessly Garth set down the plastic carrier he carried. Conscious of Eric talking to her mother a few feet away, Madeline opened its wire door and Garth reached inside for the two black-and-white kittens. They went into the large cage.

"Can you place them together?" he pleaded.

"We'll try." She looked at him with compassion. "Are you sure you want to be here?"

He set his jaw. "I need to see who takes them."

"Okay." She touched his arm. "I've always felt that way, too."

One of the store employees produced two more folding metal chairs. Madeline hadn't expected Eric to stay, but he promptly settled down behind the table with every appearance of permanence.

When he wasn't watching his son, his narrowed determined gaze rested on her. Once, when her mother was chatting with someone who'd stopped to show off their ten-week-old Sheltie puppy, Eric said in a low voice to Madeline, "We need to talk."

She turned her head to see Garth watching them. She couldn't tell what he was thinking, and when their eyes met he jerked away and crouched down to pet Chev and Ron.

"Have you talked to *him?*" she asked.

Eric's hesitation told her what Garth's reaction had been. Seeing the knowledge on her face, Eric tightened his jaw. "Yes. He's a kid, Madeline. He'll come around."

"He needs to feel secure about you," Madeline said quietly. "Right now you're all he thinks he has."

"Goddammit, he—" Eric cut himself off.

Madeline turned a bright smile on an older couple who'd stopped, oohing and aahing over the cats.

"Our daughter and her children are planning to get two kittens," the woman said. "Are any of these brothers and sisters?"

Assured that several were, the couple hurried out, promising to phone her. Garth hovered as a young woman visited all the kittens, finally choosing a small black-and-tan tabby.

"Maybe Chev and Ron won't go today," he said hopefully when the woman left with the kitten in a cardboard carrier.

"It'll only get harder," Madeline said, pretending not to notice the unhappiness that flooded his face.

He turned away quickly, and she guessed he was hiding tears.

Miracle of miracles, they placed a ten-year-old white cat named Snowman, a handsome fellow who'd come to the shelter when his elderly owner had to go into a nursing home. Snowman fought being put into the cardboard carrier, but the middle-aged woman, who'd chosen him to keep her older female cat company, persuaded him. She'd stroked him gently and talked to him in a soothing murmur until he'd purred and she'd been able to back him into the box, petting him until she'd closed the flaps.

"Poor guy, he must be frightened," she said, and smiled calmly at all of them. "I'll take good care of him. Matilda likes her Fancy Feast. Do you suppose he will, too?"

Snowman, Madeline felt sure, was going to put on a few pounds and live a pampered life.

The woman had no sooner departed than a family appeared.

"Grandma said you had kittens," the boy began, but then he spotted them. The boy and his sister dropped to their knees beside the wire cage. Their mother stopped at the table.

"Oh," the boy breathed, "look at these black-and-white ones!"

Grudgingly Garth took Chev and Ron out to be held by the boy and girl, who were perhaps ten and twelve. They cuddled the kittens tenderly, and after a bit even shy Chev began to purr. The whole while, Garth stood over them, ready to snatch his charges back at any moment.

The mother lowered her voice. "We adopted a kitten six months ago, but he wasn't in very good health from the beginning. Of course by the time we realized that, it was too late. We already loved him. We recently found out that he had leukemia, and he went downhill fast. It broke the kids' hearts.''

"That's hard," Madeline said sympathetically. "Are you sure you're ready for a new pet?"

"Oh, we've waited a couple of months. This time we decided to get two, so they'd have company when the kids are at school and I'm working. I'm a single mother," she said as an aside.

Keeping an eye on Garth, Madeline discussed Ten Lives's policies and queried the woman about how safe their home was and how much of a commitment they were prepared to make to their pets. She was satisfied quickly, but she couldn't tell if Garth felt the same.

The mother went over and visited Chev and Ron, as well. The girl looked up. "Mom, can we have them?" Her eyes held such anxiety and hope, Madeline had a welcome feeling of rightness, especially when she saw the same expression in the boy's eyes.

She looked at Garth, standing quietly now behind the family. He gazed down at the two kids for the longest time, then gave an agonized nod. His face contorted and he hurried away. Eric rose and strolled after him. On the edge of tears herself Madeline felt a stab of gratitude that Eric had stayed.

It was twenty minutes before they returned from the back of the store. Garth's eyes were red and puffy, but the tears had been scrubbed away, and he seemed not to mind his father's hand on his shoulder.

Madeline couldn't help remembering a similar scene, only Eric had been comforting her.

Garth was careful not even to glance at the cage that no longer held his two little boys. His Adam's apple bobbed. "Do you need me to stay?"

She shook her head. "We'll be fine. Garth—"

"I'm okay," he said woodenly.

"You taught them how to love." She gave his hand a squeeze. "Thanks to you, they'll have a fine life."

Tears leapt into his eyes again. He gave a jerky nod and fled.

"I'm sorry," Madeline said helplessly to Eric. "Maybe fostering was a terrible idea for him."

"No." He wrapped his hand around the back of her neck and kneaded lightly. "You're right. He did give them a chance at a fine life. But they're not the only ones who learned. He did, too."

"I hope so," she whispered.

Eric gave her a quick hard kiss. "We'll talk later," he said, a promise and a threat, and strode out.

Madeline looked over to see that her mother was dabbing her eyes with a tissue.

"So," Mrs. Howard said with a final sniff, "we've done quite well today, haven't we?"

"Yes, and we have another hour."

But the heat of the summer afternoon had brought a lull in business. Store clerks chatted quietly with one another, and the few customers who passed had carts loaded with birdseed or dog food.

It seemed a good moment to say difficult things.

"Mom," Madeline began, but her courage failed

her, and when her mother glanced over inquiringly, she said the first thing that came into her head. It turned out not to be far from what she'd intended. "There's an audition tomorrow night in Everett. It's a community-theater production."

Mrs. Howard waited, only a certain stillness about her betraying that she understood Madeline was telling her something important.

"I thought I might try out for a part." Madeline took a deep breath. "Would you like to come and watch?"

"I don't believe," her mother said unsteadily, "that anything on earth would make me happier."

Hardly aware she did so, Madeline began to align the edges of the stack of handouts. It helped, somehow, to have her hands busy and not to be watching for her mother's expression.

Even so, it was hard to say, *I might have been wrong. I'm starting to understand why your life felt empty, how you might have convinced yourself that you were making the right choices for me.*

Hoping her mother would be patient, Madeline said, "Garth doesn't want me to marry his father. He's frightened. His mother just remarried, and he thinks she doesn't want him anymore, and...well, Eric and I have discussed the possibility of not seeing each other for now. Until Garth is ready. No, let me say this," she said, when her mother began to protest. "The thing is, I'd almost convinced myself that he'd be happier with me as his stepmother even though he doesn't know it. Assuming," she added scrupulously, "that I'm reading Eric right and he's thinking of asking me."

She took another breath and went on, "Anyway, I suddenly saw how easy it is to believe you know best when you're the adult. Maybe you even do. Maybe Garth *is* wrong in not wanting me to marry his dad." At last she said it. "Maybe *I* was wrong in thinking life somehow would have been better if you'd let me be more normal."

"I don't know," her mother said, and her face held painful honesty. "I've had plenty of years to think about everything I did and why I did it. It *wasn't* all bad, truly."

"No. I know. I've been remembering. The night *Annie* opened was one of the most glorious of my life. There I was, out on the stage, singing and dancing, and people were laughing and cheering *me*." Madeline gazed into the past, a bittersweet smile touching her lips. "Of course, I thought I had the most beautiful voice in the world."

"You sang from the moment you got up in the morning." The affection in her mother's voice was new to Madeline. "You used to stand in your crib and rattle the bars and hop around, burbling. Even then, I knew you were dancing and singing."

"But I have a terrible voice."

"Not terrible…"

Their eyes met, and suddenly both were laughing.

"It was fine for an eight-year-old," her mother said. "It just…well, didn't develop into anything special."

Madeline wrinkled her nose. "I sing in the shower."

"I know. I've heard you."

And just like that they laughed—no, giggled—again. Mother-daughter. Momentarily in harmony.

The silence that fell afterward was companionable, easy. Madeline had more she wanted to say, but her mother beat her to it.

"There was a time you loved acting and modeling." Her mouth compressed. "My mistake was not letting the choice be yours when you started *not* wanting it. And yes, you were right—money was part of the reason. I had no way of earning what you could. But it was more. My life felt empty, I suppose, and your success filled it." She looked directly at Madeline. "I'm sorry," she said starkly.

"Maybe, if we'd just talked..."

"I fear that's my fault, too. Expressing feelings never came easily to me." Her wrinkles deepened. "Which I regret more than I can say. Perhaps it's what destroyed my marriage. Understanding what I do about myself, I'm not at all sure I should try again."

With new certainty Madeline said, "But something has changed, hasn't it? I know a few women whose best friends are their mothers. I've always envied them. We could try."

Tears sparkled on her mother's eyelashes. "I'd like that very much. Oh, Madeline, I am so sorry!"

Flooded with emotion, tears filling her own eyes, Madeline whispered, "And I'm sorry, too. It shouldn't have taken me so long to grow up."

They hugged, cheeks pressed together, fingers gripping hard. The embrace was awkward, but real. Mother-daughter.

CHAPTER FIFTEEN

MADELINE PARKED in the alley as always and was unlocking the back entrance to her boutique when a hand closed on her shoulder. Her heart took a wild jump and she spun around.

"Eric! God!" She pressed a hand to her chest. "You just about scared me to death."

In khakis and a heather green T-shirt, he had no right to look so handsome. Perhaps the fright had made her realize his impact afresh.

"I'm sorry. I made plenty of noise coming down the alley."

"Not enough," she said tartly.

"You haven't returned my phone calls."

"I told you I needed to think."

He turned the key in the lock, opened the door and ostentatiously handed the key back to her. "I won't accept a decision not to see me."

Her rare temper awakened and she lifted her chin. "What will you do—keep sneaking up behind me in alleys?"

Between set teeth, Eric said, "I'm not a stalker."

"Well, then, kindly don't tell me you won't accept my decision!"

The creases in his cheeks deepened. "I love you."

Her heart thumped. "What?"

"You heard me." He nodded toward the open door. "May I come in?"

In a daze Madeline said, "I...yes. Of course."

He waited for her to go ahead. She automatically flipped on the storeroom lights. A heavy damask curtain separated the work area in back from the store proper. Eric closed the door behind them, shutting out the clang of a Dumpster lid and the rumble of the garbage truck farther down the alley. Then he removed her purse from her nerveless hand and set it on a table.

"I would love you," he said, "even if you were as homely as Mudhen."

An image of the shelter cat's battered one-eyed face popped into her head. There'd been times she'd wished she were ugly.

Why was she resisting this man? "Garth..." she reminded herself, and him.

"No, let me finish first." Eric cupped her face, brushed a thumb across her lips.

She quivered. Unfair. How could she put his son first when Eric touched her this way and said the words she'd lived her whole life to hear?

"I've...learned a good deal about myself since I met you." His expression was completely unguarded, his eyes dark with emotion. "Thanks to you, I've discovered what really matters. For the first time in my life I don't just want a woman, I love her. You." His voice hardened. "I will not let you go because Garth is afraid I can't love two people at once."

"I love *you*." It wasn't what she'd meant to say.

One corner of his mouth lifted. "Yeah. I kind of figured you did."

"How arrogant."

"No." Any humor disappeared. "I've been a bastard. If you didn't love me despite my idiocy, why would you have let me have a second—or third—chance?"

"Good point," she managed.

He kissed her finally, slow, tender, loving, passion in abeyance. When he lifted his head, she had to cling to him for support. "I will marry you no matter what," he said. "We can prove to Garth that he's wrong. But God knows I'd rather have his blessing. Will you talk to him?"

"Me?" Her legs regained their strength. "Aren't I the threat? Would he even listen to me?"

"He worships the ground you walk on. You're a threat because you're 'too cool.' I quote," Eric said wryly. "He might believe you if *you* tell him you wouldn't mind having a twelve-year-old stepson around."

Madeline gazed up into those tumultuous gray-green eyes and said helplessly, "Yes. Okay."

"Take him to the shelter."

She nodded.

"Or just come to visit Mittens and Dusky. They're in his bedroom now that Chev and Ron are gone."

"He'll think it's a setup."

"It *is* a setup." Eric looked at his watch. "I've got to go. I love you, Madeline."

She nodded foolishly.

Eric grinned, kissed her again, this time with desire added to the mix, and left, the back door closing with a solid sound behind him.

I would love you even if you were as homely as Mudhen.

Madeline went to open the cash register. On the way she began to sing.

"WHY DON'T WE both spend some time in the kitten room cuddling the scared ones?" Madeline suggested brightly, wondering if poor Garth could tell he was being manipulated.

Apparently not, because he nodded. "That's cool."

"I'm glad to hear Mittens and Dusky are doing so well," Madeline said. "You're sure he's drinking water?"

"I saw him drinking again this afternoon," Garth told her. "He lapped up a whole bunch."

"Great." She opened the door to the kitten room and automatically stuck out a foot to stop an energetic youngster from scooting through on an exploratory foray. "And you're getting quite a bit of food down him?"

"Yeah, a can a day." He looked dubious. "Those cans aren't very big, though."

"But very high in protein. That should be plenty to keep him going."

The litter boxes in here had been freshly changed, and a couple of older kittens were munching on dried food. Others were piled in baskets or round sheepskin beds, while two tabbies sat on the windowsill, noses pressed to the screen.

Madeline introduced Garth to the newcomers, and they each chose one of the shyer guys for a snuggle. Garth sat cross-legged on the floor as usual, a six-week-old calico in the crook of his arm. She buried her face in his shirt, but couldn't resist his fingernails; after a moment a soft rumble came from her. The older long-haired black-and-white kitten Madeline had picked up was made of sterner stuff; she held out a couple of minutes before she gave up and purred.

Madeline waited a bit before she asked, "Have you talked to your mother lately? Is she having a good time?"

"Um...I guess." From the look on his face, Madeline suspected he hadn't asked.

What teenager cared whether his parents had a good time? Obviously it had never occurred to *her* as a teenager to wonder about her mother's happiness.

"When do they get back?"

"They *are* back." He sounded resentful. Madeline wondered how he'd feel if his mother had wanted him to cut his summer short and join her and her new husband. Would he be happy? Or assume that now his father had wanted to get rid of him?

"Will you have to move to a larger house because of your mom marrying?" she asked.

"Yeah, but probably someplace not too faraway. She said she didn't want me to have to change schools."

Madeline didn't point out that this hardly sounded like a parent trying to "dump" her kid. Instead, she mused, "I was really angry at my mother when I was a little older than you. Have I told you about it?"

He let his kitten go and began flicking a feather wand for another one. "You started to once. You said you'd tell me about it later."

Funny how much fresher in her memory those years had become, thanks to her self-examination. Faces and names came to her at odd moments; she'd remembered a disastrous date her mother had let her go on. A month ago she'd have sworn her mother had always said no.

Madeline told him about her modeling and acting past, fielding questions on what it was really like in front of a camera and admitting that no, she had never met Sandra Bullock, Mel Gibson or Jim Carrey.

"I mostly did commercials," she said. "Not very glamorous, I'm afraid."

His expression told her he agreed.

"I haven't acted in years," she told him, "but I actually went to an audition last night for a community theater. I don't know if I'll get the part, but just being on the stage and playing a role, listening to other people talk about opening nights and how Friday-night audiences are different from Saturday-night ones and hearing them tease each other about missed lines or directors who were hard on them…it just brought it all back. I don't regret giving up being a professional, but I am sorry I turned my back on friends and on something I loved doing—like acting. Not to mention rejecting my mother the way I did.''

Madeline was silent for a moment, conscious of Garth watching her. ''You know,'' she said, ''it's taken me all these years to figure out that Mom was probably doing her best.''

He frowned. ''You're not mad at her anymore?''

''I was until this summer.'' Madeline made a face. ''Truth is, I was until just a week or so ago. You want to hear the really crazy part?''

He was a twelve-year-old boy. Of course he wanted to hear the crazy part. He nodded eagerly.

''After I threw a temper tantrum and moved out when I turned eighteen, we never talked about why I was angry.'' Incredible. All those years, wasted. ''I didn't speak to my mother at all for two years. Then one day I called, but it was as if only the present existed. We've had this distant relationship ever since, like pleasant acquaintances.'' She grimaced. ''That's about all we were. We hardly knew each other! Anyway, we'd talk on the phone about once a month for five minutes, see each other maybe twice a year for really short visits. I never said, 'Mom, I'm still angry at the way you pushed me into taking modeling assignments when it meant I couldn't go to school or have friends like other kids.' Not once.''

Madeline kissed the kitten's white nose and let her go. A friendly tabby leaped to her lap to take the other's place. Madeline continued, ''And Mom never asked—not once—how I felt about my childhood or my career or her. We talked about the news or she'd tell me about getting her hair done or...oh, just dumb stuff.''

"My mom and I don't talk that much, either." Garth's voice was low now, with his head bowed over the kitten. "Not like this."

"Maybe she has something in common with my mother, who admitted the other day that she's never found it easy to talk about emotions, so she just doesn't." Madeline made a face. "I guess that explains why I'm so warped."

His head shot up. "But you're not! Not like me—" He stopped abruptly, eyes rolling like a spooked horse's.

She stared. "You? You're a great kid! Why do you think you're warped?" Was he far more depressed than even Eric realized?

Garth ducked his head. "I guess I'm not really. I just...that is, sometimes I think people don't like me that much."

Madeline could think of only one thing to do. She smiled at him with all the warmth and affection she felt for him. "I like you—a lot," she said simply. "Do you know how few kids your age would spend the time here that you have? And care so much? Garth Bergstrom, you're one of my favorite people in the world."

He stole a glance at her. Red rushed up his neck to his cheeks. "I...you're nice, too," he mumbled.

Madeline's heart began to drum. Crunch time. How to ease into it? No, she decided. Just ask.

"But you don't want me to marry your father."

Garth scrambled to his feet, shedding the startled kitten. His voice rose. "Dad told you that?"

"Yes. But I'd already guessed. You were trying so hard the other night to get rid of me."

"He shouldn't have told you," Garth said resentfully.

"Maybe not, but he did because he loves you." She held up her hand to avert an explosion. "He asked me to talk to you."

That news was no more welcome. "You came to get me today just so you could tell me all this bull…"

"No." She cut him off without apology. "I came to get you for the same reasons I have two or three times a week all summer. Because you're a big help here and because I like you."

His thin face worked as he tried to find some way to turn her declaration back against her, but apparently he failed, because after a moment he wheeled away and stared out the window.

"You know," she said softly, "I'd never thought much about having kids of my own until I got to know you. Now I understand why people do. I sort of wish you were mine."

He whipped around. "You're lying!" His tone was furious.

"No," Madeline said again. "When I was with you and your dad, we felt like a family." She waited until he met her eyes. "I love your father. I'd like to marry him. But I won't, at least not for a while, if you don't want me to. I think…for now you need to come first with him. So the decision will be yours.

I'm just asking you to think about it, and...and give me a chance.''

How feeble that sounded, the forlorn petitioner asking for his blessing! She doubted he'd believe her promise not to steal Eric from him; why would he, when he didn't believe his own father? But what other tack could she have taken? Announce she was going to marry his father no matter what he thought, but oh, by the way, we promise not to shut you out?

At his continuing silence Madeline sighed, but soundlessly, trying to avoid any suggestion of impatience. ''I'll leave you here for a while,'' she said, rising from the room's one chair. ''I'd better check messages and return some phone calls.''

Garth made no reply; only stood rigid, hands knotted at his sides. He looked so thin and vulnerable, his pale scalp still showing through what might have been a close crew cut. She hadn't yet seriously considered what asking Eric to wait would mean; right now, she ached inside for the loss of the son, not the father.

Madeline went to the door. ''I'll see you in a bit.''

''I guess it'd be okay,'' Garth said behind her, voice loud, abrupt.

She turned, startled. ''What would be okay? My leaving you here? If you'd rather do something else—''

''No.'' He faced her, squaring his shoulders. ''I mean, you and Dad.''

For an instant, she was numb. ''Are you...are you sure?''

Eric had asked her that, she remembered, countless

times, and she'd always said yes even when it was a lie.

"Yeah." The boy's expression was as stoic as if he expected her to euthanize him any minute. "I always wanted you to marry him, but I *didn't,* too." He moved uneasily. "That's dumb, isn't it?"

"No. Everyone's had the experience of wanting something and being scared of it both at the same time." She was having that experience right now. Everything she'd ever wanted was seemingly in her grasp, and she was terrified that somehow she'd lose it all.

"I'm scared of lots of stuff lately." He hung his head. "I'm a baby."

Madeline took the risk of going to him and giving his shoulders a quick undemanding squeeze. "Kiddo, everybody is scared of lots of stuff. I have this horrible feeling I've spent my whole life ruled by fear. I've never met your mother, but I'd just about guarantee that she's afraid of losing you altogether, afraid her new marriage might not work, afraid of the changes it'll bring. If you're a baby, so are we all."

"I'm afraid Mittens and Dusky might not get a home." Not as irrelevant as it sounded.

Gravely she said, "I promise we'll find them a home. Word of honor."

Garth stole a shy glance at her. "Okay."

Madeline put her hand on the doorknob. "I know you don't need another mother, but I'd like us to be friends. Can we try?"

He nodded again. "Can I tell Dad?"

"About our agreement?"

"Yeah."

She wanted to rush to the telephone and call Eric, but another few hours of waiting was a small price to pay for Garth's acceptance of her.

"You bet," she said.

She slipped out of the kitten room and closed the door behind her. Exhilaration—and fear—tingled from her toes to her fingers.

No more obstacles stood in the way. If Eric really loved her, if she was certain in her heart that this was right, nothing would stop them from promising each other forever after.

IF HE'D SAID NO, would Madeline really have told his dad she wouldn't marry him? Garth sort of liked the idea that she would have; it gave him a sense of power he didn't remember ever feeling before. Real power. Cool.

He considered the possibility of torturing his father by waiting all evening to tell him that it was okay if he proposed to Madeline. After saying good-night, he would sort of casually stop in the bedroom doorway and add, "Oh, by the way, Madeline and I talked today. I guess you can marry her if you want to."

He savored the imaginary scene for a minute. Talk about feeling powerful! But reluctantly he decided it would be too mean. Anyway, telling Dad would be like giving a really cool gift, the kind you can hardly wait until the person opens.

He wished there was some way he *could* wrap it,

or maybe some symbolic object. His English teacher was hooked on that word: *symbolic*.

He had Madeline drop him in town in front of the dime store. It mostly had kind of cheapo stuff and didn't look as if it would be full of symbols. But you never knew.

Like magic, Garth found what he wanted in the first aisle. He bought it for $2.99 and paid the clerk fifty cents to gift wrap the package.

On the way home he decided to go whole hog and cook dinner, too. That way, it could be like a celebration. He thought about inviting Madeline—not that he was a very good cook—but her presence would give away his surprise immediately.

He made a salad—that was easy—and put it in the fridge, then baked potatoes in the microwave while he broiled steaks. Once they were in the oven, he got to worrying that Dad might be late. Then they'd either have a cold dinner or a really well-done one.

But he was turning the steaks out onto a plate when Dad walked in.

His father stopped in the kitchen doorway, eyebrows shooting up. "What provoked this?"

"I just felt like doing something," Garth said nonchalantly.

His father shook his head. "I'll go wash my hands and sit myself down. Unless waiting on Dad isn't part of the deal."

"I can put dinner on the table." Garth had already set it with china from the buffet, and he'd put out the salad dressings and croutons and the sour cream—Dad bought the real thing, not the nonfat stuff Mom did.

Garth felt proud of himself when Dad's eyebrows rose again at the sight of the table. "Hey, this is nice! You make me ashamed of the way I usually slap dinner together with no frills on the eating bar. Your mother must set a better example than I do."

The table at home was always pretty fancy, cloth napkins—Mom was into recycling—coordinated with place mats or the tablecloth and even the dishes. Garth had always liked the way the two of them sat down for dinner as if it was a big deal, not something you ate in front of the TV like some of his friends' families did. That was the kind of memory he held on to when he was scared Mom didn't want him anymore.

Dad didn't push to find out why he'd gone to so much effort. Garth was glad. The present was under his chair, and he wanted to wait until after dinner.

The steaks had cooked a little too long and the potatoes not quite long enough, but despite that, the meal was really pretty good. If he didn't become a veterinarian like Dad, maybe he ought to become a chef. No, it had to be a vet so he could help animals like Chev and Ron and Mittens and Dusky.

Dad finally sighed and pushed his plate away. "So, do we have a selection of desserts tonight?"

"Would you believe ice cream or Popsicles?"

Dad yawned and shoved his chair back. "I think I'll pass. A hot bath sounds better. The meal was great, Garth. Thanks."

"I've got something for you." Garth bent over

and picked up the small package, handing it across the table to his father. It actually looked a little silly; the only paper the store had had was a kids' cartoon one.

Dad turned the package over in his hands. "A present." His brow wrinkled. "What's the occasion?"

"You'll see."

As carefully as though he planned to reuse the paper, Dad opened the package, taking out the small box. He opened it and stared inside, then lifted his head and stared at Garth.

"It's...wedding rings."

"Plastic," Garth said helpfully. "I think they'd break really easy."

"Are you...are you trying to tell me something?"

Was his father a little slow or what?

"I figured if you hadn't bought an engagement ring yet—" Garth shrugged "—I'd help you along."

Dad looked down again. He picked up the fake ruby ring and turned it slowly between his thumb and finger. A flake of gold paint drifted away.

Suddenly Dad's shoulders started to shake. Was he crying? Garth worried. Now what was he supposed to do?

And then this whoop came out of Dad, followed by another one. He was laughing! Every time he slowed down, he'd look at the ring again and laugh harder.

"They're symbolic," Garth said with dignity. "Like, with this ring, I give you permission. Or something."

Dad's face went quiet. "Forget permission. How about your blessing? I want you next to me when I say, 'I do.'"

"Cool," Garth said blithely. He might actually *enjoy* this wedding!

SHE TOOK HIS BREATH away. This dress was only a little less seductive than the green one, but she looked just as spectacular. Rust-colored and high-waisted, it floated down to midcalf; but the fabric was so insubstantial, so clingy, that the long lines of her thighs and the curve of her hips were revealed and concealed as she moved, like wisps of fog parting to reveal the sun.

Her hair was soft tonight, done in some complicated twist that still let curls cascade over her neck and shoulders. Her makeup was as beautifully done, but softer, too, less blatant.

She was no less sexy.

What the hell was she playing at?

Eric said polite things—he hoped—to her mother before escorting Madeline down the walk, under the fragrant garden arch and to the car. In its dark interior he kissed her.

Her mouth opened for his, as though she knew no other way of responding. He imagined her beside him in bed when he awakened in the morning, the way she'd instinctively turn to him, respond to his kiss, murmur with pleasure. Not just one morning, but every morning. Forever.

They scarcely talked on the way to the romantic candlelit restaurant he'd chosen for his formal proposal. Everything had a dreamlike quality, from the small box forming a lump in his suit-coat pocket to the golden quality of the early-evening summer sunlight. Her elegantly packaged beauty added to his sense of unreality; where was his Madeline?

The waiter seated them in a private alcove by the windows where they could watch the setting sun. But Eric didn't even glance at the view.

"You've dressed up again."

"Well." She smiled, teasing, flirting, laughing. "You might have tried, 'How lovely you look, Madeline.'"

He brushed that aside. "You know what I mean."

"You don't like me in this dress?" She batted her eyelashes.

His heart did a somersault. "Yeah, I like you in that dress," he growled. "You know damn well it turns me on. That's not the point."

"Then what is?" she asked innocently.

"I love you." He reached both hands across the table, crushing the elaborately folded napkins and shoving aside the centerpiece. "*You.* Not the feeling of being turned on."

Her smile trembled; her eyes were pools of green and gold and brown. "But you see, I've discovered that I can enjoy looking beautiful sometimes. I'm me, no matter what. I was so determined to learn to like myself despite how I look it's taken me fifteen years to realize that I can like myself the *way* I look. I don't have to...disguise myself."

"You can dress any way that pleases you," he said roughly.

"Admit it. This is fun once in a while."

"Oh, yeah." He wanted to make love to her right here on the spot. "It's fun."

She crinkled her nose. "Good."

The waiter approached; Eric shook his head, and the fellow faded away again.

"Garth made me dinner last night," Eric told her.

Her teeth worried her lip. "He did?"

"Gave me a present," Eric said casually.

Now he'd perplexed her. "A present?" she echoed.

"Symbolic, Garth said."

"Symbolic," Madeline repeated, looking dazed.

"Yeah." Eric let go of one of her hands to take the box from his pocket. "Madeline, will you marry me?"

"I..." Her face went completely still.

His heart almost stopped. Was she hesitating?

"Yes." Her voice was so low he scarcely heard it. "Yes, I'd love to marry you, Eric."

His hand tightened in a spasm on hers. "I wish we were home. Alone."

If eyes could reveal a soul, hers did. "I wish we were, too."

Committing to memory that look, the kind a man could live for, he handed her the box. "From Garth. His symbol."

She opened it, took out the gaudy plastic ring and gravely slipped it on her finger, as if he'd given her real rubies, real gold. Gazing down at the ring with a tender smile, she said, "I love your son."

"He's pretty cool, isn't he?" Eric grinned crookedly. "He gave me his permission. Or blessing. I didn't try to distinguish."

Still she admired the ring. "I will treasure it always."

"Carefully. It's losing paint."

A giggle escaped. "Oh, dear."

"Tomorrow, we'll go choose one for you to wear. I figured maybe Garth could come with us. Unless you'd rather he didn't."

She flashed him a glorious smile. "I would love him to come."

"Shall we order so we can eat and get home sooner?"

"Whose home? Mine, with my mother? Or yours, with your son?"

Eric swore. "How about a very private back road?"

Humor quivered at the corners of her mouth, although her eyes held the darker shimmer of passion. "That sounds very intriguing. Since we *are* engaged..."

"I love you," he said, the declaration scraping a throat that suddenly felt raw. These weren't words that should be said lightly; they had to hurt.

"Yes. I love you, too." Madeline looked back at the ring. After a moment she said musingly, "Do you know—my dress is symbolic, too."

He had no trouble understanding that one. "Of all you can be. When you choose."

"Very nicely put," Madeline said. "I chose *you* very wisely. Just think, no more vet bills."

"But eleven cats on our bed every night."

"Oh, I'm *very* fond of cats." He'd die for a smile like this one. "Cats, and you," Madeline murmured.

"Ditto," he said.

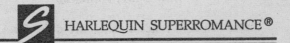

HARLEQUIN SUPERROMANCE ®

COMING NEXT MONTH

#762 THE AUSTRALIAN HEIRESS • Margaret Way
Margaret Way is a romance legend—one of the most
popular romance writers ever published. We're proud to
welcome her to Superromance with this dramatic and
distinctive story. Camilla Guildford is the Australian
heiress—daughter of a powerful financier. But she hasn't
inherited the fortune everyone *thinks* she has. Instead, her
father's death has left her with an unexpected legacy of
bitterness. She blames one man for her father's decline.
Nick Lombard. *Can you fall in love with your enemy?*

#763 FATHER FOUND • Judith Arnold
The Daddy School
What does a guy do when he finds a baby on his doorstep?
Especially when it might be his? Jamie McCoy turns to
nurse Allison Winslow for help. He attends her "Daddy
School" to learn how to change, feed and burp his daughter.
But that's not enough for either his daughter or for Jamie.
They need Allison for far more important things....

#764 THE LITTLE MATCHMAKER • Muriel Jensen
Matchmaker, Matchmaker
Eight-year-old Jason is worried. His grandparents are
threatening to sue for his custody—and he thinks they might
win. So he runs away, leaving his mother, Beth, frantic and
his grandparents raising hell. Enter Ethan Drum, town sheriff.
Ethan finds Jason hiding in the woods and rashly promises
that if he can do anything legal to help, he will. But he hasn't
counted on being introduced to Jason's grandparents as
Beth's fiancé!

#765 ONE MORE RODEO • Lynnette Kent
Jeff Buchanan never understood why Mickey York walked
out on him the day of their wedding. At first he was hurt—
he and Mickey had been best friends since childhood and
were as close as two people could be. Then he was angry.
Finally anger turned to concern as time went by and there
was no word of Mickey. Now, ten years later, she's back
and he wants an explanation. But Mickey's guarding her
secret. Is she also guarding her heart?

*Welcome—for the second time—
to the Silver Dollar Ranch,
near Tombstone, Arizona*

You may have met Morgan Bodine and
Jasentha Cliffwalker in *She Caught the Sheriff.*
Now this is their story—

IN THE ARMS OF THE LAW (#759)
by Anne Marie Duquette

Morgan Bodine is part-owner of the Silver Dollar; he's also
Tombstone's acting sheriff. Jasentha is busy studying the bats
that live in the caves on Bodine property. Morgan and Jaz
loved each other years ago, but it was a love they weren't
ready for.

Are they ready now? They'll find out when a stranger comes to
Tombstone, threatening everything they value most....

Available October 1997
wherever Harlequin books are sold.

HARLEQUIN SUPERROMANCE®

You've told us how much you enjoy our
9 Months Later stories! These are romances
about new parents—and new babies. Now
Harlequin Superromance is pleased to
offer you double the reading pleasure...

Two men named Zach—two men who weren't
expecting fatherhood in *any* guise.

Two babies on the way—whether their
mothers are ready or not!

Two special books you won't want to miss—
by *two* of your favorite authors.

September 1997—**LAURA'S BABY** (#756)
by Rebecca Winters

October 1997—**JUST ONE NIGHT** (#760)
by Kathryn Shay

You'll find them wherever Harlequin books are sold.

HARLEQUIN SUPERROMANCE®

the Daddy school

Three wonderful new books from
Judith Arnold

**Sometimes…a man needs help learning to be a dad.
That's what The Daddy School is all about.**

November 1997—*Father Found.* Cynical journalist
Jamie McCoy literally finds a baby on his doorstep. For
the first time in his life he needs help—in the form of
Allison Winslow, who runs The Daddy School. Soon he
simply needs Allison.

December 1997—*Father Christmas.* A hard-bitten cop is hot
on the trail of thieves—who turn out to be the precocious
children of a powerful lawyer. But neglecting his own son
wasn't part of the plan, and it takes the help of Allison's
partner, Molly, to teach him the true meaning of Christmas.

January 1998—*Father of Two* features the precocious
youngsters introduced in *Father Christmas.* Of course
there's romance as well as hijinks as two lawyers butt
heads over cases and kids.

THE DADDY SCHOOL
Don't skip it!

Available wherever Harlequin books are sold.

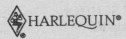